Double Dog Dare You

Lacey Black

Double Dog Dare You

Cover Design by Melissa Gill Designs

Editing by Kara Hildebrand

Proofreading by Joanne Thompson & Karen Hrdlicka

Format by Brenda Wright, Formatting Done Wright

Published in the United States of America.

ISBN: 978-1-951829-07-0

Chapter One

Royce

Unknown: *It was horrible. H-O-R-R-I-B-L-E!*

I stare at my phone, at the mystery number I just received a text message from. It's not completely rare to receive them at nine at night, but it is a little odd to get one from a number not programmed into my phone.

Before I can reply, another message pops up.

Unknown: *Why do men feel the need to talk about their penis sizes on a date? On a FIRST date nonetheless.*

Color me intrigued, as I glance down at my own naked crotch, a smirk spreading across my face.

Me: *Because it's a favorite amongst all appendages?*

Thanks to a freaked out woman at work, I had to shower the moment I got home to wash the vomit off my leg. I toss my wet towel into my hamper and grab a pair of shorts. The entire time, watching for a reply from whoever is on the other end of this chat. I'm already smiling when my device lights up.

Unknown: *It's only a favorite with them. No woman has ever been excited to get a dick pic, Sabrina. None. Ever.*

I snort a laugh, my fingers already flying across the screen.

Me: *I think you've been receiving the wrong pics of dicks then.*

I fire it off, a burst of pride sweeping through my body as I preen like a proud papa bear. My dick is glorious, if I do say so myself. Any woman who gets a picture should be honored to receive it. A solid nine inches, thick and straight. A unicorn amongst guys, if you will. Many a lady friend has complimented me repeatedly about how impressive my cock is. You know, screaming my name over and over again.

There's no greater compliment than multiple orgasms and hollering the Lord's name.

Unknown: *Not true. The dicks worth photographing are all taken or attached to a cocky manwhore, who has every intention of shoving his dick in every vajayjay this side of the Mississippi.*

Again, I snort, because she's not wrong. Guys like me aren't looking to settle down, at least not yet. We're having too much fun playing the field, or as my mystery texter said, shoving our dicks into available vajayjays. And let's be real here. Life is about having fun, living it to its fullest. Why muddy the water with commitment and monogamy?

Take my brother, Rueben, for example. The asshole went to a class reunion last fall as single as you can get, met up with an old friend, and is now engaged to be married. Why? He's essentially cutting off his own balls and handing them to one woman to carry in her purse for the rest of his life.

I shiver at the thought.

Don't get me wrong, I like Cricket. A lot, actually. She's funny and smart and loves to give my brother hell. That alone is a key selling point in her favor. But the one woman thing for the rest of your life? Yeah, not for me.

Me: *Variety is the spice of life...* *inserts smiling devil emoji*

Unknown: *Who are you and what have you done with my BFF?*

I almost tell her who I am and that I haven't done anything to her friend—yet—but I keep it to myself. This is too much fun. Before I can respond, she adds:

Unknown: *Anyway, I'm calling it a night. I need to drown my sorrows in tequila and wake up in the morning, pretending this night never happened. Here's to not remembering this date with Gill.*

Gill? Well, no wonder the date sucked with a name like Gill. I can almost guarantee that guy measures in at just under five inches but boasts about a solid sixer. He's probably a stockbroker or insurance agent to boot.

I focus in on her reference to tequila. The last time I did shooters of it, they were out of the belly button of a petite redhead named Candy, who I met at a tourist bar on Parkway. I live and work in Gatlinburg, in the heart of tourism USA. While I prefer the small dive bars on the nights I'm looking to have a few drinks and be alone, it's the busy bars and restaurants in downtown that I frequent when I *don't* want to be alone. Bachelorette parties, girls' trips, and divorce celebrations all have one thing in common: single ladies looking for a little no-strings fun between the sheets. Or in the shower. Hell, even against the wall in the VIP bathroom at the club.

That's where I come in.

Me and my nine inches of earth-shattering fun.

Unknown: *Talk to you in the morning, Rina.*

I'm nothing but smiles as I send my reply.

Me: *Night, sweetness. Looking forward to it.*

I toss my phone on my bed, suddenly wishing it would light up again with another message. That's not a feeling I'm used to. Desire, sure. Excitement, definitely. But this feels more like...longing. A desire and excitement all wrapped up together, and not in a sexual way. In an 'I want to talk to her some more' way, which is absolute fucking madness, considering I don't even know who she is.

Part of me wants to get dressed and head to town, find a new willing friend to get lost in for an hour or two. But another part, the chunk that's outweighing the power of my cock, tells me to throw on my running shoes and go pound the pavement for a bit. That's the part that overrules the sex-fueled piece of my brain and has me reaching for my favorite runners and slipping on a T-shirt.

I do a few stretches in my front yard and get ready to go. I start down the hill where my small cabin is situated and make my way to the road. Most of these roadways are more of a single lane until you get down to the base of the mountain. That's one of the things that attracted me to Gatlinburg when my mom and brother relocated here: the scenery. It's like being secluded away from the action, even though houses are somewhat close together.

My cabin sits on the side of the Great Smoky Mountains, facing downtown Gatlinburg. I love the lights and the sounds that float my way without actually being in the city. My space is a single bedroom, loft-style home with the biggest shower and Jacuzzi tub known to man. In fact, besides the view, it was the selling point that tipped the scale. Do you know how many women will fit in that shower?

The answer is five.

Comfortably.

Plus me.

No, I didn't screw them all in the shower. This isn't a cheesy porno. But I did enjoy the company of one particular lady later that night, after her friends partied in my hot tub, showered, and left.

Did I mention they were all in their suits when they showered together?

See, not a cheesy porno.

My pace picks up as I reach the bottom of the mountain and start to make my way through the side streets. Running in Gatlinburg is a great workout. There's not a single road that's flat or straight for any reasonable length of pavement, and some of the inclines are fucking brutal. Like the one that'll take me home. Going back up the mountain, especially at the end of your run, is never an easy feat.

I glance at my watch and notice I'm already three miles in and barely breathing hard. After my time in the Army, physical fitness and endurance was such an engrained part of my day, I kept the routine going. Running, some light weight training, and kayaking are my favorite ways to keep in shape, and I do all three as much as possible.

As I make my way down the road through a small grouping of houses, a shadow sweeping across a front porch catches my attention. When I'm right in front of the house, a loud thud sounds, followed quickly by, "Shit." The voice is soft and feminine, yet laced with authority. No-nonsense, of sorts.

I find myself slowing my pace and stopping completely when I reach the short sidewalk that takes me to the front porch. "Is everything all right?" I ask, spying the shadow crouched over.

She quickly stands up and looks my way. The light is behind her making it difficult to see her features, but I can tell she's a tad on the short side with curves for days. "Hello?" she whispers, taking a step to the edge of the porch.

The sound of her voice makes my cock start to thicken in my shorts.

That's never happened before. Never have I gotten an erection from a voice alone. Usually it's what the voice is saying that has me firing on all cylinders and raring to go.

"Uhh, sorry, I was just passing by and heard a noise. Just checking you're okay," I answer, making sure I stay at the edge of the street. The last thing I want is a jealous boyfriend to come out with a shotgun and a pissed-off attitude.

Unfortunately, that's happened before.

"Oh," she replies with a slight chuckle. The sound is like Viagra. "I dropped my drink."

I can't help but laugh. "Ahh, well, that's cause for the use of profanity," I justify.

"Yeah, especially because it was the last of my tequila."

The mention of the hard liquor reminds me instantly of my mystery texter. "Well, shit. Your day just got a whole lot worse," I tease.

"No kidding," she replies with a deep sigh. "I guess that means I'm done drinking for the night."

"Or you could head down the street to the twenty-four seven liquor store and restock," I suggest, a smile on my face, even though she can't see it in the darkness of night.

"I could, but I've already taken off my shoes," the woman replies, lifting her leg up knee-level and wiggling her toes. Even though I can't see detail, I'm suddenly wondering what color those toes are painted, if they're ticklish, and what exactly they'd look like hitched over my shoulder.

"And taking off your shoes is equivalent to taking off your bra at the end of the workday, am I right?"

She barks out a laugh, the sexiest sound I've ever heard, and makes me smile even wider. "I guess that's true."

I'd love to ask about said bra, find out whether or not that's already off too, but I figure that's probably pushing it. I don't know this woman, nor anything about her. Could have a husband inside or at the very least, a boyfriend. A woman with those kinda curves and a laugh that can erect a cock faster than the opening BJ scene in a skin flick, definitely isn't single.

Damn.

"Well, I should probably let you figure out what you're going to do without the rest of your tequila," I say, lifting my hand in a departing wave.

"Yeah, probably off to bed in a state of sad despair," she replies with a giggle.

My cock jumps at the sound, and I almost groan.

Then she steps forward, the outdoor security light illuminating the woman for the first time. Blonde hair the color of sunshine and the most beautiful set of blue eyes I've ever seen. Even from about twenty feet away and the darkness around us, I can see the sapphire hue blazing brightly. She has high cheekbones and the sexiest pair of lips I've ever seen.

And I've seen my share of lips.

"Thank you for coming to my rescue," she replies, her smile captivating.

"Well, I didn't do anything," I tell her, the whole time wondering if she can hear the loud pounding of my heart in my chest. "Maybe another time I'll save the tequila," I add with my own grin.

Her smile remains on her lips as her fingers wrap around the porch post. All sorts of dirty images parade through my mind like a movie, most prominently, my cock playing the role of the lucky post. "Good night," she whispers, her sweet voice like a cool breeze that washes over my fevered skin.

"Night," I reply, throwing her a second wave before taking off again. It's uncomfortable running with a hard-on, but I ignore it. It's not like I can do anything about the state of my hardness right now anyway.

I reach the end of the road and head to the right. It'll loop back around and spit me out on the main roadway. From there, I'll work my way back up the mountain and toward home. To my little slice of solitude and peace.

Just as I reach the base of the mountain, my watch alerts me to a text message. It's my brother, of course, who's a night owl. He has some cyber security job for the government that he can't talk a lot about, and I find I talk more to him late at night than any other time of day.

Rueben: *Hot date tonight?*

I push through my last half mile uphill, relieved when I reach the point to start my cooldown. Hands on my head and sucking in greedy gulps of air, I walk the rest of the way to my house and plop down on the front yard. I stretch my legs and back, relishing in the pull of the well-used muscles. My mind returns to a certain blonde with blue eyes and the *muscle* I'd like to use on her…

Finally, when I'm good and stretched, I unlock the door and grab my phone to fire off a reply to my little brother.

Me: *Why, jealous since you've locked yourself in on one pussy for the rest of your life?*

The bubbles appear immediately. I grab a bottle of water from the fridge and head out to the back deck. As soon as I prop my feet up on a chair, his message appears.

Rueben: *Why would I be jealous of you? When you find the right woman, none of that bullshit matters anymore.*

Me: *I call bullshit. I mean if you like BJs and the girl you're marrying thinks it's gross, how can you say that's the best option?*

Women are like cars. You have to test drive. Lots of test drives, my friend.

Rueben: *There's no way we're related. You're a sick individual.*

I snort and finish off my bottle of water.

Me: *Think whatever you want, but my dick isn't anywhere near hibernation like yours.*

Rueben: *Who said anything about hibernation? We just had sex twice tonight. Once in the shower and then out on the back deck.*

I whistle at his reply, a wide smile on my face.

Me: *Twice in one night? I taught you well, young grasshopper.*

Rueben: *You didn't teach me jack shit except what our neighbor Mrs. Hanson sounds like when she's coming.*

I bark out a laugh that echoes up the mountain and through the trees. Ah yes, Mrs. Hanson. A young newlywed that might have taken a few rides on my cock at the tail end of my senior year in high school. She was twenty-four, maybe? And her husband worked long hours.

Me: *She got lonely.*

Rueben: *I still have no clue how her husband didn't find out.*

Me: *You and me both…*

I don't have an excuse for sleeping with my older and very married neighbor except I was young and dumb. She was flirty and had a pool. One day after school, I went over to pick up something for my mom and found her lounging by the pool in a teeny bikini. What's a young, horny eighteen-year-old to do when he has sex on his brain twenty-four seven and an opportunity presents itself on a silver platter?

Yeah, not my proudest moment, but at the time, I thought I was king of the world.

Now, if I get the hint that a woman is married or in a relationship, I'm out of there. The last thing I want is the drama that accompanies that. You want to cheat? Fine. Enjoy. But don't use me to do it.

Rueben: *Anyway, I'm off to bed. Lunch later in the week?*

Me: *Sounds good. You're buying.*

Rueben: *Wouldn't expect any less.* *eye roll gif*

Me: *Later*

I toss my phone onto the table and lean back in the chair, gazing up at the stars. There's nothing better than Tennessee nights in the mountains. They sure beat the hell out of southern Illinois where I grew up.

My phone pings with a text, and I wonder if it's my mystery woman. I should definitely tell her she has the wrong number, but I'm having a little innocent fun. If she texts me tomorrow, I'll let her know I'm not Sabrina. When I glance at my phone, I see a work-related message from one of my employees.

Damn, not her.

In the meantime, I guess I'll just sit here and think about the woman down the mountain with striking blue eyes and blonde hair that looks soft enough to tangle my fingers in it.

Chapter Two

Quinn

It's a gorgeous night.

And *that* was one gorgeous man.

His features were shadowed by the light, but I could still see enough to make my heart flutter in my chest. Dark hair, firm, stubbled jaw, and a smile that did a number on my trusty cotton panties in a shockingly short amount of time. I don't even know who he was, but he did more to my libido than the last three dates I've had...combined.

I slip back inside my house and set my empty glass on the counter. I can't believe I actually spilled the only alcohol I have in my possession. I'm not a drinker really, and am surprised I even found it in the back of the cabinet, covered in a thin layer of dust. Sabrina brought it over a few years ago after I broke up with Malcolm. Ice cream and margaritas do a broken heart good.

My mind goes right back to the mystery man out for a run. I saw him coming down the street. That's actually when I dropped my glass and spilled it. That moment he crossed through the light of the streetlamp. Thank God it was a heavy tumbler or I'm sure the glass would have shattered like...well, a glass. Probably a cheap one, but you understand my analogy. Anyway, I saw a man running my way, his long, muscular legs carrying him so effortlessly up the slight incline of my street, and my heart actually skipped a beat. If I were in the medical field, I may have been concerned by the palpitation, but since it started back up again and warmth flooded between my legs, I figured I was fine.

Damn, I wish I had more tequila.

Instead, I grab my bag and return to the porch, drinkless. There are a few reports I need to review before Thursday's board of education meeting, as well as pick a winner for our monthly Student Inspiration Award. As the principal of Grace Private School, I've implemented many programs for our students to participate in throughout the school year. They vary from volunteer work outside of school to different options while in school, in addition to the standard sports and clubs.

This particular award is presented to one student nominated by a teacher who has shown leadership and personal growth throughout the previous month, and the reward is of their choosing within the community, within reason, of course. Last month's winner wanted to ride go-carts at a local outdoor facility, which I granted. The month before was a special pizza luncheon to share with her entire class. I happily purchased those pies, and even threw in cookies. That leaves me to pick this month's winner.

I start reading the nominations, focusing on the reasoning for the nomination, instead of the name and their reward request. Already, one stands out above the rest. An individual who has volunteered in another class during his study hall and spent time reading to younger students, who has worked hard and brought a struggling math grade up to a B plus. A young man who works part time after school at a local hotdog stand because he befriended the owner, who's older and in poor health. I'm smiling as I award Logan Hendershot the Student Inspiration Award for this month.

That's when I look at his reward request.

Ziplining down the Smoky Mountains.

Say what?

I've never taken a student ziplining, never thought it'd be even a possibility. How am I going to submit this request to the superintendent? There's no way he'd allow it, right? I mean...it's ziplining for goodness sakes.

I toss the paper on top of the pile and massage my throbbing temple.

Ziplining.

Seriously?

Who wants to suspend themselves from a rope and dash down the mountain at rapid speeds? Not a sane person, that's for sure.

Sighing, I really regret not having that drink now. Maybe I'll take the gorgeous stranger's advice and drive over to the liquor store. I mean, I barely had two sips before I dumped the rest of it on the porch. Well, at least I don't have to go with him. I mean, I've always paid for the reward, but never actually participated. And his parents might not even sign off on the request, so maybe I'm getting myself all worked up over nothing.

I close my eyes and take a deep cleansing breath. I'm definitely in need of a yoga class right about now. Between the long day at school, my ancient cell phone breaking and losing all of my contacts, and then my crappy first date with Gill, a security guard at Dollywood, I'm feeling a little tense. And not in the good way as a result of seeing Gill's flaccid penis in live Technicolor on his cell phone screen.

I shiver.

Who whips out a picture of their soft dick and just shows it to a woman they've just met?

Apparently, Gill the security guard does.

I snort a laugh.

It wasn't even a nice soft penis. It was small and wrinkly and sat sadly between his hairy thighs like a baby mole.

Deciding to pack it up before I give myself nightmares, I slip back into my house and secure the front door. I should definitely try to figure out my new phone, but I just don't have the patience to deal with a new smartphone, especially when the Blackberry I've had for nearly seven years worked just fine. Until it didn't. And because my device was so old, it wouldn't upload anything into my Cloud account, including photos and contacts.

Good thing I had Sabrina's number memorized.

Instead of dealing with my phone and the reports due on Thursday, I decide a long hot bath is in order before bed. It'll give me an opportunity to try out that new jasmine bubble bath I found at a little shop at the edge of town. Then, and only then, might I be able to put this horrid day behind me.

Tomorrow will surely be better, right?

***

Me: *I think I'm going to need some sort of class to figure this new phone out.*

I set the device on my counter and fill my coffee cup. I still don't know how anything works really, but at least I can send a text. A text I'm sure will go unanswered for at least another hour. Sabrina isn't exactly a morning person like me. In fact, she doesn't understand why any rational person would even want to get up at five in the morning, let alone comprehend it's the most perfect time of the day. The sky is still dark and calm, while the city sleeps beneath it. Wildlife is starting to rise and scrounge for breakfast. Other morning people like me are turning on coffee pots, inhaling the sweet aroma of brewing the first cup of Joe. It's the most glorious time of day.

My favorite.

I'm surprised when the phone chimes a response. Setting my cup down, I smile at her reply.

Sabrina: *I may have to agree with you there.*

Me: *What are you doing up?*

Sabrina: *It's the best time of the day.*

Me: *Seriously? Don't make fun of me.*

Sabrina: *I would never. If you're not up and running by six, you've already missed the best part.* *insert shocked face emoji*

"The sunrise," I whisper aloud, confused by her response. Sabrina is a night owl, so why the hell is she acting like mornings are her thing?

Me: *Don't mock. It's not becoming.* *insert laughing emoji* *insert fishing pole* *insert birthday cake*

What the hell? How did I do that?

Sabrina: *What does that mean? Are you having a fishing party that you're inviting me to?*

I snort out a laugh.

Me: *Me? Fishing?*

Sabrina: *Might be fun...* *insert big fish emoji*

Me: *I thought you hated to fish. The smell, the worms, the sunburn because you always forget sunscreen.*

Sabrina: *Do I?*

I roll my eyes.

Me*:* *You know you do. Your pasty complexion is no match for UV rays.*

Sabrina: *I see...*

I grab a slice of wheat bread and pop it into the toaster. While it does its thing, I grab the jar of apple butter from the refrigerator and slather it on nice and thick when breakfast pops up. Two bites in, my phone chimes with another text. I can't help but wonder if maybe she's just going to bed...

Sabrina: *Can I tell you something?*

Me: *Of course.*

Sabrina: *It might upset you a little.*

Now, the hairs on the back of my neck stand up. Sabrina has a brilliant mind, but sometimes she acts before she thinks. It's one of the reasons she lost her job at a clothing boutique in town. Not all customers like being told their new dress makes their ass look bigger than a double-wide.

Me: *What did you do?*

Sabrina: *It's not so much me, but you...*

Me: *Me? What did I do, Sabrina?*

Sabrina: *This isn't Sabrina.*

That gives me pause. Not Sabrina? What does that mean?

Me: *I don't understand.*

Sabrina: *My name is Rigsby and you texted my phone by accident last night. I don't know a Sabrina.*

Suddenly, I start laughing. I take a bite of my breakfast before my fingers move over the image of the keyboard on my screen.

Me: *Ha, ha, very funny.*

Sabrina: *I'm not joking. My friends call me Rigsby, my last name, and I live in Gatlinburg. I moved here a few years back. I'd happily send a pic, but I know you're not a fan of dick pics...* *insert winky face emoji*

I stare at the screen in horror. No way I've been texting some random guy when I thought I was messaging Sabrina, right? I mean, I know I lost all of my contacts when my ancient phone died, but...

And then a picture message pops up on the screen. With shaky fingers, I click on the download and wait for it to complete. When it does, I bust out laughing. There on my phone is a picture of a crotch—covered, thankfully, in cotton sweatpants—and it most *definitely* isn't Sabrina's.

It's very male and very...large.

And not even hard.

My entire face bursts into flames as I gape at the image. Why is this image of a stranger in sweatpants better than any dick pic I've ever received?

Sabrina: *Believe me now? I'm sure your friend isn't sporting... *inserts eggplant emoji**

I can't stop the giggle.

Me: *No, I'm pretty sure she isn't. I can't believe I've been texting a stranger.*

Sabrina: *Well, if it makes you feel better, you don't feel like a stranger anymore.*

Weird, it doesn't. I click on the name at the top of the phone and edit the information. I delete my best friend's name and replace it with a new one. Rigsby. When it updates, I go back to our text exchange and read it all with fresh eyes. He never led me to believe he was Sabrina, that I can tell. Rigsby spoke to me as himself, just failed to actually confess his real identity.

Rigsby: *Well, you probably need some time to come to terms with the fact your new BFF is a hot dude, and I have to head to work. I'll talk to you later.*

Me: *You're not just going to delete me?*

Rigsby: *Hell no, I've added you to my phone. We're official.*

Me: *Official what?*

Rigsby: *Official besties. I'll get us necklaces after work. Bye!*

I can't control the smile on my face. Why am I smiling? I don't even know who Rigsby is.

I set my phone down on the counter and finish my cold toast. As soon as my mess is cleaned up, I gather my stuff and head out the door for school. I'm always in my office by seven getting as much done as possible. You never know how many interruptions you'll receive during a typical school day, both from students and teachers.

The day passes in a flurry of gathering final bids to have the gym floor redone and making sure the bus drivers' contract is renewed with our transportation partner. Throw in an assembly on making healthy choices and an early dismissal, and I've never been happier to be pulling into the yoga studio on Oak Street. I've been coming here for a little over three years now after attending a class with Sabrina. I was hooked by my first downward dog.

I grab the bag I keep in my trunk with extra workout clothes and head inside the small building. Crystal, the owner, is there to greet me with a wide grin as I slip past a few students congregating off to the side, and head into the locker room. A quick change of clothes and I'm set. My hair is already up, in a no-nonsense bun. It's my hairstyle of choice during the week, unless I have something lined up.

Like a date.

And even I try to limit those to only when necessary during the workweek.

With my mat and water bottle, I head out and start to stretch.

"I can't believe I didn't hear from you last night," Sabrina bellows as she flops on the floor beside me. "I'm assuming the lack of communication meant it went well, and you were indisposed," she adds with a giggle.

"That or he was an axe murderer and I was his latest victim," I whisper-yell as I reach for the toes on my right foot, stretching out my leg.

Sabrina seems to stop and consider it. "Well, considering you're not chopped into tiny pieces, I take it the date went well." She gives me her trademark grin.

Exhaling a deep breath, I reply, "No, it didn't go well." I glance around and confirm no one is too close. "He whipped out his phone and showed me his dick before we even finished the appetizer," I huff.

Sabrina's eyes widen, almost comically, before she bursts into fits of laughter. "Shut. Up. You're kidding me, right?"

I stretch my left leg, feeling the burn as it spreads from my calf to my butt. "I wish I were," I mumble, sticking both legs out and reaching for my toes.

She leans in and asks, "Was it a nice one?"

I laugh without humor. "Uhh, no, Sabrina, it was definitely *not* a nice one. It was...you know what, I'm not even getting into this with you right now."

"Why not? I want to know the details," she insists, conducting her own stretches beside me.

"No, believe me, you don't. It wasn't a pretty one, Rina."

She just looks at me with sad eyes. "He was so cute though."

"Yeah, apparently cute doesn't equal impressive penis."

Crystal heads to the front of the room to start our group stretches. Sabrina and I follow along, but I'm unable to focus on anything with my best friend chirping beside me. "I can't believe you didn't let me know last night."

I huff. “I did.”

She glances at me, a confused look on her face. “No, you didn’t.”

I roll my eyes. “I know *now* I didn’t, but at the time, I thought I did.”

Sabrina stares at me with a blank look on her face. “That makes no sense.”

“Remember how I told you my Blackberry finally broke? When I went to the store to get a replacement, it wouldn’t even backup anything, but I thought that was okay because I have all the main numbers I need memorized.” I push up from the floor and stretch out my back.

“Okay,” she encourages me to continue.

“So, I programmed in your number when I got home from my date and sent you a message. Turns out, it wasn’t your number.”

Sabrina gets into our first position and holds it for a count of ten. As she exhales slowly, she asks, “So who’s number was it?”

The moment I suck in another breath, I reply, “Some guy named Rigsby.”

Her eyebrows pull together. “That’s a horrible name.”

“His last, he said.”

“That’s hideous. I bet he’s ugly. Probably five foot eight with a potbelly and bad toupee.”

“I don’t think so,” I reply before I can recall the words. After the photo he sent, I’m pretty sure there’s no potbelly. I’m pretty sure there’s not an ounce of fat on him anywhere.

I can feel her eyes on me but refuse to look her way. Instead, I close my eyes and try to concentrate on relaxing, on my poses, and on letting the tension of the day go. Instead, the moment my eyes are closed, I see Rigsby. Well, specifically, I see the image he texted me this morning in his gray sweatpants. It wasn't a dick pic, but it wasn't *not* one either. It was...wow. I don't know what it is about a pair of well-hung sweatpants that does weird things to female libidos everywhere.

"Why did you just get this weird look on your face?" she whispers.

Opening my eyes, I glance her way. "What look? And why aren't your eyes closed?"

"You had this look like someone just gave you a double scoop ice cream cone on a hot summer day."

"You're dumb," I tell her, closing my eyes so she can't tell how right she was.

Sabrina giggles softly. "And you're into him."

I huff out another deep breath. "That's absurd. I don't even know him." I change positions with Crystal, trying to ignore the chirping bird at my side.

"No, but you want to," she singsongs, mirroring my pose and exhaling.

When our class comes to an end, I hop off my mat and roll it up, grabbing my water bottle and bag. "Give me your phone," Sabrina says.

"Why?"

She rolls her eyes dramatically at me. "I'm going to program in my number—the *correct* one, silly." I reach into my bag and pull out my fancy new phone. "Wow, look at you! Stepping into the twenty-first century," she teases as she taps away at the screen. After only a handful of seconds, she hands it back. "Done."

I slip it back into my bag. "Thank you."

"Now, you'll actually text me and not some strange guy. Unless, that's your thing now."

I'm already shaking my head. "No, definitely not. That was a one-time accident."

She just grins. "We'll see," she sings, following me through the front door. "Wanna grab dinner later this week?"

"Sure" I reply, unlocking my car with my fob. "I have a board meeting Thursday night, but am free this weekend."

Sabrina pulls a face. "Of course you are. Saturday night it is! Maybe, I'll invite those two guys from the coffee shop down the block to join us," she says, waggling her eyebrows. "They're so flirty."

"Stop. Just us."

"We'll see," she repeats before sliding into her own vehicle and driving away.

I toss my bag into my car and climb in, hating the warmth filtering through the vents instead of cool air. I contemplate stopping for some takeout, but ultimately decide to just head home. A long shower and maybe a southwest chicken salad are what's in store for me tonight. Plus, reruns of *Friends*.

As I pull into my short driveway, something at the front door catches my eye. There's a brown bag there. I climb out and glance around, not really sure what I'm looking for, but when I don't see anything out of the ordinary, I slowly make my way up my steps. The paper bag is wrinkled and twisted closed at the top. Carefully, I reach down and retrieve it, surprised by how heavy it is. There's a note on the paper bag, scrolled in penmanship that rivals a physician's.

So you can take your bra off. Enjoy!

Deciding to go ahead and open it out here, I pull apart the twisted paper and glance inside. A hearty laugh pulls from my chest as I reach in and remove the bottle of liquor. The man from last night. He's the only one who would have left me this gift.

Smiling, I unlock my door and slip inside, anxious to open my new bottle of tequila.

Chapter Three

Royce

I'm gearing up for the final run down the mountain of the evening. The last group took off about ten minutes ago, which means they should be hitting the second platform now. I make sure my harness is secure and glance over at Charlie, giving him a thumbs-up. He releases the brake and lets me push off the platform. "See you at the bottom," I holler.

"Later, Rigsby."

The initial fall is always the best part.

I take in my surroundings, enjoying the hell out of the unobstructed view. The sun is dipping low behind the tree line and the air is starting to cool. It's a beautiful night, a perfect one for Parkway. Tourists will be out in droves tonight, drinking and hanging. It's been a few weeks since I hit up that scene, so maybe I'll head into town tonight after my run, find a new friend to entertain.

When I think of my run, I picture her.

The woman on the porch.

The one I dropped off a bottle of tequila to earlier today. I talked myself out of the gift at least a dozen times, yet for some reason, I couldn't stop myself from writing a note on the bag and setting it in front of her door. She wasn't home at the time, but I still felt like there were eyes everywhere. Gatlinburg isn't exactly small, but we still look out for our own.

When I reach the first landing, I make the adjustments myself, telling the attendant to head on down as soon as I take off. It's part of our nightly ritual. I always make the final run down the mountain, and as soon as I'm past, the employees shut down their stations and wait for the UTV to pick them up.

I continue down, loving the freedom that comes with ziplining. It was part of the attraction to the company I work for when I moved here. Rueben was doing his internet cyber security stuff, Mom got a job right away at a bakery, and I was on the hunt for the biggest thrill-ride I could find. Elevate was looking for someone with management experience, but settled when they met me. The only experience I had was jumping out of a plane a few times a year in the Army. But they appreciated my passion and drive, and with some proper training, they ended up making me manager of this outfit.

I love it.

As I make the final descent, my mind flips back to the text messages from this morning. The employees are gathering on the ground below me, watching my approach, and I can't help but wonder if my new texting friend is a fan of thrills. The women I meet in town usually talk a big game about excitement and fun—I mean, most of them are about to embark on some no-strings nookie. The moment I tell them what I do, their eyes light up like firecrackers. There's just something about my job as a zipline instructor that makes the panties melt away.

Well, that and my lady-killer grin.

The moment my feet hit the final platform, my team is beside me and helping me teardown and store my gear. We go through the closing process, piece by piece to ensure the area is secure and safe before everyone clocks out for the day. I head into the office to finish a little paperwork and send some emails, the part of the day I dread the most. I'd much rather be up on the mountain, with the wind in my face and nature all around me. This is the part of the job that gives me hives.

I notice right away today's numbers are slightly down compared to yesterday, but that doesn't faze me. It's the middle of the week. You never know what the weekdays will bring. All I know is this weekend will be busier than hell. The weather looks absolutely perfect, with light winds and warm temperatures. Perfect for ziplining.

Jill, the office assistant, helps keep things in here going on a day-to-day basis, but it's my job to finish. I sign off on a few orders and send them in to corporate, along with the final numbers for today. Just as I'm wrapping it up and logging out of my computer, my phone pings with a text.

I grab my phone, surprised by the disappointment that sweeps through me when I see my brother's name. Not that I don't want to talk to my brother, but I was a little hopeful it would be a certain wrong number texter.

Rueben: *Cricket is working some event on Saturday night. Wanna grab a few drinks at Pork's?*

Me: *Absolutely. He serves the best burgers.*

Rueben: LOL! *You're always hungry. Meet you there at 8.*

Me: *Deal.*

I shove my phone into my pocket and lock up the office. There are a few employees hanging around the back lot, so I throw them a wave and climb into my truck. As soon as I do, I retrieve my device once more and send the message I've been contemplating all day.

Me: *As much as I like seeing Bestie listed amongst my contacts, how about a name to put with it?*

I'm not sure if she'll reply or if I'm blocked at this point. Maybe I'll never speak to my mystery texter again, and she'll never experience a *real* dick pic. Though, admittedly, I've only sent one in my life and it was when I was nineteen and dumb. I prefer my lady friends to experience my cock up close and personal.

As I start the truck, those familiar bubbles appear, making me grin.

Bestie: *Like Tami with an I?*

Me: *Depends, is that your name?*

Bestie: *Oh, you wanted my name? You're going to have to be more specific next time. You just said a name.*

Me: *You're right, I did. But Tami with an I?*

Bestie: *You don't think I could be a Tami with an I?*

Me: *I didn't say that at all, but the last Tami with an I I knew was...friendly.*

Bestie: *So she was easy?*

Me: *Friendly.* *insert winky face emoji*

Bestie: *Same thing.*

I bark out a laugh and back out of the parking spot. When I reach a stop light, I notice the screen light up again. Against my better judgment, I glance at the message.

Bestie: *Maybe you need more classy names in your life like Margaret, Elizabeth, or Monica.*

I snort as I glance up and see the light still red. My fingers fly across the screen.

Me: *Dated a woman named Maggie a few times. She was a yoga instructor and dancer. Very bendy.* *insert grinning devil emoji*

Bestie: *insert eyeroll gif* *Of course you did! I probably don't want to know what kind of dancer either.*

I burst out laughing because she's right. She probably doesn't want to know.

A horn honks behind me, and I realize the light changed to green. I throw my phone on the passenger seat and finish my drive home, all while ignoring the phone that lights up and dings with each reply. The moment I pull into my driveway and park the truck, I reach for the device.

Bestie: *No response?*

Bestie: *I must be right, you're not replying.*

Bestie: *Though, I can't say much for her flavor of dancing, but I can vouch for yoga. Amazing for flexibility and core strength. I go a couple of nights a week.*

Now my vivid imagination is working overtime as I picture my faceless texter bending over and posing in all those crazy yoga positions. I've never tried them, but I enjoyed the hell out of watching Maggie give a naked demonstration.

Over my cock.

Which is now getting hard at the thought of Bestie doing her own demonstrations.

I grab my keys and type out a reply.

Me: *Sorry, was being a responsible driver and not texting while driving.*

Bestie: *I'm proud of you, Rigsby. Texting while driving is bad.*

I wave at my neighbor up the hill and slip inside my cabin. Fuck, I love this place. Mine's not quite as big as my brother's but I don't need a lot of space. While his sports three bedrooms, I opted for a much smaller scale log cabin. My home is an open floor plan with a spiral staircase that leads to a huge loft with gaming tables I was able to pick up for a steal from a cabin resort that was looking to upgrade. It has a pool table, foosball table, an old Pac-Man arcade game, and a bar. I spend a decent amount of time upstairs, but not nearly as much as I thought I would.

Downstairs, you'll find a large kitchen with eat-in dining room, living room with stone fireplace, bathroom, and a single bedroom. I bought it from an older couple, who was moving to an assisted-living community. They struggled with the winter snow and ice and didn't feel safe traveling down the mountain any longer. I came along at the right time and took their little cabin off their hands.

Speaking of hands, I make a quick adjustment to the contact and fire off a message.

Me: *Just got home.*

Bestie Tami with an I: *I'll let you go get something to eat.*

Me: *Workout first, dinner second.*

Bestie Tami with an I: *Ewww, workout.*

Me: *That's right, you're a yoga girl.*

Bestie Tami with an I: *I am.* *insert smiling face emoji*

Me: *Later, Bestie Tami with an I!*

Bestie Tami with an I: *You're weird. Goodbye.*

I toss my phone on the kitchen counter and slip into my bedroom to change into running clothes. I should probably head to the gym tonight, but quickly nix that idea. It's been a long day and the last thing I want to do is fight over who's using the free weights next. Plus, Selena will most likely be there, and I'd rather not deal with her brand of crazy right now.

After changing into a pair of thin shorts, tank top, and my favorite running shoes, I head out to do a little stretching before my run. When my feet hit the pavement, I consider my options. Usually, I switch up my route every time, but tonight, I'm not sure I can. I'm being pulled in the direction of a certain blonde's house. She wasn't there when I dropped off the tequila earlier, and I might be a little hopeful she'll be there tonight.

Probably stupid, but I've never been accused of being a smart man when it comes to the opposite sex.

I zigzag through the streets, my body already soaked with sweat as I approach the familiar street. My breathing is even as I stride toward the cute little house along the roadway. My eyes are searching without actually looking; it's a technique I've perfected when out at the bar. A way to check out a woman without blatantly staring. I keep my pace steady, even though I'd like to slow down. I don't want to pass it too quickly, but there's really no reason for me to stop.

I'm not *that* guy.

Even if I did deliver a bottle of liquor to her doorstep earlier in the day.

Just as I'm right in front of her short walkway, I catch movement in my peripheral vision, followed by the sound of a screened door slamming. "Funny meeting you here again."

I stop, unable to help myself, and turn to face the woman. Her hair is up in a bun that reminds me of a schoolteacher back in the day. Of course, Mrs. Hutchinson was a million years old, and this woman is anything but. I'd say she's right around my own age, actually. Her eyes are bright, and her lips hold a smile as she steps to the edge of the porch and into the light.

Before I'm able to formulate a reply, she adds, "I suppose you're the one I should thank for the gift?" She holds up a tumbler with what I assume is the tequila.

Placing my hands on my hips, I suck in a deep breath of oxygen. "I felt bad you spilled yours."

She grins. It makes my cock twitch in my shorts. "Well, it wasn't necessary, but since you bought a much better brand than my friend, I'll accept your gift." She lifts the glass to her lips and takes a sip.

Lucky fucking glass.

"I've had the cheap shit before and that's no way to drink on a Tuesday night. Or Wednesday night, for that matter," I tell her, taking a step forward, but maintaining my place off her property.

"I'm not much of a drinker any night of the week, actually. Last night was a rare instance. It would be my luck that I spilled what little I had left."

"Well, then luck must be on your side that I happened to run by in your time of need," I reply with a grin, flirting a little bit.

She snorts an unlady-like noise. "Time of need, huh?"

"Most definitely. I'm all about providing services to damsels in distress." I go ahead and throw her my lady-killer grin, just to prove the point.

The woman barks out a laugh. "Oh, I'm most certain you are." She clears her throat. "Beautiful night for a run," she adds, glancing up at the early night sky.

"The best," I confirm, but instead of following her gaze, I keep my eyes locked on her. She's stunning. The blonde beauty is wearing a black tank top and little red shorts. And her feet? I almost groan when I realize they're bare again. I have no clue what's going on with me, but I have this crazy urge to do dirty things to those feet.

"How far do you run?" she asks, leaning against the porch for support, her glass placed on the railing.

"Five to seven miles, depending on the route," I confirm. My eyes are drawn to her slender fingers as she slides one along the rim of the glass.

"That's five to seven miles farther than I'd want to run," she replies with a giggle.

Fuck.

It takes everything I have to suppress my groan. I can tell my dick is getting hard, and there's nothing I can do to stop it. If I'm not careful, she's liable to see real quick-like how she affects me.

I shoot her a smile and slightly turn my body to help camouflage my growing erection. "It's not something I particularly enjoyed until the military. Then, it was beat into my head every day, and now, it's just part of my daily routine."

"What branch?" she asks, seeming intrigued.

"Army. Twelve years and three tours," I tell her, wishing she'd invite me to join her on the porch.

Her eyes light up with something. Respect, maybe? "Wow, thank you for your service."

I just nod, never really knowing what to say when someone says that to me. Since it's clear she's not going to invite me to join her, I decide this is the perfect out for me. "Well, I should probably get back to my run and leave you to your drink."

She watches me for a few long seconds before replying, "Thank you again for the bottle."

"You're welcome. Let me know if you need anything else. I usually run this route two to three times a week," I tell her with a smile.

When she returns it, it feels like lightning striking through my veins. "Good to know, kind sir." She gives me a little wave of those delicate fingers, and like the dog I am, all I can think about is how amazing they'd look wrapped around my cock. "Safe running."

I toss her a wave in reply and take off down the street, feeling her eyes on me the entire way. Before I reach the end of the block, I can't help but turn around, jogging in place. The beauty is standing right where I left her, watching me. Her head is leaning against the porch post, her glass poised almost to her lips. I swear I see a smile over the glass, but I can't be certain from this distance. All I know is she is still there, those bright blue eyes observing my every move.

Throwing another wave, I turn back around and continue on my way, a wide grin on my face as I go.

Chapter Four

Quinn

I finish off my little amount of tequila, feeling pretty damn good. My body has the start of a nice buzz, even though it's not something I normally welcome. I don't usually enjoy the feel alcohol has on me. The impairment isn't welcome. But with this smooth tequila, it's not so bad. Of course, it could also do with the buzz the stranger gave me as well.

I almost missed him. I was literally walking out the door when he was running by. The moment I saw him, my breath caught in my throat and a shiver swept through my blood. He has a body made for running…and for something else too. Something that makes me tingle between my legs. I could feel his eyes on me the entire time he stood at the edge of the roadway, an appreciative glance that didn't feel demeaning or dirty. It was like he was savoring me with his eyes, slowly and delicately.

The invitation was on the tip of my tongue to ask him to join me. Why? I have no clue. I don't know this man from Adam, but do you know what? I wanted to. I wanted to ask him to my porch, to share the swing and a drink of tequila. Only then, I'm sure it wouldn't have ended with a leisurely drink on my porch. The way his eyes devoured me, I'm sure it would have moved right into the bedroom, and I would have gone willingly.

But that's not my MO. I don't sleep with men I don't know, despite how incredibly gorgeous they are in the moonlight. I have a strict five-date rule, and I'm not about to break said rule for a hottie with sparkling eyes and a cocky grin. Even if that hottie has stubble on his jaw that would no doubt cause the most delicious burn against my thighs.

He's not my type, however. With his charismatic boyish charm and his devilish good looks, he's the one to promise an epic, memorable night of sex but will leave before first light, trailing broken hearts as he swaggers away. He's most definitely the kind you take home for the night, not home to Mama. This man screams Mr. Good Time for Now, while I'm looking for Mr. Forever.

Two very different men.

I slip back into my house and set my glass in the sink. I'm not exactly sure why I had the drink, let alone finished it. As I told Mr. Tall, Dark, and Devastatingly Handsome, I'm not a drinker. Last night was a rare instance, and when I found the bottle on my porch earlier, I felt like I owed it to him to try out the liquor. I mean, he did spend money on it, right? Why just slip it into the cabinet above the fridge, only to pull it out on special occasions?

Now, the little bit I had in the glass is gone and I can feel the warmth spreading through my veins. I'm certain that's from the booze. Well, maybe seventy-five percent from the alcohol and twenty-five from the man. Fine, most likely fifty-fifty, but no more than that.

I grab my bag and pull out everything I need to review before tomorrow night's board meeting. You know, all the stuff I didn't complete last night. There are a few reports and some teacher requests for me to submit, but not too much. I go over the statement I prepared earlier regarding Seth James, a young man who was caught smoking in the restroom during lunch. Even though I had to place a call to his parents, I didn't suspend him, as expected. I gave him the punishment of three after-school detentions, as well as a community service project of his choice. I could tell he wasn't happy at all, but he didn't balk. At least not with his parents sitting beside him.

My final piece of work for the evening is to type the congratulatory email to Logan Hendershot for the Student Inspiration Award. In the email, I attach the form his parents will need to sign off on for the reward he has chosen. Ziplining. A shiver of nerves sweeps through me.

As soon as his email is complete and sent, I pull up ziplining companies for Gatlinburg and the surrounding areas and am not too surprised by the quantity I find. There are billboards and advertisements everywhere for numerous companies in the area. The one that jumps out is Elevate, rated very high for safety and experience, as well as recipient of an award for Best Zipline in the state of Tennessee.

I read up on the entire experience, from start to finish, from their website, even watching a few of their posted videos. I'm about to click through the photos when my phone chimes, alerting me to a text message.

Sabrina: *I. Am. Bored.*

Me: *Aren't you supposed to be working?*

Sabrina: *Yes, and it's dead. No one is here.*

Me: *I'm sorry. I hope it goes by quickly.*

Me: *Hey, can I ask you something?*

Sabrina: *YES! Please talk to me!*

Me: *Have you ever been ziplining?*

She doesn't text back. Instead, my phone rings a few seconds later.

"Hello?"

"Ziplining? Are you high?"

I chuckle. "Uhh, no. I'm just curious."

Sabrina exhales, and I can almost picture her sitting behind the counter of the small boutique she works at, twirling her hair like she does to give her hand something to do. "Yeah, I went with Rusty, that guy I dated a few years ago. He was all about the thrills. Why? You thinking of going?"

"Wait, wasn't he the guy who took you to the dinner show and got a little freaky under the table? And to answer your question, no, not me. The student who won my Inspiration Award chose it as his reward."

My friend is already chuckling. "Uh, yeah, that guy. He had...magic hands. So one of your students wants to go? Fun! You'd probably like it, actually."

I just can't see myself doing it. "Really? The thought of dangling from a wire, flying down a mountain doesn't sound that appealing."

Now she's full-on laughing. "Oh, I was joking. You'd hate it with a passion. It's something you can't control."

"I don't need to control everything."

Wrong. I do.

"Riiiiiiight..."

"Just because I prefer to have schedules and systems for everything, doesn't mean I need to control them," I huff.

"Hahahahahahaha! Okay, if you say so."

"You're mean," I retort.

"Only because I'm honest," she replies softly. "Listen, Q, I'm not saying it's all bad. You are who you are, and I love you despite it. Someday, you'll find a man who loves your checks and balances as much as you do."

"What's wrong with being organized?" I ask, glancing down at my Google calendar with a detailed list of tomorrow's workload.

"Absolutely nothing. Honest. Do you want to know what I think?"

Trying to be annoyed with her, but not really finding the gumption, I ask, "Are you going to tell me anyway?"

"Yes, I am," she says brightly. "I think you need someone to offset your organizational skills with a little mess."

"That makes no sense."

She snorts into the phone. "Oh, but it will. Someday, when the right guy comes along, he's going to wreck your perfect little pie charts and not use the proper detergent to fabric softener ratio with the laundry."

"That sounds horrible! Why would you not make sure you have the right balance? It helps with wrinkle control, as well as freshness."

"You're impossible," she mumbles. "And I look forward to the day he folds your towels wrong."

I huff, wishing I still had a drink. The thought of someone *not* folding them the right way makes my head spin. "The best way to maximize cabinet space is to fold them in half longways, twice, and then three times, Sabrina. It just makes sense."

Now she's laughing hard. At me. "Oh, believe me, I know exactly how you fold towels. I tried helping that time you were sick. I vividly remember the detailed video you sent me the following morning, requesting me to do it the right way next time."

"And there wasn't a next time," I remind her, annoyed that I answered this call.

"Right, because I wasn't touching your precious towels again."

"I just don't understand someone who folds them all willy-nilly style. There's no consistency." She just starts to fold and however they end up, that's how she puts them in the cabinet. Like a monster.

"Anyway, I'm not sure why we're talking about your towels," she starts.

"Because you brought them up," I interrupt.

"My thought is this. You listening?" She pauses dramatically, for effect, I'm sure. "Go ziplining. It'll be good for you."

"You're crazy," I scoff. "I'm not even sure why we're friends." Even though I really do. She might not meet me eye to eye on everything, but she's the one person who is always in my corner, even when times are hard.

She giggles now, the sound of a bell chiming in the background. "We're friends because of my solid, sage advice. Listen, I gotta go. We actually have a customer. Think about it, 'kay?"

"Fine," I grumble. "I'll think about it. Now, go. Work."

"Love you," she replies, blowing kisses into the phone before hanging up.

I exhale and set my phone down. I met Sabrina in high school. We were as different as night and day, and I'm not even really sure how we became friends. Well, that's not true. I remember the day she walked into my calculus class and sat behind me. She asked to borrow a pencil and hasn't let me alone since. We started hanging out after school, me working on my homework and her dreaming about boys, and before I knew it, we were as close as siblings.

As different as them too.

But I can't imagine my life without her in it.

Just as I'm getting ready to power down my laptop, I notice an email in my inbox. It's a response to Logan's letter of congratulations from his parents. I click on it, smiling when I read their boastful reply. They attached the release form, which relieves the school and me, as administrator, from any liability, and included a note about his birthday. It's Saturday, and they wondered if it was possible to do his reward then.

I blink at the screen.

Three days.

They agree to bring him to the site and sign any permission forms that need signatures. Basically, I'd just need to be there to meet them and take photographs. I head to Groupon and search for availability on ziplining, pleased to find a deal for Elevate. I fill out all of my personal details and pay, which then sends me to a reservation page for the company. Several dates and times are blacked out already, but I'm grateful to find a spot available for two o'clock this Saturday. I click the time and accept, receiving their confirmation screen a few seconds later.

There. Done.

I reply to the Hendershot's email with the good news about Saturday afternoon at two, hoping it fits with their schedule. Their acknowledgement is almost instant. They agree to meet me at Elevate by two o'clock for Logan's ziplining adventure.

Sighing, I log off and power down my computer. As I make my way to the kitchen, I set my phone on the counter and grab a bottle of water, taking a hearty drink. I really should eat some food to soak up the alcohol in my stomach. As I make a quick ham and cheese sandwich, I keep glancing at my phone, as if it's taunting me. When I'm halfway through my dinner, I finally walk over and grab it.

Me: *Have you ever been ziplining?*

Rigsby: *What kinda question is that?*

Me: *A serious one?*

Rigsby: *We live in the mountains, Bestie. Who hasn't been ziplining?*

Me: *Uhhh, me?*

Rigsby: *Why do you keep answering my questions with a question?*

Me: *In all fairness, I was the one who asked the original question.*

Rigsby: *I'll give you that. Are you serious about never ziplining?*

I return to my sandwich and take a bite before typing my reply.

Me: *Yes, I'm serious. I might be taking someone this weekend though.*

Rigsby: *What does that mean? You're going?*

Me: *No, one of my students earned it as a reward. I'm taking him Saturday afternoon.*

Rigsby: *I hope you're taking him to Elevate. They have the highest safety rating in the area. Plus, I can vouch for the staff. They're topnotch.*

Me: *That's where I have a reservation.*

Rigsby: *Good deal. What time?*

Me: *Two*

He doesn't reply right away, so I take the opportunity to finish my sandwich. Paired with a bottle of water, I don't feel the effects of the tequila any longer. However, now that I'm relaxed, exhaustion starts to settle in. My body is tired, my mind even more so. This is one of the times I wish I had a hot tub or Jacuzzi for relaxation, but even though they're crazy popular in the area, especially amongst tourist cabins, I've never really felt the need to own one.

A bath with lavender bubble bath will suffice.

Me: *I'm off to relax. Night.*

He replies right away.

Rigsby: *Do you own a dog, Bestie Tami with an I?*

Me: *That's random.*

Rigsby: *I've been thinking of getting a dog.*

Me: *What kind?*

I take a seat on one of the stools at my counter and try to picture myself as a dog owner. As a child, I wanted a dog, but we lived in town, in a small apartment complex with two other families, us being on the top floor. I remember begging my parents for a dog when I was about eight, swearing I would take care of it every day. Of course, my child idea of taking care of it and the reality of caring for a dog were two totally different things. We settled on a cat because it didn't require multiple trips outside a day from the third-floor apartment with no elevator, and while I was perfectly content with Miss Kitty, the desire to get a puppy has never gone away. I just ignored it as an adult, convincing myself I was too busy with work to properly train one.

Maybe someday.

Rigsby: *Something that likes to be outside, enjoying nature with me.*

Me: *Oh that's right, that running garbage you mentioned.*

Rigsby: *LOL Yes, that garbage. I'd love to take my dog with me. But he'd have to be something big and manly, like a Lab or a Shepherd.*

Me: *Oh! A chocolate Lab! They're so cute. That was one of the pups I had picked out when I was younger.*

Rigsby: *A good choice too. Labs love the outdoors.*

Me: *I'm not too much of an outdoorsman though. I'd probably be better off with something like a cockapoo or a morkie.*

Rigsby: *insert shocked face emoji* *WTF is that????????*

I giggle as I type out my reply.

Me: *A cocker spaniel poodle mix and a terrier maltese mix. My friend's parents have a morkie and it's so stinking cute!!* *insert heart-shaped eyes face emoji*

Rigsby: *Those sound like little ankle biters. Nothing manly about those, Bestie. I'm disappointed.*

Me: *Why?*

Rigsby: *It means we'll never settle on a dog together.* *insert winky face emoji*

My heart gallops and suddenly stops beating altogether in my chest. Together?

Rigsby: *I should let you get back to your relaxing. I'm going to search local pet shelters for a manly dog to adopt.*

Me: *Aww, good luck!*

Rigsby: *By the way, are you relaxing in a hot tub? I'm trying to visualize right now, you know, maybe naked? A bottle of wine?* *insert grinning devil emoji*

I bark out a laugh and shake my head. Men.

Me: *No hot tub for me.*

Rigsby: *Damn. I guess I'll just picture you in a bathtub instead. Naked. Lots of bubbles.*

Me: *You're incorrigible.*

Rigsby: *I'm a dude. Guaranteed that I'm thinking of someone naked twenty-four seven, Bestie.*

Me: *Good to know, I guess.*

Rigsby: *Well, I've got one, just so you know. It's available anytime you want to relax. Swimsuit optional.* *insert winky face emoji*

Me: *Of course you do…*

Shaking my head, I can almost picture him now, sitting back in his hot tub with half a dozen women. He's definitely a player, a man who could probably charm the panties right off a nun with little to no effort. Rigsby is a natural flirt and probably reaps the benefits of it nightly.

Before I can talk myself out of it, I go ahead and send my own flirty farewell message.

Me: *I'm off to my bath.*

Me: *Naked.*

Me: *With bubbles...*

Then I quickly exit the texting app, plug my phone into the charger on the counter, and head off to the bathroom with a grin on my face, ignoring the insistent chimes of his replies.

Chapter Five

Royce

"How's my favorite oldest son?" my mom asks, when she sees me standing at the counter at Sweet Treats Bakery.

"No need to throw in the word oldest. I know I'm your favorite, regardless of birth order," I tease.

She gives me a warm smile and shakes her head but doesn't rebuff my claim. There's no use. She knows I won't listen to it anyway. "This is a pleasant surprise," she says, as she wipes her wet hands on a towel and comes to the counter.

"Rueben called and is bored, so he's meeting me," I tell her, noticing Vivian, a woman a few years younger than me, staring at me with one of those grins. The one that says she's definitely interested in a little no-strings fun if I'd give her the slightest inkling I was willing. And not that I'm *not* willing, but I refuse to sleep with my mom's coworkers, despite how hot they are. That's a whole kettle of fish I'm not interested in getting into. Like sleeping with my own employees.

Not happening.

I throw Vivian a wink and a grin and return my attention to my mom. It's more flirtatious than an invitation, but I'm not sure she knows the difference. Mom glances over her shoulder and just shakes her head.

"What?"

She sighs. "Oh, nothing, Royce Daniel Rigsby. Nothing at all."

"Why are you middle naming me?"

"When are you going to settle down with a nice woman?" she huffs, crossing her arms over her chest and giving me a glare that means all business.

"Vivian's not nice?" I ask, knowing I'm prodding the bull. If I'm not careful, I'll get the horns in the form of a lecture from Jackie Rigsby.

Mom's gaze is pointed. "Don't sass me, Royce. You know what I mean. I'd like grandkids someday before I get too old to enjoy them."

Now it's my turn to roll my eyes. "You're fifty-eight. Hardly too old to enjoy grandkids," I argue. "Besides, I'm not the one getting married, Mom. Why don't you bug Rueben with your desire for grandkids?"

Just then the bell on the door chimes behind me. "You don't think I haven't mentioned it to him too? At least he's getting married," she says, her face softening with a smile as she looks over my shoulder. "To a wonderful young woman."

"I'm pretty sure that means I'm her favorite," my brother whispers in my ear, earning an elbow to the gut.

"That's not at all what she said before you walked in." I shrug and glance up at the menu.

Sweet Treats is a bakery first and foremost, but lately has added panini sandwiches and homemade side salads to the menu. Mom is usually in back, taking care of baking fresh breads, cookies, pies, and even cakes. It's also where I indulge in my cream cheese bars obsession. Ever since I was a little boy and Mom baked her first pan of strawberry cream cheese bars, I've been hooked.

"It's always the rotten sibling that continually draws the attention to the fact he's the favorite one," Rueben replies, pulling out his wallet.

"Put that away," Mom says, waving her hand dismissively.

"We don't come here so you can buy us food," he states, which is the truth. We come here because the food is excellent, service quick, and we get to see Mom.

"It's Rueben's turn to buy. Take his money," I tell her.

Mom just shakes her head and grabs a pen. "What would you boys like?"

"I'll have the turkey ranch panini with a side of coleslaw and a blueberry smoothie," I tell her, stepping aside so my brother can add his.

"I'll have the same but with a mango smoothie and also a chicken salad croissant with pasta salad and an iced chai tea with vanilla."

"Jesus, good thing you're buying if you're eating that much," I tease.

"Cricket is joining us." Just the mention of his fiancée's name brings a smile to his face. I've never been jealous of my brother, but there's something in the contentment and happiness I see on his face that causes a little bubble of something to rise in my chest.

Pushing it aside and refusing to dissect it, I say, "Of course she is. You can't go anywhere with your *girlfriend*."

"*Fiancée,* asshole. Get it right."

"Go sit down, both of you," Mom says as the door opens, and a small group of customers come in. "Maria's in back. I'll see if I can sit with you for a few minutes."

"Don't forget to collect his money!" I holler to her back as she slips through the swinging doors that lead to the massive kitchen.

"Hey, Royce," Vivian's singsong voice fills the room as she steps up to the vacant counter to collect the next group's orders.

"Hi, Viv," I reply politely.

Before I can slip away to join my brother, she asks, "Busy day today?" She pops her gum and juts out her hip in an attempt to look seductive.

"Not really. I'm off today," I confirm.

She leans forward so the group at the counter can't hear and presses her arms into her chest, causing her tits to protrude from her bakery V-neck shirt. "I really wish I was *off* today." She adds a wink, just for good measure.

I chuckle at her innuendo and give her one of my cocky grins.

Just as I start to reply something teetering on dirty, my brother hollers, "Royce, get over here," saving me from probably making Viv an offer I can't take back.

"Bye, Viv," I reply, turning and heading toward my brother, noticing her instant pout before I completely turn my back on her.

When I slip into my seat, he says, "Knock it off."

"What?" I ask innocently.

"Pssh! You know exactly what you're doing. Don't sleep with her," he whisper-yells so no one can hear him.

"I wasn't going to," I defend.

And I wouldn't. I can't. Not when my head is full of images of my blonde stranger on the porch from last night. It's hard to think of anyone else but her, which to be honest, is throwing me off my game. Add to it the parting comments from the other woman I've been randomly texting, and I'm a practically a walking hard-on today.

"What's going on with you?" he asks, knowing me too well.

"Nothing," I reply as Savannah, one of the bakery's part-timers, delivers our drinks.

"I call bullshit." He gives me a pointed look as he takes a drink of his smoothie.

"Where's Cricket?"

"Don't even try to change the subject. What's going on with you?" he asks with a little more authority. He's not going to let this go until I talk.

Exhaling loudly, I lean in so the entire room doesn't hear me. "I met someone."

His eyes go wide in shock. "Really?"

"Yes," I tell him, but to be honest, I'm not really sure which woman I'm talking about.

"And…"

I shrug. "And it's still pretty early, man." I'm not about to tell him I don't even know either of their names. "Can you just let me figure it out?"

"Okay, sure. Just know I'm here if you need me," he states. My hazel eyes meet his, and I nod in understanding and appreciation.

"Hey, guys!" Cricket sings as she enters the bakery and makes a beeline for our table.

"Hey, babe," my brother practically coos the moment his fiancée slides into the chair beside him, his lips meeting hers in greeting.

"Hi, Royce." Cricket is all smiles as she takes the empty seat across from me.

"Cricket. You come to your senses yet and ready to leave him for the better Rigsby?" I tease.

Rueben growls almost immediately, making me laugh. "You do that on purpose," Cricket chastises with a laugh.

"Is Royce bothering you, Cricket?" Mom asks, as she approaches our table with a tray of food.

"What? Why am I the guilty party automatically?" I ask my mom, enjoying the way her hazel eyes sparkle with laughter.

"Because I know you, Royce."

I reach over and take the food before she can serve us. She may work here, but I hate she has to do that. I instantly notice a fourth plate, so I scoot over to the chair against the wall, freeing up the closer seat for Mom.

"How are you, Jackie?" Cricket asks, as she dives into her pasta salad.

"Wonderful, dear. How's work?" she replies before taking a bite of half a ham panini sandwich.

"Busy. Our awards night and fundraiser is Saturday," my brother's fiancée replies.

With a mouthful of food, I ask, "Do you need a date? I'm free Saturday night." I barely get the offer out before I'm kicked in the shin under the table. "Ouch, fuck!" I grunt, dropping my food to rub my leg.

"Serves you right, dick," Rueben replies casually, as if he didn't just use his fucking boots to try to break my shin.

Giving Cricket a pointed look, I ask, "Do you see how mean he is?"

She smiles wide and giggles. "I believe you had that coming, Royce."

"My boys have always had a knack for pushing each other's buttons," Mom murmurs.

"Oh, Jackie, my mom and sister are coming down next weekend to go dress shopping. Can you go too?"

Out of the corner of my eye, I watch as Mom offers her a wide smile. "I'd love to go with you, dear. Thank you for inviting me," she replies, reaching over and squeezing Cricket's hand. She glances back at me. "Big plans for the afternoon?"

"Actually, I thought about adopting a dog," I tell my family between bites of my slaw.

"Really?" my brother and his fiancée both ask at the same time. Rueben's is more skeptical, while Cricket's is definitely excited.

"That'll be fun," Mom agrees.

"I've been wanting one for a while now, and I figured now is a good time, since the weather is still decent. Training a dog in the winter would suck," I state.

"And Rueben can help you when you're at work and the puppy needs to be taken outside," Cricket chimes in, causing her fiancé to gape at her in surprise.

"What?" my brother asks, sounding offended.

She shrugs and turns her eyes on me. "He can practice now for when we get a puppy."

"Say what?" he barks without a touch of bite. "Since when are we getting a puppy?" Cricket just smiles sweetly and bats her long eyelashes. I watch as she leans over and whispers something in his ear. His eyes widen and his cheeks turn pink as a wolfish grin spreads across his lips. "Apparently, I'm getting a dog too," he says eagerly, making me laugh.

"What kind are you looking for?" Mom asks.

"I'm not exactly sure. There's a few on the county's Humane Society page I'd like to look at."

"Well, bring it by when you decide."

"Us too!" Cricket adds between bites of her sandwich.

We finish eating just as Mom is summoned back to work by the growing lunch crowd. I clean up our mess on the table and slip up to the counter to tell her goodbye. I place a kiss on her cheek as she hands me a small white bag. "What's this?" I ask, my mouth already watering for whatever treat is inside.

"Must you ask?" she deadpans.

"Strawberry cream cheese bars?" I ask, like a kid who just received permission to go into a candy store.

She nods in reply. "One strawberry and one peach," she says with a wink.

"I knew I was your favorite!" I bellow, just loud enough for my brother to hear.

He steps up and reaches for the second bag in her other hand. "Oh, look at that. A bag for her real favorite son," Rueben says, as he leans over and kisses Mom's other cheek.

"You two." Mom glances behind us. "Cricket, this one's for you," she says, reaching behind the counter and grabbing a small platter of treats.

My mouth drops open. "What the hell?"

Cricket just giggles and steps forward. "At least now we know who the *real* favorite is. Thank you, Jackie. I'm sure everyone will love these back at work."

"Good." Mom looks over to me and my brother and adds, "Now, go. I have to get back to work. Be good, boys."

"Bye, Mom. Love ya," I reply as I head for the door, my brother and Cricket hot on my heels.

I find my brother's vehicle parked beside mine when we get outside, Cricket's SUV on the opposite side of that. He takes her dessert tray and places it on the passenger seat before pulling her into his arms and kissing her soundly. For a second time, something clenches in my chest, almost choking the air out of my throat. I have to look away.

"Make sure you send me that puppy pic, Royce," Cricket demands with a playful grin.

I return her smile, but not for the reason she's probably thinking. My very first text exchange with my new friend comes to mind, the dick pics she apparently received. Our exchanges are playful and fun, something I'm not used to having with the opposite sex outside of the bedroom.

"Will do," I reply with a wave, climbing into my truck.

Pulling out of the lot, I contemplate my next move. I have a few loads of laundry to do at home, but for some reason, my truck doesn't head in that direction. Instead, I find myself off toward the address I saw online. It takes a little longer to get there, considering it's the tail end of the noon hour, but when I finally do, I'm a mixture of nerves and excitement.

I shut off my truck and just sit there, staring at the large brick building with images of cats and dogs on the windows. Is this really what I want? A dog is a big commitment, one I can't take lightly. Not only could there be extra time with training, but my daily schedule would be altered to accommodate a dog. Plus, I don't have anything. I'd need food, bowls, a bed, and crate. I'd need to register him with the city, possibly deal with groomers, and keep up with his vet needs. Hell, I don't even go to the doctor myself. Am I ready for this responsibility?

The answer is yes.

I've been thinking about it a long time now, and always tell myself "someday soon." Well, as I open the door and climb out, "someday soon" is today.

The moment I pull open the front door, I can hear barking coming from the back. The front room is pet-friendly with bright yellow walls and old brown chairs. There are photos covering the walls of happy families with their new dogs or cats as they prepare to take them to their forever homes. A young man sits at the counter, a grin on his face as he places the phone on its cradle and turns to me. "Can I help you?"

"I was wanting to check out some dogs today." My heart is pounding in my chest like a jackhammer.

"Awesome," he sings, spinning in his chair and coming around to meet me with his hand extended. "We'd be happy to help. I'm Landon, the manager. Come have a seat." He grabs a clipboard and pen and leads me over to the old chairs.

We go through a few questions about what I'm looking for, Landon smiling the entire time we talk. "Oh my gosh, I'm so excited. We have a handful of larger breed dogs that would be perfect for you. Would you like to go back and see them?"

"Absolutely," I reply, standing up and wiping my sweaty palms on my jeans.

Why am I so damn nervous?

Seriously, I wasn't even this anxious when I went to pick up my junior year prom date, who just so happened to be a senior with well-known oral skills. She proved it about halfway through the dance in the parking lot too.

Landon leads me through a door and the barking becomes louder. We pass a large room with a handful of cats inside. Some are sleeping, one is eating, and a few play with toys. I instantly think back to my conversation with Bestie and the cat she said she had as a child. She would probably get a kick out of seeing them all.

We proceed through another doorway and find a wall of kennels, two high. They're all separated by a metal frame for stability, with smaller dogs on top. "So why don't you take a walk along this wall and let me know if you'd like to see any of the dogs. There's a sign on the front that tells you their breed, age, and name," Landon instructs, stepping back and giving me space.

I slowly walk along the wall, checking out each dog, including the smaller ones. I can't help but smile. There are pups of every shape and size, every color and breed. Some lounge and sleep, while others are spinning in circles in excitement at seeing a person. Tails wag eagerly and a few even bark when I approach.

A medium-sized dog with big floppy ears gives me those puppy eyes, and a bark of laughter slips from my lips. "Bucky has the face down pat," I say over my shoulder to Landon, who lingers off to the side.

"Oh, he does. He's been here about two months, but I know his day is coming soon."

I nod and keep walking, recognizing this decision is much harder than I expected. I suddenly realize if I were able to take them all and give them a loving home, I would. In a heartbeat. Unfortunately, that's not an option for me, so I keep walking until I reach the empty kennel at the end.

Suddenly, a loud bark pulls my attention behind me. When I turn, I see a large mix breed dog, wet from a bath, sitting in the middle of the floor. He's on a leash with a shelter volunteer next to him, trying to dry him off. A smile instantly spreading across my face, my heart galloping around in my chest.

I squat down on a knee, and something flashes in that dog's eyes. He takes off like a bullet from a gun, pulling free from the volunteer, and running right for me. He hits me with a wall of wet dog hair and rains kisses down all over my face. I don't even know when I started laughing, but I am, petting this big, hairy dog with a tail so wild it would probably hurt if you were hit by it.

"Royce, meet Jack," Landon says, as he walks up beside me and reaches for his leash. "He was just enjoying a bath and apparently couldn't wait to be dried off to say hello."

My face hurts from smiling so widely as I scratch behind his ears. "Landon, I think I'd like to take Jack home with me today."

Chapter Six

Quinn

I start to wonder if this meeting will ever end. After I've given my principal's report, I sit back as they go through different committee reports and school correspondences, including the latest financial statement. We're a private K-12 school, funded through tuition, fundraising, and grants and have been very fortunate to have maintained a balanced budget for several years. Of course, it helps having alumni benefactors who've left money to the school in trusts and wills.

When the meeting finally draws to a close, a few board members come over to talk. As anxious as I am to get out of here and throw on a pair of lounge pants, my attention is required here. I spend a few minutes chatting with Mrs. Louise Seymour, a retired faculty member of our school, as well as Mr. John Billingsly, the president of the board. Both are anxious to start working on a plan to upgrade the old wooden bleachers in the gymnasium with something a little safer and easier to retract. It's an expense that will be great but needed.

"I'd like to present estimates to the board next month, Quinn. It's something that's been on our list of future repairs, and now that the school heating project is complete, I feel this is a worthy next plan for our fundraising efforts," John says as he adjusts his tie.

"I agree. I can start working on gathering estimates and have some available for the board at our next meeting," I confirm, making a note in my planner.

"That would be great," he agrees, offering a hand to shake.

When he walks away, Louise gives me a smile. "You're doing a fine job, Quinn."

Louise was the outgoing history teacher when I was hired as her replacement at Grace Private School. We were able to work together throughout that summer, her offering precious guidance to a young educator, straight out of college. I learned so much from her and often leaned on her for advice regarding lessons and projects. I was a very hands-on teacher and loved bringing history to life in the classroom setting. She was also the one who recommended me to the board for the principal position three years ago.

I had a newly earned master's degree in education and eager to use it. When our principal received an offer at a larger school upstate, he left big shoes to fill within these school walls, but I've enjoyed the challenge. It's definitely a much more rewarding job than even I could have anticipated.

"I think the meeting went well," Louise says, her voice still holding the hint of authority it had in her teaching days.

"I agree."

"You're doing an exceptional job, Quinn. I'm proud of you," she adds with a warm smile.

I've always looked to Louise for the advice in this field. My own mother is a homemaker, while my dad works as a mechanic. Neither really knew much about my profession of choice, even though they've been supportive my whole life. That's why I gravitated toward Louise when it came to matters of my career.

"It's been a joy to serve the board and students in this capacity. You know, after I enrolled in those night classes for my master's, a few times I wondered if I was making the right choice. I mean, did I really need to accumulate more debt in my early thirties when I still had some from college? But now, even with that mountain of student loans, I'm so thankful I proceeded with the schooling. This is definitely the job for me," I state openly.

Louise just smiles that familiar, warm grin, reaches over, and squeezes my arm lightly. "Like I said, I'm proud of you, Quinn. You are absolutely the right person for this job," she says, causing a hard lump to form in my throat.

"Thank you," I whisper, emotions grabbing hold and refusing to let go.

"I should be on my way, dear. Maybe we can meet for lunch soon?"

"I'd love that, Louise. I'll call you first of next week to set it up?"

"Sounds wonderful. Take care, dear," she says, as she pulls me into a hug. It's familiar, her rich floral perfume tickling my nose and making me smile.

I watch as she exits the meeting room, followed by the few lingering board members. When I'm finally alone, I breathe a deep sigh and kick off my kitten heels. It's been a long day, working over thirteen hours, only breaking long enough to grab a takeout crab salad from the deli down the street. Then it was right back here, preparing for tonight's meeting.

It only takes me about twenty more minutes to wrap everything up and shut off the lights. I make sure my office is secured, slide my shoes back on my feet, and head out the side door that leads to the staff parking lot. As I'm walking to my car, my phone chimes with a text in my purse. My guess is it's one of two people, and the thought of it being from Rigsby has my heart fluttering in my chest like a butterfly. I force myself to leave my phone where it is until I'm secured in the cab of my car. Then, and only then, do I pull it from my bag and click on the message app. The moment I see the name, I smile.

Rigsby: *I have someone I'd like you to meet.*

Me: *Is that your intro, and then BAM, dick pic?*

Funny, because suddenly an image pops up on the screen and starts to download. My heart skips a beat at the prospect of actually getting an inappropriate picture from Rigsby. Something tells me, I wouldn't be at all disappointed.

But it's not the image I was expecting. Instead, I see what can only be described as a smiling dog. A bubble of laughter spills from my lips.

Rigsby: *Meet Jack, as in Jack Daniels.*

Me: *Oh my goodness, that face!!!* *insert heart-shaped eyes emoji*

Rigsby: *He's got a lady-killer smile, what can I say? It was like we were meant to be together.*

Me: *I don't have a wide knowledge about dogs. There's definitely German Shepherd in him, right?*

Rigsby: *Yep, Shepherd and golden retriever.*

Me: *So tell me about it! How did you know to pick Jack?*

Rigsby: *Well, Jack picked me. They had about two dozen dogs and each one would have probably worked, honestly. When I got to the end of the row, Jack was coming out of a bath, soaking wet, and jumped at me. He licked me straight across the face. I knew he was my dog.*

Me: *That's seriously the sweetest thing ever.*

Rigsby: *He's two and belonged to a state trooper. She was killed by a drunk driver while helping a disabled car about four months ago. The shelter said the owner's dad tried to hang on to him, but he lived in a small apartment and it wasn't a good fit for Jack long term.*

Me: *That's terrible.*

Rigsby: *I'll admit, the story choked me up a little.*

Me: *Have you gotten him all settled?*

Rigsby: *Yep. We went to the pet store and I bought my next paycheck's worth of dog stuff. When we got home, he went out and marked his territory for about ten minutes before even coming inside the house. We went for a long run too, which was interesting. I've never ran with a leashed dog before, and he was very interested in sniffing everything.*

Rigsby: *Plus, there was a squirrel incident, but we're not getting into that tonight.*

I laugh out loud and scroll back up to see the photo of the dog. He's sitting on a porch, his tongue dangling from the side of his mouth, with a new red collar on his neck. I scan the background and see a pretty stellar view of the mountainside. I can't help but wonder if that's Risgby's home and where exactly it's located.

Rigsby: *Anyway, I just wanted you two to meet. When I told him you were my Bestie, he didn't seem to take too kindly to the insinuation that he's my number two.*

Warmth spreads through my veins. How can that be? I've never even met this man, yet here I am, getting all schoolgirl excited about the prospect of my sudden high ranking, even though I know it's complete bullshit. A man like this is way too charismatic, too flirty. If I'm at the top of his friends list, I'm probably in the company of about a dozen other women.

Me: *It's still early in your relationship. I'm sure he'll shoot past your never-met-before bestie in no time.*

Rigsby: *I'm hurt you'd insinuate I'd just replace you the moment I get a dog.*

I can't help but giggle. It's a relaxed, light sound, one that always seems to come easily when I'm talking to him.

Rigsby: *You know, we could remedy that. I could send you a pic, one that's not of my dick. Unless you want me to send one.* *insert winky face emoji* *insert eggplant emoji*

A gasp slips from my throat at the prospect. Do I want to see Rigsby? Well, yes, actually I do, but I'm not sure that's for the best. And no, I'm not talking about down under. Although, I wouldn't mind seeing that image either. But there's something fun about the mystery of talking to him and not really knowing who he is. Is he gorgeous (that's probably a yes) or have a potbelly and live in his mother's basement? I'm not leaning that direction, not after the sweatpants photo.

Rigsby: *I can see you're considering my offer. Just let me know when to send you the pic. Dick or otherwise.*

Me: *You're incorrigible.*

Rigsby: *I know. You tell me often.*

Rigsby: *Well, time to take Jack out for his nightly bathroom break. TTYL*

Me: *Did you really just type TTYL? Are you a thirteen-year-old girl?*

Rigsby: *LOL! No, I'm just a lazy guy.*

Me: *I'll let it pass, but be careful so your teenage girl doesn't show again…*

Rigsby: *You sound like my brother.*

Me: *He sounds smart.*

Rigsby: *He's not. He's a terrible nuisance.*

Me: *Spoken like a true sibling. Older or younger?*

Rigsby: *I'm older by two years.*

Me: *I wish I had a sibling.*

Rigsby: *None?*

Me: *Nope, only child.*

Rigsby: *Sometimes, I'd say you were the lucky one, but I admit, I'm glad to have my brother. He's my best friend.*

I can't help but smile at the sentiment. That's exactly how I imagined it would be to have a little brother or sister. Someone who annoyed me to the point I wished I was an only child, but then to have a person who's like a best friend, who always has your back, who's a call away when you need to talk or veg out with Chinese food.

Me: *Should I be jealous?*

Rigsby: *Naw, he's not nearly as pretty as you.* *insert winky face emoji*

Me: *You've never even seen me!*

Rigsby: *My imagination has been working ever since you sent me that accidental text Tuesday night, Bestie.*

Why am I smiling so big?

Rigsby: *OK, I really have to go. Jack is standing by the back door glaring at me.*

Me: *LOL! Goodbye.*

I set my phone down in the cup holder and turn the ignition. As I head out of the empty parking lot, I'm still grinning like a lunatic, wondering what I've really gotten myself into with this man. It should probably bother me more than it does that I'm so friendly with a stranger, but he doesn't feel like one. Even only a few days into this weird texting exchange, he feels more like a friend I've known for years.

Someone I can banter with.

Maybe even flirt with a little.

Harmless.

I've never been one to engage in flirting, my personality a little more reserved. Yet here I am, doing just that so freely. Even though it's nerve-wracking to step out of my comfort zone with guys, it's been fun to flirt a little. And not just my mystery texter, but with the runner too. There's definitely some attraction there, and it appears to not be one-sided. I've caught him checking me out.

My lips turn upward in another grin.

Look at me.

Having fun.

***

"I can't believe it's a Friday night and you're shopping," Sabrina grumbles from behind the counter as I browse a selection of leather handbags.

Slip Into Style Boutique is empty on this Friday evening, which means my best friend can turn off her filter. "Why not? Is Friday not a good time to buy new clothes?" I ask, finding a gorgeous red leather handbag with black stitching.

I can feel Sabrina's eye roll all the way over here. "You're supposed to be out, having dinner, getting laid."

Now it's my turn to roll my eyes. "Maybe I just wanted to visit with my best friend for a little bit this evening."

She steps around the wide counter and approaches, a mischievous grin on her pale face. "I was going to text you later. I have excitement to share."

"Do tell," I reply, checking out the inside of the handbag. It has a soft gold liner with a few pockets, perfect for my phone, ink pens, lip balm.

"We're going on a date," she boasts proudly.

My wide eyes meet her happy ones. "A what?"

"Remember earlier in the week, I told you I was going to ask those two guys from the coffee house down the street to join us for dinner?"

Dread fills my entire body as I gape at my best friend. Wait. *Former* best friend. "What did you do?" I whisper.

"I invited them to have burgers and drinks with us tomorrow night, and they accepted."

"Sabrina," I whine, stomping my little black kitten heel on the industrial carpet. "Why?"

"Because you need to have some fun, let your hair down," she practically demands as she steps aside to straighten the wallets. "And because they're totally cute," she adds with a wiggle of her eyebrows.

"How old are they, Rina? Seriously? That one with dark hair looks like he just graduated college."

My best friend shrugs her shoulders and moves about the display area. "Early thirties?"

"I'm thirty-eight. Thirty. Eight. I have no business going out with anyone born in the decade after mine," I reply, trying to wrap my head around the fact she thought this was a good idea.

"Oh, stop," she says, placing her hands on her hips and giving me a pointed look. "You don't have to marry him, Q, just screw him. Younger men have fabulous stamina." She's really excited about this.

"I don't think so."

"You're going and that's final. I'll take the younger one, and you can have Lance. He's the manager and probably a little more your type."

I take the handbag and set it on the counter. The sudden stress calls for a new bag. "I can't believe you're making me do this."

"Oh, I'm makin'," she says, coming around the counter to ring up my purchase. "This is a great color and very bold for you. I'm proud."

"It's so pretty and soft."

"And tomorrow night, you'll have dinner with pretty Lance and hopefully, he'll be all sorts of hard."

I groan at her dirty pun as I pull my wallet from my purse. "Where are we going?"

"Pork's. I'll pick you up before seven."

With my debit card in hand, I reply, "I can meet you there."

Sabrina's already shaking her head. "Heck no. If I pick you up, there's no way you can weasel out of it."

I scoff at her comment, but don't deny it. There's no use. I would totally skip the dinner or "accidentally" forget. Exhaling a deep breath, I finally ask, "Is this like a *date* date?"

Her eyes soften as she glances up. She knows my track record with dates lately. Most of them don't make it to a second one, and the ones who do never get to the magical fifth date either. It's been so long since I've had a fifth date, I barely remember what sex feels like. I think my last bedroom encounter was Paul, my boyfriend of two years. We were at the critical impasse—move in or let go. Sadly, it didn't hurt as bad to let go as I expected it to.

"No, honey, not a *date* date. It's more of friends hanging out. Pork's has the best food, so we'll grab some sandwiches and a few drinks. It's a Saturday night so there might even be a band later. Plus, a seven o'clock meet-up gives us plenty of time to end the evening early, if you don't feel it's going well."

I give my friend a relieved smile. "Thank you." I reach for my bag and add, "I guess I'll see you tomorrow before seven."

"Sounds good," she says through a yawn.

As I head to the door, I stop and turn around. "Oh, I almost forgot, I have that ziplining thing tomorrow afternoon with Logan. He's so excited for his reward."

"Are you going with him?"

I shake my head. "No way. I'll be much happier with both feet on the ground at all times."

"Have fun, and wear something cute!" she hollers, as I head out the door and toward my vehicle.

When I slide behind the wheel, I do a quick catalog of my closet's content. There's a lot of business professional and business casual attire and not a whole lot of anything else. There's my lounging around the house outfits of leggings, shorts, and tees, but I would never wear those on a date. I usually wear black slacks and a nice shirt. Simple. Classic.

But I won't be able to wear that to Pork's. That place has more of a blue jeans and boots feel to it. Sighing, I back out of my parking spot and head home. I'm sure there's something in my closet that won't make me look like a schoolteacher.

Right?

Chapter Seven

Royce

I glance at today's reservation schedule for the thousandth time, wondering who Bestie is. There's a handful of people planned for the two o'clock session, but these names mean dick to me. The reservation could be under the boy's dad's name or even his name. I could drive myself completely fucking insane trying to figure out which of these six names on the schedule could be associated with my mystery texter.

I made sure to set up the schedule so I was the guide and training the two o'clock group. There's eight total in this session, six individuals and two couples. They should be arriving anytime to start the paperwork process. They're instructed to arrive at least fifteen to twenty minutes early, especially during weekends where traffic is heavier and tourism is high.

As I make my way down to the front office, I pull out my phone.

Me: *Are you excited?*

Bestie Tami with an I: *For???*

Me: *Ziplining*

Bestie Tami with an I: *I'm not ziplining today, just accompanying a student.*

Me: *Too bad. It's a pretty awesome thrill.*

Bestie Tami with an I: *I'll take your word for it.*

Bestie Tami with an I: *I should probably go. I just got here and see my student.*

I can't help but glance ahead to the office, where a handful of people stand or sit at one of the picnic tables.

Me: *Enjoy*

Slipping my phone back into my pocket, I don't even fight the grin on my face as I make my way around to the side of the office. I step inside and head to Jill, the employee taking care of the front end of things today.

"Hey," I say, as I take the clipboard she's already handing to me.

"Hi, Royce. We have seven already signed in. The last two are filling out the paperwork now. Should be another minute or two and you can head up."

"Why seven? I thought the schedule had eight?"

Jill shrugs. "One of the two-for-one coupons only had one check in."

I glance out at the group, my eyes drawn instantly to a blonde. Even from behind, I can't take my eyes off her. She's wearing khaki shorts and a polo shirt in a Kelly green color and her hair is pulled up high on the top of her head in a ponytail. There's a professional air to her, even as she visits with a high school aged boy and who are probably his parents. The sound of her laugh floats with the breeze and through the open windows, desire rushing through my blood like a tidal wave.

I'm completely enthralled.

"Which group only had the one check in?" I ask, my eyes still stuck on the blonde beauty.

Jill steps up beside me and scans the crowd. "That boy and his parents checked in," she says, pointing to where my eyes are locked. "By that woman with the green shirt."

A slow smile spreads across my lips at the prospect of going to speak to her. I grab the clipboard, which contains their coupon for two, and give it a quick scan before heading out into the sunlight. As I approach, I slip my sunglasses into place, but hide my eyes enough that everyone around me can't tell I'm checking her out.

"Logan Hendershot?" I ask as I step up behind her.

"That's me!" the tall, lanky boy says, raising his hand in the air like he's asking a question in class.

The blonde turns around with a smile on her face and completely steals my breath. "It's you," she whispers, her eyes wide beneath aviator shades.

I can't help but laugh. "Wow, I wasn't expecting to see you here," I say to the woman I met earlier in the week. The woman from the little white house. The one who dropped her glass of tequila and prompted me to go out and purchase her a new bottle. She's here.

What are the odds?

"What are you doing here?" she asks, glancing around before her eyes land on my Elevate embroidered polo shirt.

"I work here," I answer, lifting my name badge lanyard up so she can see the photo and name.

"Royce," she whispers and a shot of lust bolts through my blood, landing square in my groin.

Our eyes meet again, smiles spreading across our lips. "You're taking a trip today?" I ask, stepping forward a little. Not too close to where I'm invading her personal space, but close enough to smell the vanilla and jasmine on her skin. It's intoxicating.

"Oh, no, not me," she says, shaking her head as if to reiterate her emphatic words. She steps to the side and places a hand on the boy's shoulder. "This is Logan Hendershot, and he is my Student Inspiration Award winner for the month. The reward he chose was to go ziplining," she says, smiling up at the student beside her.

Something prickles in the back of my mind as I consider her words. It's weird. When we were chatting in front of her house, we never discussed ziplining or her job. Yet, this conversation sounds oddly...familiar.

"Well, Logan, you're going to have a great time," I tell the boy as I shake his hand. Turning to his parents, I add, "We'll take good care of him." Both mom and dad seem nervous, but eager for their son's experience. Turning back to the blonde beauty, I ask, "Are you going on the second pass?"

She glances up at me with ice-blue questioning eyes. "Excuse me?"

"The second pass. The deal you purchased online was for a double experience," I tell her, trying not to stare, but failing miserably.

The look on her face is almost comical. "Oh, uh..."

"Yes! You can come with me, Miss Michaels. Please?" Logan pleads with the woman before me.

"Logan, I don't know," she replies, wringing her hands together nervously in front of her.

I step forward and reach out, unable to stop myself from touching her arm. Her skin is warm and soft and does bad things to my cock in front of present company. Yet, I'm unable to actually drop my hand. Just that slightest touch makes me feel grounded and calm. "You'll be safe the entire time, I promise. It's an experience like no other."

She's wavering, clearly at battle with herself here. On one side, it's not her thing. Even with every safety measure in place, this woman likes control. But I also can see her desire to do something...fun. Something unsafe. Something that makes her feel alive and free. That's why I go for the kill. "Double dog dare you."

Her eyes go wide as I lay down the gauntlet and issue her the challenge. A moment ago, I sensed she was about to decline, but now, I see the fire. The excitement. She opens her mouth and our eyes lock once more, she whispers, "Okay." Her smile mirrors my own and I feel it strike my chest with the force of a thousand arrows. It pierces my soul, cracking the tough exterior, and sending sunlight filtering through those crevasses for the first time in...well, ever.

"Let's get you signed in," I state, handing her the clipboard. There's a slight tremble in her hand as she takes the board. When she reaches for the pen, our fingers touch, a gentle graze that sparks electricity through my limbs.

As she fills out the form, I turn to address the rest of the group. "Good afternoon. I'm Royce and I'll escort you up the mountain today. We have beautiful weather with clear skies for your trip. The entire process will take less than two hours. We're almost set to head up, so if you'll head over to the UTVs over there," I say, pointing to the roadway behind the office, "We'll be ready to get started in just a few minutes."

When I turn back around, the beautiful blonde is watching me with assessing eyes. "Here," she says, practically throwing the clipboard at me nervously.

A wide smile spreads across my face. Glancing down, I see the name printed across the top line. Quinn Michaels. Feminine. Regal. Beautiful. Like her. "You're going to have the time of your life, Quinn. Trust me."

She swallows hard, searching my eyes for any signs I'm bullshitting her, before she finally nods in agreement. "All right. Let's go."

Logan waves to his parents, who have their cameras ready to go. We make our way to the UTVs where Justin is waiting by the second one. He has three guys and a woman with him, and it's the first time I really stop and take in the rest of the group. They're all men, with the exception of two women. One has her hand nestled in a man's on the other UTV, and the second woman is walking beside me.

Suddenly, reality hits me like a bolt of thunder.

Quinn is Bestie.

My Bestie.

She has to be.

My heart beats wildly in my chest as everyone climbs on the UTV. Logan and two guys slide on the back, while Quinn hops on the seat beside me. When everyone is buckled in, we take off, heading toward the mountain. I slip easily into guide mode, telling them all about our experience and the Great Smoky Mountains. Quinn holds onto the "oh shit" handle like she's afraid I might bounce her out of the open vehicle.

My mind is reeling as we proceed up, making our way to the first landing. I need to find out more, engage her in conversation so I can determine for a fact whether or not she's Bestie Tami with an I. "So you're a teacher?" I ask, recalling how she told me she was taking a student ziplining.

"I'm a principal, actually," she says, the blonde hair of her ponytail blowing gently in the breeze.

"And you're here because he won a reward?" I ask.

"Yep."

"You've never been ziplining?"

"No way. It's not really my thing," she says softly, glancing my way out of the corner of her eye.

"Why'd you choose Elevate?" I ask casually, even though I feel anything but.

"The reviews were outstanding online and it has stellar safety ratings," she replies, looking out at the gorgeous landscape. "A friend told me you were the best."

The corner of my lip turns up. "Your friend sounds very smart."

I can feel her roll her eyes as she turns back to me. "He's annoying at best," she sasses, making me bark out a laugh. When I glance her way, she's grinning and taking me in. Our eyes lock, and I expect her to look away, but she doesn't.

When we finally reach the top of the mountain, I park in my designated spot and turn off the engine. We're about to lock up personal belongings before we go over the procedure for ziplining and get them outfitted in their harnesses. I have only a little window to confirm my suspicions.

"We're about to lock up any extra personal effects in a lockbox that I'll take back down the mountain with me. Any items inside will be at the main office where you signed in to claim," I tell them, as I lead them to the small building we have set up for our operation. "There'll be a clear pouch attached to your harness. You'll be able to place a small camera or cell phone inside and still use them on your trip down."

I reach in my pocket, making sure I'm standing beside Quinn. "Oh, excuse me, I need to send a quick message."

I type out a quick message, reminding myself to breathe.

Me: *Ready to go ziplining?*

The moment I click send, my heart climbs into my throat. My heart completely stops beating when I hear a chime coming from the pocket of Quinn's khaki shorts. I watch, helpless to say or do anything, as she pulls it out and smiles. That smile. The most gorgeous, easy-going grin I've ever seen.

She glances up and says, "I'm so sorry."

I give her a tight grin. "No worries. Go ahead and reply," I tell her with a shrug.

Her full lips turn upward, and her fingers fly over the screen. I make sure to stay close so she can hear my phone when she replies. A moment later, my phone notifies me to a text. She glances up and meets my gaze, but I don't think she truly catches on yet.

Bestie Tami with an I: *They talked me into going. Can you believe that?*

Quinn goes to slide her phone back into her pocket as I type out my reply. There are so many ways I can go with this, but I realize I don't want to string her along. I don't want to play games.

Me: *You're going to love it. Oh, and you look beautiful in green, Bestie.*

Send.

Just as her hand leaves the device, it chimes again. She glances around, specifically at Logan, and I wonder if she's going to read the message. I can tell she's professional, and part of that is not texting someone while you're in the company of others. But curiosity gets the better of her as she carefully slips the phone back out and reads the message.

I know the moment she sees my words.

Her eyes widen and dart around, as if she's trying to find out where Rigsby is and how the hell he knows she is wearing green. I keep my eyes trained on her, and the moment they meet, it's like the lightbulb goes on. We just stare at each other for a minute, neither really knowing what to say. Finally, I extend my hand. "Nice to meet you, Bestie Tami with an I. I'm Royce Rigsby."

She gasps, her beautiful mouth falling open as she gapes at me. Quinn doesn't move for several long seconds, and I start to get a little sweaty under the collar, wondering if she's about to leave me hanging or bolt. Her soft blue eyes search mine, and after what feels like the world's longest ten seconds, she finally places her much smaller hand in mine and squares her shoulders. "Quinn Michaels. Nice to meet you, Rigsby." Her voice is strong and so fucking sexy.

I can tell she's still in a state of shock over the revelation, mostly because I'm feeling it too. I hate that we can't just sit down and talk, but unfortunately, now is not the time. I have a job to do, so that's why I release her hand, step to her side, and turn to face the group. "Welcome to Elevate. Justin and I are going to go over all of the safety measures in place, as well as give you a quick tutorial on today's adventure. Let's head over to the shed, so we can give you the experience of a lifetime."

Turning to Quinn, who's gone stiff and a bit pale, I add, "I'd love to visit with you afterward. I think we have a lot to talk about."

She makes a noise in agreement. I place my hand on her lower back and gently guide her to the group.

I spend the next twenty minutes going over the spiel I can recite in my sleep, making sure to pay close attention to Quinn. She listens intently, like she's making mental notes on every do and don't I mention, but doesn't make eye contact. Logan wears a smile the entire time, especially when we start outfitting everyone in their harnesses.

Quinn takes my final harness and slides her feet into the holes. Justin is making sure Logan's is tight and fits properly, while I take great pleasure in doing the same for Quinn. She maneuvers it into place and gazes up at me under long eyelashes. I keep my eyes locked on hers as I reach around her waist and secure the belt. Then, I slip the other latches into place and give them a tug, my arms grazing against hers, the backs of my hands sliding against her abdomen. When I know she's good and secure, I finally glance down and take in my handiwork.

"You've done this a time or two," she says, a teasing tone in her angelic voice.

"A few times," I confirm with a smirk. "But you're definitely the prettiest I've ever had my hands on." With a wink, I turn and step into the center of the group.

I clap my hands and smile at my group. "Are you ready?"

Cheers echo through the trees as Justin takes one zipline and I take the second. They line up across from each other, with the couple going first. Justin secures the female onto the line, while I do the same. Everyone stays back, yet watches with excitement-filled eyes as we get them ready for the first leg of their ride.

"Just sit back and enjoy the ride. Our team will take care of you," I tell them, nodding to Justin, who radios down to the next platform that runners are on the course. "Ready?" I ask with a wide smile. If I'm not out on the line myself, this is the next best thing. The eagerness, the thrill I see reflected in their eyes the very first time they run the mountain. "Three, two, one..." I countdown, and they're off.

Their laughter and screams of delight fill the air as we watch them dart down and to the left, heading toward their first platform. I turn to glance back, catching sight of Quinn in the back, peeking around the side of another guy. I give her a reassuring smile as our next twosome steps up to be secured to the line.

We proceed through the group, waiting until the previous runners get to the second platform before sending the next group. This gives my team enough time to make sure the platform is clear before their next visitors.

When we're finally down to two, Quinn steps up with fear in her eyes. It's not a complete terror—I've seen that before here—but more of a nervousness. She's able to walk and talk, and that's definitely a good thing. As she steps up beside me, I can't help but reach out and place my hand on her arm. "You ready?"

She just gazes at me and swallows hard. Then, she takes a deep cleansing breath and says, "I'm ready."

"You got this, Miss Michaels," Logan says beside her, while Justin makes sure he's secure and safe.

"I'll see you at the bottom, Bestie," I tell her, throwing her a cocky grin.

"Are you really Rigsby?" she whispers, her eyes searching mine.

My hand brushes a piece of hair that falls out of her helmet. "I really am. I had no idea Bestie was you until we started talking and things started adding up. You said you were coming to Elevate, and well, I made sure to put myself on the schedule for this group."

"You really had no idea?"

"None," I tell her honestly. "I was chatting with this fun woman via text and then happened to meet this gorgeous woman on her front porch around the same time." I toy with that sprig of hair, loving the way it softly moves through my fingers. "I still can't quite believe you're actually the same woman."

She chuckles in disbelief. "No kidding." Her eyes meet mine once more. "What are the odds?"

"I'd say we were destined to meet, Bestie Tami with an I. Now, I'm going to send your cute ass down the mountain for the ride of your life. Keep your eyes open and enjoy, okay?"

She nods and glances at her student. "You ready, Logan?"

"I'm more than ready! I can't wait to do this," he says, practically bouncing where he stands.

I hear the cue to send the runners come over my walkie-talkie. "Alright, go ahead and have a seat in the harness," I tell them. An idea pops into my head and I quickly pull out my cell phone. "Hey, both of you look this way and smile," I say, taking a few pictures of them right before they head down. Shoving my phone back into my pocket, our eyes meet one last time. I step up to the switch that releases the brake and start the countdown.

"Three…two…one…"

And then I let them go, sailing down the side of the mountain.

Chapter Eight

Quinn

I want to scream, but when I open my mouth, nothing comes out. I'm stuck in some parallel universe with breathtaking views and steep mountain terrain. It might actually be the most beautiful sight I've ever witnessed with my own two eyes.

"Holy crap!" Logan bellows beside me through his laughter. "This is amazing," he adds, turning and glancing my way.

I snap out of my fog to return his wide smile. Reaching down, I grab the pouch and open my photo app. I don't start snapping pictures of our beautiful surroundings. At least, not yet. First, I aim my device at Logan and take photo after photo of his very first zipline ride. I watch as he leans back, extends his arms out to the side, and enjoys the fall. It's the most serene and spectacular experience to witness. Then, I turn the camera area and take a selfie—something I *never* do—to document this momentous occasion.

Before I know it, we're reaching the first platform stop. There's a gentleman there to greet us and get us situated for the next run. It happens pretty quickly and professionally, and all I need to do is sit back and take it in.

"You good, Logan?" I ask, glancing to the student beside me.

"Miss Michaels, this is pretty much the best day of my life," he announces with tears in his eyes. "Thank you for making this the greatest birthday ever."

My own eyes get a little misty as I gaze over at the young man. "You earned this reward, Logan. You're working hard in school and outside of it, and that hasn't gone unnoticed. You have a bright future ahead of you," I tell him.

His face practically splits in half with his smile as we get the cue to make our next run. The view is just as spectacular as we fly over a small stream and see wildlife frolicking around. It's hard to believe I've ever had reservations about ziplining, because this is an experience I'll treasure forever.

By the time we make it down the mountain, my face hurts from smiling and I have dozens of photos as keepsakes. When my feet hit the final platform, I see Rigsby—or Royce, as he happens to be—standing off to the side, taking photos with his phone. He slips it into his back pocket and makes his way toward me. There's a swagger in his walk, a confidence he possesses that seems to seep from his pores.

He takes the steps two at a time and is right in front of me moments later. Royce turns his attention to Logan and asks, "Well? How was it?"

"Dude! That was amazing! More than amazing, it was...just..." Logan struggles to find the right words, making Royce laugh.

"I totally get it, man. I come down the mountain every night that way. Now that you have the bug, you'll always find a reason to run a line, and there are definitely some beautiful ones around the world."

Logan's eyes are alive with excitement as he drinks in every word Royce says. "That's so cool. Where have you ziplined?"

"Colorado and New York in the United States, as well as Puerto Rico and New Zealand."

The young boy's mouth practically drops to his shoes. "Seriously?"

"Yeah, I was in the Army and was fortunate to catch some amazing sights while serving our country."

"Wow, that's badass," Logan replies. His parents are near the platform and wave.

"Go on down, Logan, and I'll be there in a second," I tell him, watching as he takes off to show his parents the photos he took.

"Well?" he asks when we're alone on the platform.

"It was pretty amazing," I concede with a grin.

"Told ya," he replies, bumping his shoulder into mine. "Here, let's get that harness put away." Royce reaches over and unclips the buckles. Once again, his hand brushes against my side accidentally, but not in an inappropriate way. Though, when he gives me that cocky smirk, I wonder if it was intentional after all.

"I should head over and talk to Logan's parents one last time and grab my keys from the office," I state.

He glances over my shoulder, taking in the happy birthday boy and his parents. "Do you have a few minutes to talk afterward?" Royce shoves his hands into his pockets casually and rocks back on his heels.

"Umm, sure."

He nods, and while I head down the stairs to where the Hendershots wait, Royce cleans up the gear from our run down the mountain. Logan is animatedly telling his parents about his trip, showing them photo after photo of the scenery. "Thanks, again, Miss Michaels. Today was awesome," he says when I join the group.

"You're most welcome. Can I send your parents these photos I took of you?" I ask, pulling my phone back out of my pocket.

"That would be great," he replies, reciting his cell phone number so I can forward the pictures.

After we visit for a few more minutes, and I confirm his mom received what I sent her, I head to the office to retrieve my keys. I locked my purse in my trunk, since I had already paid when I booked the experience. I wanted to have my hands free to document his trip. Little did I know, I'd be dared to join Logan by the very man who has been monopolizing my thoughts.

When I grab my keys from the woman at the counter, my phone chimes with a text message. Pulling it out, I spy a series of photos, but not from Logan. From Rigsby.

The first one is of Logan and I as we get ready for our trip down the mountain. I don't know how Rigsby—or *Royce*—snapped this photo without my knowledge, but he managed. But it's the second one that has a bubble of laughter spilling from my lips. Royce is standing to the left of the frame with a big, goofy grin and a thumbs-up, and there in the background is me, gazing out over the mountain with every ounce of nerves I felt showing on my face.

"That's a horrible picture," I mumble, shaking my head.

"I think it sums us up perfectly." The voice comes from behind and very close. I can feel his body heat pressed up against me, and for one fleeting moment, I wish he were actually touching me.

Glancing over my shoulder, my eyebrows pull together. "You being all silly and me looking like I'm terrified?"

His chuckle reaches into my chest and soothes my soul. "Not gonna argue the silly part, but I was talking about your beauty," he says, as he points to a picnic table off to the side.

I feel the blush from his words start at my chest and creep up my neck. Taking the seat across from him, I fumble with my keys before setting them down on the tabletop. An awkward silence fills the air, as if neither of us knows what to say.

"So I'm sure you're just as shocked by this as I am," he starts, strumming his thumb on the pitted wood. "What are the odds?" The grin he gives me instantly makes my panties damp.

"Very slim, I imagine. I am still trying to wrap my head around the fact you're Rigsby." I glance up from watching his hands to staring into his eyes. They're hazel with a dark ring around the edge and flecks of gold sprinkled throughout the irises. His eyes are actually beautiful in a unique way.

"Well, like I said earlier, I'm Royce Rigsby, but most everyone here calls me Rigsby. I've been the manager of Elevate for a few years now. I was born and raised in southern Illinois and after I left the Army, I moved here to be with my mom and brother. My birthday is March twenty-third, in case you want to buy me a gift," he says with a wink, "and I think running is fun. I like to play soccer, but think golf is the most boring game on the face of the planet, and I truly despise, with a deep passion, pineapple on pizza."

"With a resume like that, how can you be single?" I ask with a laugh, but deep down, I'm serious. Why hasn't a woman snatched up this man? He's funny and clearly a family man, if moving to a new state to be closer to his mom and brother is an indication. He has a decent job and can support himself. Plus, he's probably the most gorgeous man I've ever seen with my own two eyes.

Royce just shrugs. There's something that flashes in the depths of those hazel eyes, but he covers it up too quickly for me to determine what it was.

"There's nothing wrong with that," I reply, though I'm not really sure we're talking about the same kind of fun. My fun consists of a good book and a bubble bath. By the way he naturally flirts and exhumes sexuality, I picture his fun a little...dirtier.

"Why are you blushing?" he asks, the corner of his lip turned upward in a half-smirk.

"No reason," I stammer, willing the warmth in my cheeks to subside. "It's warm out here."

"Mmhmm," he sings before throwing me a wink. "So tell me about you, Bestie Tami with an I, which I knew wasn't your name. You didn't feel like a Tami."

"Known a lot of Tamis, have you?" I tease.

"A few."

Damn, that cocky grin makes me want to...kiss him.

"Anyway, you now know I'm the principal of Grace Private School, which I love. You also know where I live, which is a little creepy," I add with my own wink.

"And that you like tequila."

"Actually, I really don't," I reply, barking out a laugh when his face registers his surprise. "That night was a particularly rough one with a horrible date, and well, I'm not much of a drinker at all. My friend, Sabrina, left that bottle at my house a while ago, and I felt I needed something to calm my frayed nerves."

"And then you spilled it."

An easy giggle slips from my throat. "I did. I barely tasted the first sip before I dropped it."

"Because some hot stud was running by and got you all flustered?" he asks, waggling his eyebrows suggestively. Only, he has no idea how close he is to the truth. Not that I'm going to tell him that.

I shake my head and smile. "Awfully full of yourself there, Royce."

He stares across the table at me, the faintest smile playing on his lips. "I like it when you say my name."

"Royce?"

His smile widens. "It sounds better on your lips than from any other pair I've ever heard."

Even though I'm returning his grin, I shake my head and glance down at my hands. "You're too charming for your own good."

"So does that mean you want to hang out with me later?"

I almost say yes. Like right away, no hesitation, but then I remember the plans I made with Sabrina. "Actually, I'm not available tonight."

"Hot date?"

I open my mouth, but no words come out.

When I shut it quickly, he adds, "That's a yes."

"It's an I don't know what it is. My friend, Sabrina, invited me to dinner. Apparently, there's these two guys who work at a coffee shop down the way from the boutique she works at, and she invited them to join us. It's not a date."

Royce gives me look. "Oh, sweetheart, the moment those guys take one look at you, it'll be a date." When I don't reply, he reaches over and swipes a lock of hair off my forehead that has escaped from my ponytail, much like he did earlier up on the mountain. "I kinda like the way you blush."

And cue an even deeper blush...

"How is Jack?" I ask, steering the conversation away from my later plans.

Royce gives me a hard laugh and shakes his head. "He already owns my place. I came out of my room this morning for work and found him lying on his back on the couch with his paws up, airing out his balls," he tells me, painting a vivid photograph.

The giggle slips from my lips so effortlessly, so quickly. "It is warm out."

He's already shaking his head as he picks up a leaf from the table and tosses it to the ground. "Not that warm. He just likes showing off his junk." He glances down at his watch. "I hate to cut this short, but I have to get back to work."

A sadness sweeps through me, one I wasn't expecting, as we get up from the picnic table and stand side by side. "Well, it was nice to officially meet you, Royce," I say, extending my hand.

The moment his skin touches mine and wraps around it, an electrical charge courses through my blood. My nipples tingle and blood swooshes through my ears, a reaction I've never experienced from a handshake. "It's nice to officially meet you too," he replies, his eyes drinking me in as if I were a cold glass of water on a hot summer day.

Nervously, I glance down, breaking our eye contact. Yet, I can still feel them on my skin like a caress, heating my skin with every passing second.

"Thanks for choosing Elevate, Quinn." Something in the way he says those words lets me know he's not just talking about the ziplining.

"You're welcome. Maybe I'll see you around?" I ask, hoping I was able to hide the tinge of desperation I suddenly feel.

The grin he sends me causes butterflies to flutter in my stomach. "Oh, Bestie Tami with an I, you can guarantee it."

Then he steps forward, and I swear he's going to kiss me. The breath catches in my throat, and I realize suddenly how badly I'd like Royce to kiss me. So bad, in fact, I find myself leaning in just the slightest. His eyes darken as they drop to my lips. My tongue snakes out, nervously wetting my bottom lip.

When he leans in, I'm disappointed his lips only graze against my cheek in a featherlight brush, but the damage is done. I catch a whiff of his earthy, musky scent that causes wetness to surge through my body, landing between my legs. His big hand wraps around my upper arm, holding me steady with just the slightest touch.

"Have a good evening, Quinn," he whispers, his voice sounding raw and raspy.

I nod, suddenly unable to find my words. He releases my arm, allowing me the opportunity to grab my keys and phone. I try to ignore the tremble in my fingers. I give him a smile before turning and heading off toward the parking lot, the feel of his eyes with me the entire time.

***

"Oh my God, the hot guy is Rigsby! Rigsby is the hot guy!" I holler into the phone the moment my best friend answers.

"Well, hello to you too, Q," Sabrina giggles, as I suck in a deep breath of air, and groan.

"I'm serious, Rina. What am I going to do?"

"First off, you can start at the beginning because I have no idea what you're going on about."

Sighing, I flop back on my bed, right on top of the shirt I picked out to wear tonight. "Rigsby, Sabrina. I met him," I whisper.

"The texting guy, right? How did that happen? Tell me, tell me," she asks, completely enthralled.

"His name is Royce Rigsby, and he works at Elevate. He figured out who I was based on our texts because I told him I was going there," I tell her without stopping to breathe.

"Okay, so how does this hot guy play into it?"

I groan, thinking back on the two times I saw Royce standing in front of my house when he was out for his run. "There was this guy, earlier in the week, who ran past my house. I dropped my tumbler of tequila and he stopped to make sure I was okay."

"*You* were drinking tequila?"

"Would you focus, please? Yes, I decided to have a few sips because that was all that was left in that bottle you left. Well, I saw him running, and oh my goodness, Rina, I'd never seen a more gorgeous sight than that. Long strides and a muscular, yet lean body. And don't get me started on his face. Even from a distance, I could tell he was breathtakingly beautiful. I ended up dropping the glass and spilling my drink."

"I'd have dropped my panties," she says, almost absently.

I snicker, because it's such a Sabrina reply. "Anyway, when I came home the next day from work, there was a bottle of tequila sitting on the porch."

"Okay, so a hot runner gave you a bottle of tequila. Did you give him your cookie in return?" she asks.

"Sabrina," I chastise.

"It's a legit question, Q. So tell me the rest," she instructs.

"So when I went to Elevate today, it was the hot runner guy who was taking us up the mountain. He's Rigsby, or Royce."

She's quiet for a few long seconds before she whispers, "Did you have sex on the mountain?"

I growl in frustration. "Seriously, Rina?"

She sighs. "I'll take that as a no. Bummer, because I'd totally love to hear the details on that one."

Glancing at the clock, I realize I need to jump in the shower. "I'm gonna go so I can get ready."

"I'll be there at six fifty. Oh, and wear sexy panties. Or no panties at all!" she adds quickly.

"Goodbye, Sabrina," I reply on a sigh before hanging up my phone.

I glance at my best pair of jeans, which are a tight pair of skinny ones I've only worn twice. I'm pairing them with a deep purple top you can see through, a black tank underneath, and the only pair of four-inch spikey black heels I own. I usually wear two-inch kitten heels all day or flats, but I've decided to give this night out some real effort. I'm even going to wear my hair down and use that special curling iron Sabrina got me for Christmas last year that adds big, soft curls.

Why am I doing this?

Not because of Lance or the other coffee house guy, whatever his name is. Because something inside of me cries out in feminine despair. I'm so used to professional attire and buns in my hair, I just want to feel like a woman tonight. A pretty, sexy, single woman.

Even if it's completely out of my comfort zone.

After a thirty-minute shower, where I scrubbed, shaved, and lotioned every part of my body, I slip on my clothes and start my hair and makeup. Again, that's something else I've always done just basics on, but tonight, I'm going with a smoky purple shadow and extra layers of mascara. Instead of my usual lip gloss, I choose a dusty rose-colored lipstick and add a second layer.

By the time I'm finished, my doorbell is ringing, announcing Sabrina's arrival. She lets herself in using the spare key I gave her and makes a beeline for my bedroom. "I swear to God, if you're wearing yoga pants and a—" she says, but stops the moment she steps inside my bedroom. "Holy shit, Quinn."

I glance down at my outfit, suddenly worrying my gut is spilling out over the top of my jeans or my makeup resembles that of a hooker's. "Is it bad?" I ask, my eyes wide with worry.

"*Badass*! Holy shit, you look so hot! Those guys are gonna be eating out of the palm of your hand," she says as she comes all the way into the room, and I take in her appearance. Sabrina's wearing a pair of black skinny jeans with strappy sandals, as well as a black Johnny Cash fitted tank top with rhinestones. Her raven hair is pull up in a high, sleek ponytail that cascades down her back. Her makeup is dark, her lips painted a deep red wine color. She's gorgeous, as always.

I glance down at my outfit, feeling completely out of place. Running a shaky hand down my side, I turn back to look in the mirror. "You sure?"

"Abso-fucking-lutely, Q. No way are you going home alone tonight," she replies, a wolfish grin on her gorgeous face. "Girlfriend's getting lucky tonight," she sings, reaching out and grabbing my arm. "Let's go. I want to keep them waiting, but only a few minutes. You ready?"

Exhaling, I let her lead me through my house and out the front door. "I suppose."

And just like that, we're off to Pork's for a Saturday night out.

Chapter Nine

Royce

I park my truck in the lot next to Pork's and turn off the ignition. I don't spy my brother's vehicle yet, but I'm a few minutes early, so I'm not worried. I step up to the heavy wooden door, the old country music filtering through the doorway the moment I give it a tug. The familiarity of one of my favorite joints hits me as I cross the threshold, my eagerness for dinner and drinks with my brother front and center.

"Hey, Royce!" Lana hollers from the bar, offering me a warm grin. The moment she says my name, half a dozen ladies turn and lock their eyes on me. It's something I'm used to, and I'm not just being cocky. Ladies love me. What can I say? I'm a sexy motherfucker.

"Eating or drinking?" Wendy, a waitress I may have slept with when I first discovered this place after moving to town, asks as she approaches. She gives me a smile, but it lacks the fuck-me vibe the others are throwing my way. Wendy's married now and not interested in taking a trip down bedroom memory lane with me.

"Eating, Wendy. Rueben's on his way," I tell her, as she points to a high table along the front wall. "Thanks," I add when she sets two menus down.

"The usual?" she asks, not bothering to get out her pad to write it down.

"Yep," I confirm before she turns and walks away. Her ass is nice in her tight jeans, but I realize it's not the ass I'd like to be looking at. The image of Quinn in her proper khaki shorts is etched in my mind like an engraving on a piece of gold. It ain't going anywhere.

I open the menu, even though I don't need it. I already know what I'm having, but it helps me pass the time until my brother gets here. It also keeps my hands busy, so I'm not tempted to pull out my phone and text Quinn. She's on her *date* tonight, or whatever you want to call it. Even if she doesn't think it's one, the guy she's meeting will no doubt disagree.

"Sorry I'm late," my brother says, as he slides onto the pub chair across from me. "I was working and lost track of time."

I snort. "You're always working." It's the truth. My younger brother by two years is one of the hardest working guys I know. He's always on his computer, monitoring security threats for the government. It's some big fancy job he was offered last fall, and he hasn't looked back since. He gets to work from home, which is pretty great, and has only needed to travel twice in the last year. Both times Cricket, his fiancée, was able to go with him.

Rueben shrugs and pushes his glasses up on his nose. "Not always," he replies absently as he looks over the menu.

"Glad to hear it. I'd be disappointed if you were. You gotta get your dick wet every now and again," I tease.

Rueben rolls his eyes. "You mean like you?" Without even glancing up from his menu, he asks, "How many was it this week? Two? Three women?"

My gut churns with his insinuation. Mostly because he's right. Not about this week, in particular, but in general. It's nothing for me to go out and find a lady or two to keep me company. Hell, a year or two ago, it was pretty much a given. Every night, out with friends and taking home whoever was willing. Sometimes I'd see them again, sometimes not, but I never felt guilty about it.

Until now.

I think about Quinn and how my body responded each time I saw her. Sure, it was a given because of how stunningly beautiful she is, but it was also more than that. I was drawn to her smile and laugh almost as much as I was her ass and legs. For the first time, I really see the whole package, and not just tits and ass.

"Actually," I start, clearing my throat and wishing I had my drink, "there haven't been any this week."

I feel his eyes on me, but I keep my gaze down. "Seriously? You sick?"

Shrugging my shoulders, I reply a quick no as Wendy drops off my beer and turns to my brother. "Same for you?"

"Yep."

I take a pull from my bottle and scan the room. "No, I'm not sick," I answer, setting my beer back down on the table. "Maybe I'm just taking a break."

When Rueben doesn't reply, I glance across the table to find his wide eyes locked on me. "Wow, never thought I'd see the day."

"What day?" I ask, picking at the label on my beer.

"The day where a woman who catches your attention actually keeps it." The asshole gives me a cocky smirk as Wendy sets his bottle in front of him.

"What are we eating?" she asks, grabbing her notepad.

"Burger and fries," I answer.

"Same," Rueben says, slipping his menu behind the napkin holder. "You've already told me you met someone. Tell me about her," he adds the moment Wendy takes off to place our order.

An uneasy feeling settles in my stomach. Technically, Quinn isn't anyone to me. She's someone I've been randomly texting, and I can count on one hand how many times we've met in person, including the times we didn't know who the other one was. Sighing, I know he's not going to let this go until I give him something. "Her name is Quinn, and she's a principal at a private school in town."

Rueben takes a drink before asking, "How'd you meet her?"

I open my mouth, but not sure how to reply. Do I tell him about the accidental texting or the front porch meet? Even telling my brother how I met this girl seems complex. This is exactly why I don't do relationships. They're too complicated with strings and expectations. The fun fizzles out the moment feelings get involved.

I decide to start at the beginning. "She sent me a text that wasn't meant for me."

"No shit?" he asks, a grin that mirrors mine spreading across his face.

"She thought she was sending a message to her best friend, but it turns out she had the number wrong."

Rueben grins. "The ol' wrong number trick, huh?"

"Well, I'm pretty sure it wasn't a trick, since neither of us knew each other beforehand. We've texted all week. It's been fun and easy to talk to her. Anyway, while I was out for a run, I met this woman standing out on her front porch. She was the most beautiful woman I've ever seen, Rueb. Like straight out of a magazine, yet not in that overdone way. Know what I mean?"

He smiles across the table. "I know exactly what you mean," he says, no doubt talking about his fiancée.

"Turns out, they're the same woman. The one who sent me a text accidentally is the same lady I saw on her front porch."

He blows out a low whistle. "No shit?"

"I kid you not. I met her officially at Elevate today," I answer as Wendy delivers two plates of burgers and fries, each with an extra side of their homemade barbecue sauce. We didn't request it, but she knows us well enough to know our order.

"Thanks, Wendy," I reply, as she lifts up my bottle to find it nearly empty.

"Another, Rueben?" she asks my brother as she reaches for his beer.

"Yes, please."

She heads off to grab us another round, while we make up our burgers. I slather on barbecue sauce and add the two deep fried onion rings to my sandwich before pressing my bun down, loving the tangy sauce that oozes out the sides. I grab two fries—because they must be consumed in pairs—and slide them across the burger masterpiece, coating them in barbecue.

"So what now?" he asks between bites of his own western burger.

I shrug. "Not sure. I mean, I wouldn't mind spending a little time with her," I start, only to be interrupted by Rueben.

"You mean in bed?"

Opening my mouth, the words I thought would fly out aren't what I actually say. "Maybe on a date." I can feel his shocked eyes bore into me from across the table, so I keep my focus on my fries and barbecue sauce. When I glance back up, I find him grinning like the jackass he is. "What?"

"You like this girl."

I finish chewing my bite before I add, "Yeah, I do."

"Good. Mom will be happy to see you in a relation—"

"Stop right there. I didn't say anything about a relationship, Rueb. I like talking to her. I like making her smile."

"The fact that you didn't say you like fucking her first speaks volumes, Royce."

I stare over at my brother, really considering his words. I know he's right, but I'm not letting him know it. Instead, I go with, "I didn't say I didn't want that," throwing in a cocky smirk. Because, yeah, I do want that too...with Quinn. "Tell me about Cricket's event."

Rueben starts right in on telling me about the Moonlight Mountain View event happening in the heart of Gatlinburg. Cricket's job has something to do with publicity and tourism, and even though I may not understand it completely, she's fucking killing it. Elevate partnered with the Chamber of Commerce with online promotion, and our business went up thirty-five percent over the last year. Our already full schedules were becoming packed, with reservations pushed out months in advance.

"She's helping man a kid's activity booth near Hollywood Star Cars Museum. I guess they're letting the kids go in for free tonight," he says, finishing off his sandwich.

"You ever been there?" I ask as I polish off my fries.

"Twice. They have the Batmobile there, man."

I roll my eyes at my brother. When we were kids, he was the biggest Batman freak ever. He spent all of his time watching the old Adam West episodes and owned every Batman remake on DVD. "Of course they do," I mumble.

Twenty minutes later, Wendy stops by to take away our plates of food and bring us a third beer. The place is starting to fill up now, a band sets up on the open side of the large room. Within the hour, Pork's will be filled to capacity with locals ready to have a good time.

Rueben is on his phone, no doubt texting Cricket, if the grin on his face is any indication, so I lean back in my chair and take in my surroundings. All of the tables are full, including the booths in back. It's darker back there, with low lighting hanging over each table, but even through the dimmer light, I'd recognize that blonde hair anywhere.

Quinn is here.

Sitting at a round booth in back is the very woman I've been fantasizing about since she left Elevate this afternoon. Fuck, probably since I saw her standing under her porch light. She's sitting on the inside with another woman with long, dark hair. Each has a guy on the outsides of the booth. The one beside Quinn has his arm extended over the back of the booth, but I can already tell by her rigid posture, she's avoiding his touch.

Fuck that.

Fuck him.

"You okay?"

I turn quickly to my brother. "What?"

"You just growled like a dog. You all right?" he asks loudly, concerned eyes locked on mine behind his black-framed glasses.

My eyes return to the woman across the room as if she were a piece of metal and my eyes the magnet. I'm drawn to her, desire swirling in my gut and landing squarely in my cock. "See that woman over there?" I ask my brother.

"The dark-haired one?"

"No, the blonde beside her." When he mumbles his acknowledgement, I say, "That's Quinn."

"The one on the date over there?"

"It's not a date," I tell him, but it sounds weak, even to my own ears.

"Then what is it?"

"She said her friend set it up with two guys from a coffee shop," I tell him without removing my eyes from Quinn. She smiles politely, but it's not the natural, easy grin I've seen a handful of times this week.

I take another drink of my beer, suddenly wishing it was something stronger. The urge to walk over there, throw her over my shoulder, and carry her from the building has never been as strong as it is right now. I toss back and finish off the rest of my brew, hating the weird bout of jealousy rolling through my body.

Suddenly, I see her say something to the guy beside her. He slips out of the booth, her right behind him. When she stands, he's close—too fucking close—and Quinn practically has her back pressed against the corner of the seat. She slips away, heading toward the back hallway where the restrooms are located.

"Hey, I'm gonna hit the head," I tell my brother without looking his way. His nose is practically pressed against his phone screen anyway and probably wouldn't even have noticed if I hadn't say a word.

Quinn slips into the restroom, so I hang back in the dark hallway and wait. A few females head my way, bright smiles on their painted lips the moment they see me. The brunette is wearing a short skirt with a tight tank top, her heels too high to be comfortable. "Hey," one sings with a seductive little wave as she walks into the restroom, her giggling friend hot on her heels. There's an enthusiasm in that wave, an invitation to join her.

A week ago, I may have taken her up on that unspoken offer, but not today.

When the door closes behind them, I sigh in relief. The last thing I need is Quinn to walk out and find those two draped all over me like a cheap cloak. I take a deep breath and position myself directly across the wall from the restroom door. A small group of ladies exits, but Quinn isn't one of them.

After what feels like forever, the door finally opens and out she comes. She's glancing down at her phone and not really paying attention to where she's going. She turns to head back to the dining area, so I quickly ask, "Sending anyone in particular a text?"

Her wide blue eyes slam into mine and a shiver slips down my spine. I get my first good look at Quinn Michaels since I noticed her at Pork's. She's wearing tight, dark jeans that hug her curves like a second skin. Her top is a deep purple and I can see the dark tank she wears underneath it. Her long, blonde hair is down with big, soft curls that make my fingers tingle to run through it. And the sexiest fucking pair of simple black heels adorn her tiny feet. She looks unbelievably gorgeous, and I know I'm not the only one to have noticed.

"What are you doing here?" she asks, a hint of a smile on those full, plump lips.

The duo from earlier exits the bathroom and stops and stares at Quinn. I reach over and gently grab her arm, guiding her away from the doorway. I can feel eyes on me, but Quinn's are the only set I care about. "Having dinner with my brother."

My eyes feast on her once more, taking in the hourglass shape of her abdomen and the delicate swell of her breasts. Blood is pumping to one concentrated area, my cock swollen and hard in my jeans. Glancing back up, I find her eyes sweeping across my chest. "How's dinner with your friends?" I hate referring to the douche canoes in the booth as friends, but it's better than calling them outright self-indulged assholes.

Blue eyes swirl with desire. "Good. Sabrina…is here. There. Out there," she says nervously, pointing toward the dining area.

The moment I step forward, she takes one back, but not in a fearful way. She's using the wall to help hold her upright. Placing my hand on the wall beside her head, I toy with a curl of hair that hangs over her shoulder, loving the softness at the tips of my fingers. When my eyes lock on hers, I hear the hitch in her breath and watch as her tongue slips out and wets her lower lip.

"Are you having fun?" I ask, leaning in just ever so slightly and inhaling her subtle fruity perfume.

"Yes." The word comes out a squeak as she gazes up at me with lust-filled eyes.

I let the outside of my finger graze against the side of her neck. "Even with that guy sitting beside you? The one who can't take his eyes off you?"

She swallows hard. "Not really. He's not my type."

"That's good, Bestie," I reply, giving her a cocky little grin.

"Why?" she asks with the slightest lift of her chin, blue eyes following my every movement.

I lean in, filling my senses with her intoxicating floral shampoo, as I whisper, "Because you're going home with me."

Chapter Ten

Quinn

Because you're going home with me.

As I make my way back to my table, Royce's words keep repeating over and over again, an intoxicating melody of seduction and desire. I'm not even sure how I'm able to walk, to be honest. My legs are like cooked spaghetti noodles as I carefully make my way toward Sabrina.

"You okay?" she asks the moment I slip back into the booth.

Lance slides back in after me, but I pay him no attention. "What? Why do you ask?"

"You're all flushed," she observes as I reach for my glass of water, a slight tremble to my hand.

"I'm great," I insist, the words coming out a bit higher pitched than normal.

I can feel eyes on me, but not hers. Royce is near, his gaze like a caress. Sabrina looks up, a knowing smile spreading across her face. "Well, well, well," she whispers as she watches Royce walk past our table. "Who is that yummy drink of water?" she whisper-yells so only I can hear.

I suck down more water, suddenly wishing it were something a little harder, and begging for it to help cool my overheated body. I've been burning up since my eyes met his in that darkened hallway. Not to mention the instant wetness between my legs when he backed me up against the wall. My body is humming, alive, with a reckless desire I've not quite experienced before.

"That's Royce," I whisper, grateful Lance and Decker are having their own conversation and not paying us any attention.

"Royce? *The* Royce?" she asks, casually turning to glance behind her to where he's now sitting with his brother.

"Yep, that's him," I mumble, sucking air when I reach the bottom of my water glass. I set it back down and fumble with the straw, just to give my fingers something to do.

My eyes seek him out again and meet his across the room. His brother looks a lot like him, just a slightly skinnier version with dark glasses. They have similar features and the same hair color. From where I sit, even if I didn't know them, I can tell they're related. His brother leans in and asks him a question, yet Royce never takes his eyes off me, even when he leans toward him and answers.

"Holy shit, Q, I think you could get pregnant from the way he's looking at you. Are you up on your birth control?"

I roll my eyes and glance to my friend. "Stop it."

"I'm serious. He's...smokin' hot. You two would have beautiful babies," she adds before sucking down a long swig of her fruity drink. "You should have another," she tells me.

"Can I get you another drink?" Lance asks, drawing my attention back to him.

He's not a bad looking guy, honestly. He's not nearly as tall as Royce, nor as muscular. He's wearing a pressed short-sleeved button-down shirt with a blue and gray plaid print, which is tucked into his stylish jeans. He looks nice.

But Royce looks hot.

He plays the bad boy.

His black T-shirt is fitted and tight, yet not in that cocky, self-absorbed way. It stretches across his broad chest and arms perfectly, hitting right above a tight ass in a pair of worn, dark blue jeans. My mouth waters from all the way over here.

Realizing Lance asked me a question, I turn toward him and reply, "Oh, no thank you. I'm driving Sabrina home tonight," I tell him, ignoring her chuckle beside me.

"If you're sure," he replies, glancing toward the hallway I had just exited. "I'm going to use the restroom." Lance slides out of the booth and I swear I can breathe again.

There's no spark. From the moment they sat down at our booth this evening and Lance shook my hand, there was nothing there. No sizzle of attraction, no desire for something more. Dinner was nice, but the conversation was a little forced. He seemed attentive, asking questions about me, my family, and my job, but kept turning everything back on him and the coffee house. He's tried to touch my shoulder casually, placing his arm across the backrest of the booth, but his touch just isn't right. It's not the one I crave.

My eyes find those hazel ones again across the room, and desire touches down in my stomach like a tornado. He places the beer bottle to his lips, and I swear I can feel the caress all the way over here. I've never before found watching a man drink to be sexy, but here I am, ready to climb across the table, throw my panties on the floor, and ask him to have his wicked way with me.

Patrons be damned.

I have to look down, break the connection of our eyes before I spontaneously combust from the heat burning through my veins.

"Oh my God, he's coming over here," Sabrina whispers, causing my eyes to fly back to Royce once more, confirming he's moving this way. He moves with the gait of a jungle cat, watching, calculating, and focused with every move he makes, and right now, he's fixated on me.

"Evening," he says, as he takes the seat vacated by Lance just a few moments ago.

I can feel Decker's curious eyes bounce between Royce and me, but I can't bring myself to look his way. I'm trapped in Royce's gaze, intoxicated by the scent of his cologne. Someone whimpers, and with a sharp elbow to my side from Sabrina, it hits me the noise came from me. The grin Royce gives me is potent. You can tell he's used to flashing it when the proper time warrants it.

Like now.

"Dance with me." His voice is low and gravelly, just barely heard over the country song coming from the band in the big room.

My eyes widen, and I glance around. For what, I don't know, but when they return to the man at my right, I feel every ounce of restraint I possess fly right out the window. My body sways toward him, completely on its own, as if he's the piece I didn't even realize I was missing.

"She'd love to," Sabrina says beside me, shoving her pointy-ass elbow into my side once more.

"Ouch! Stop it," I hiss, glaring at my friend. Her knowing, wide grin lets me know she's not sorry at all for jabbing me.

The song suddenly changes to a slow, seductive beat. Shock waves race through my body as his hand slides lightly down my arm, leaving a strip of goosebumps in its wake. "What do you say, Bestie. Care to let me lead you around the dance floor?"

"I'm not sure that's the best idea," I tell him, catching Lance's approach out of the corner of my eye.

He leans in just a hint and inhales. "I think it's the second best idea I've had all night."

"Second best?" Sabrina asks, totally absorbed in our conversation.

His lips curl upward in a way that makes me think of sex. Hot, sweaty, dirty sex. I try to cross my legs, but the ache burns fierce with no alleviation in sight. With his eyes locked on mine, he answers, "I'm just really looking forward to going home tonight."

It's so hot in here, I swear ice in my veins wouldn't even extinguish this burn.

"Uhh, can I help you?" Lance asks, standing right beside Royce.

Royce doesn't even give him a glance. "Well, Bestie?" He leans in and whispers, "Double dog dare you."

My hand is placed in his without any direction from my brain, encouraging him to slip out of the booth, me in tow. I glance up at Lance, who's clearly confused about what's going on. Sabrina saves me from having to answer his unspoken question by saying, "That's her friend, Royce. She promised him a dance."

Guilt sweeps through me as I'm led to the dance floor. I know I'm not dating Lance or even here with him, but still, I don't want to hurt him. I think he'd agree there's nothing between us, but that doesn't mean I want to rub it in his face how badly I'm attracted to another man. I'm not that kinda woman.

Any worry I had about Lance is rushed from my head as Royce pulls my body flush with his own. He's so much taller than I am, probably close to nine or ten inches, yet we seem to fit together like puzzle pieces. His hand pressing into my lower back, his thumb gently moving up and down, creating soothing friction with just the slightest touch. We start to sway in beat, and I realize instantly, he's got moves. Even just through a basic slow dance, I can tell by the way his hips rock, and his body follows.

If he can dance this spectacularly to music, can you imagine what he'll do between the sheets?

Yeah, I'm already picturing it too.

I sort of feel like an amateur in his arms, but he doesn't let me falter. Royce is the expert here, and I'm just along for the ride. The song moves from one slow ballad to another, this one originally performed by Tim McGraw and Faith Hill. It's about wanting someone, needing them, even when they're not with you. How they're all you can think about until you finally give in, because they're exactly who you need. I feel this song all the way down to my toes. I feel the beauty of their words mixing with want, the pain colliding with the passion.

When he opens his mouth, it's not for the reason I expect. He sings along to the words of the song, his voice low and smooth like butter. It melts me from the inside out and makes my knees weak. I've never known a man who can sing, not like this. My cheek moves, resting against his chest as the vibrations of his singing echoes in my ear. I'm pretty sure my panties are completely soaked at this point, my body humming with energy and desire.

As the song finally comes to an end, I lift my head and gaze into his eyes. There's a conviction there, a resolution, as if he knows exactly how this night is going to end. And you know what? I know how it's going to end too. I couldn't walk away now if I tried. It's a combination of the way his eyes burn into my soul and the heady words he spoke in the hallway. The way he came over and basically claimed me as his without so much as a care in the world.

Like we're destined to happen.

"You here with Sabrina?" he asks.

I nod and bite my lip, hating that response because it makes me sound so cliché. But I actually bite it to keep from just throwing my arms around his neck and plastering my lips to his.

"Ready to get out of here?" His hands slide around my sides and to my arms in the softest caress ever.

Am I ready to go? With Royce? I'm certain there's only one thing on his mind right now, and it so happens to be the same thing on mine. If I leave with him, I'll be in his bed as quickly as he can get me there. I'll give in to all this reckless lust that's been swarming me like bees and refusing to subside.

I've never felt this way before. Never have I left any place with a man for the sole purpose of sex. Never broken my strict five-date rule. Never worried about the status of our relationship before we crossed the line. But here I am, knowing there is no relationship, no dates. This means one thing and one thing only.

Sex.

And while I should be shocked by my behavior, my response to him, and the fact I'm even considering this, I'm not. Not at all. It feels too good to be anything but right. I'm not just outside of my comfort zone, I don't even see where it is. It's just me and him and the desire to give in to what we both want.

I have no idea what tomorrow holds, but tonight, I want to be reckless.

Tonight, I want Royce.

With every ounce of determination I possess, I lift my chin and look him square in the eye. "I'm ready."

He takes my hand and backtracks us through the dance crowd. I notice right away his brother is gone. I'm not sure if he's in the restroom or has left the building, but Royce doesn't seem concerned. He leads me straight to my table, where my best friend visits with Decker, their heads tilted toward each other in an intimate way.

Apparently, I won't be the only one going home with someone tonight.

I realize Lance isn't at the table and glance around. The bar is full now, the noise escalating as people try to be heard over the band. When I step up to our booth, Sabrina looks up with a knowing grin on her face. "Hey," she practically sings as I reach for my purse. "Going somewhere?"

"Uhh, yeah," I stutter, unable to look at Decker, even though I feel his eyes on me. Royce places a hand on my lower back, and I can't stop my body's reaction to sway in his direction. I look once more to the empty seat where Lance sat.

"Lance met a friend," Sabrina says, pointing just over my shoulder and to the left.

When I turn, I find him totally engrossed in a conversation with a shorter redhead. I can tell by their body language and the way she giggles, she's totally into him. A weight I didn't even know I was carrying seems to lift. Lance notices me, whispers something to the woman beside him, and walks my way.

"Hey," he says, with an easy smile. He looks up at Royce and extends his hand. "Lance Roman. I don't think we've officially met."

"Royce Rigsby. Nice to meet you," he replies, shaking his hand.

Lance looks back at me, then over my shoulder once more. "It was nice meeting you, Quinn."

"Nice to meet you too," I state, noticing the redhead watching our every move.

"If you're in the area, stop by the coffee shop sometime and say hello."

"I'll do that. Thank you for having dinner with me this evening."

He nods and quickly makes his retreat back to the redhead. Royce chuckles behind me, a low noise that goes straight to the apex of my legs. His hand spreads wide on my back, and I can't help but wonder what that hand will feel like...*elsewhere*. My body tingles, my nipples are hard, and I'm surrounded in warmth from just the touch of his hand. I don't even care that my heels are starting to kill my feet.

"You okay?" I ask my best friend. I've never left her in a bar alone. Never. We've always had each other's backs, and if she were to ask me to, I'd stay until she is ready to leave. That's what friends do.

Sabrina gives me a wink and a Cheshire cat grin. "Oh, I'm more than okay. You two have fun now," she says with a wave of her delicate fingers.

"If you're sure," I reply.

She glances at Decker before throwing me a wink. "I've got plans." Then she turns her attention right back to him and laughs at something he says.

Realizing there's nothing to do but leave, I reach inside my purse for some money for a tip. Our meals were already paid for, and we had been paying for the drinks as we received them, not that I drank anything but water after my one and only alcoholic beverage. Before I can pull a ten out of my pocketbook, Royce drops a twenty on the table and reaches for my hand.

"You didn't have to do that."

He shrugs, almost as if he's embarrassed. "I don't mind."

"Well, thank you," I state, dropping my wallet back into my purse and slipping the strap over my shoulder.

"Ready?"

I nod, my throat suddenly thick and dry. He guides me through the masses, reaching down and retaking my hand in his. I glance at the table he once occupied, only to find another couple in the seats. "Did you brother leave?" I ask as we get to the door.

Royce chuckles. "Yeah, his fiancée called and wanted him to stop by the event she was hosting. He's completely whipped where she's concerned."

We push through the door and into the warm night air. A shiver sweeps through my body, but not for that reason. His hand is still wrapped around mine, the musky scent of his cologne tickles my nose, and a hum of sexual desire surrounds us like a bubble. Yet, as we approach his truck, the bubble pops and reality sets in.

I'm about to go home with a stranger.

No, I know he's not technically a stranger, but the truth is, we *have* only known each other for less than a week. I've never done anything like this, and can't quite understand why I am now. I could try to analyze and dissect it, but I'm not sure I'll really find the answers I'm looking for.

When he opens the door, our eyes meet. I can see the change in his instantly. They go from hungry to worried. "Are you okay?" he asks, still holding my hand, but doesn't move.

"Uhh, yes?" I'm not sure why it comes out a question, but it does. Royce picks up on it right away. I can see his wheels spinning in his head as he tries to figure me out.

"I have an idea."

"Okay?" I ask, nervously.

"Grab your phone and text Sabrina." When I just look at him in question, he squeezes my hand and gives me a reassuring smile. "My address is 1402 Cliffside Lane. It's about three miles from here.

My name is Royce Daniel Rigsby, middle name after my dad, and you already know I work at Elevate. My brother is Rueben, and he lives in Pittman Center, and my mom is Jackie. She works at Sweet Treats Bakery, across from the Target."

I can only smile at his effort to alleviate some of the nerves I have. It's as if he can read my mind and understands my pause.

"And I want you to know if you tell me no or to stop at any point, I will do it immediately. I'm a guy, but not a bad one, Quinn. I would never take advantage of you." His eyes burn with seriousness and honesty as he gazes down at me under the moonlight. I'm very much aware of how good-looking he is, but it's more than that. I believe him. He's not just trying to get me in bed. He wants me to feel safe and in control.

And I realize, I do.

I know I'm in good hands with him.

Probably the best hands I've ever been in, if his dancing is any indication.

That's why I step forward, pressing my chest to his. I can hear his sharp inhalation. His hands move to my back, positioned very low, his fingers dancing along the globes of my ass. I'm pretty sure he's not breathing, and to be honest, neither am I.

Wrapping my arms around his waist, I say, "Let's go."

Chapter Eleven

Royce

I'm practically bouncing like a girl with excitement but trying to play it cool. I can tell Quinn got a little spooked back there. I could feel the tension roll through her body, the closer we got to my truck. That's why I told her all that personal shit about myself. I don't want her to feel anything but completely relaxed, and maybe a hell of a lot of anticipation. I may not know her well, but what I do know is enough to give me pause and really try to keep my cool. She's never done this before.

Quinn isn't someone I can just throw over my shoulder and go barreling toward the bedroom. Though, I do see a certain light in her eye whenever the bad boy in me comes out. Specifically, in the hallway. I knew she was interested, even if she just gave me a shy grin and headed back to her table, a little extra swing to her hips and a sassy gleam to her eye as she turned around and made eye contact once more.

As I pull out of the parking lot of Pork's, I reach over and grab her hand. She links her fingers with mine easily, but I can still feel the tension in the air. It's sexual, laced with a touch of nervousness. If I'm being honest, that part is present on both of our accounts. I've never been this anxious to take someone home with me. Not like I am with Quinn.

She's sharp as a tack and beautiful and funny, a combination I rarely see in a woman. Sure, I've met my share of beautiful ladies, but Quinn is more. She's sophisticated and proper and has this untouchable air to her. Yet, here she is.

With me.

I know I have to take it slow. I also know, even though she's told me twice she wants this, I'm not about to assume she's all-in, and I won't push her. In just a short amount of time, her opinion of me, of how I act, means something. I'm not sure what, nor am I in any headspace to dissect it tonight, but it's there, niggling at the back of my neck.

"So tell me about this school you work at," I say, realizing it's not just to fill the time and get her more comfortable, but because I really am curious. Weird. I've never cared too much about what a woman does for a living.

She smiles, and I can feel it wash over me like a ray of sunshine filtering through the glass. "It's a private school over on Fairman with small class sizes. I started off as a teacher and ended up going back to college for my master's. At the time, I wasn't sure how I wanted to apply my degree, but one of my former colleagues sort of championed for me to apply for the position. I'm glad I did because I find it even more rewarding than teaching, which I absolutely loved."

"That's awesome. The world needs more educators like you," I tell her, giving her hand a little squeeze.

"Well, it's not easy now. There are so many rules and regulations in place that didn't quite exist a few years back when it comes to paperwork. It's hard when the people putting together these guidelines have never taught in a classroom a day in their life."

"I'm sure," I reply, as I turn onto my road and start heading up the mountain. "But you care, and that's big."

"And there's a teacher shortage everywhere, so schools have to make difficult decisions. They're cutting extracurriculars and clubs, combining classes, and enlarging the student to teacher ratio to an alarming number. We're very fortunate at our school to not yet be affected by those problems. Our faculty is loyal and the families happy with the education we provide."

I pull into my driveway and put my truck in park. Turning her way, I give her a smile. "I'm proud of you."

Even through the darkness, I can see her blush. "You don't even know me."

"Not intimately, but I'm learning a lot about you, Quinn. You're dedicated to your job and want the best for your students and the school. It's admirable."

"Oh, well, thank you," she stammers, glancing around to break the seriousness of my gaze. "So this is your home?"

I look out the windshield, trying to see my place through her eyes. The bushes are freshly hedged and the yard trimmed neat. There's a glider rocker on the front porch that the previous owner left and a potted plant my mom placed by the front door when I moved in. I put a lot of pride into this place, and it's perfect for me. I hope those little touches reflect in how she views my home.

"This is it," I reply as I shut off the ignition. "Want to go inside?"

Why do I sound so nervous?

Quinn nibbles on the side of her lip and glances back out at my house. When our eyes meet again, there's a deep resolution there. A confirmation. My cock twitches within the confines of my denim jeans, the burn of her blue eyes seeping into my bones as she nods.

I grab my keys and hop out of the truck. She has the passenger side door open when I get there and places her hand in mine as she hops down. Her legs look a million miles long in those damn jeans and heels, and I can see the curve of her tits under that purple top. I almost throw her against my truck and kiss the ever-loving hell out of her.

But I don't.

Yet.

The security light beside my front door clicks on the moment we reach the steps and Jack starts to bark. Her eyes light up as she glances my way. "I almost forgot about him." There's an eagerness, a giddiness in her words, and the moment I unlock the door, she practically bolts inside.

My laugh fills the living room as she falls to her knees right in front of Jack's crate. "Oh my gosh, he's so pretty," she coos, sticking her fingers through the wire. My dog instantly starts licking her hand, his tail thumping so hard against the side of the container I'm afraid it's going to move.

"Jack prefers handsome," I tease, even though my dog seems all too happy to be called pretty. Actually, I'm fairly certain it has more to do with the stunning woman showing him some attention than the fact she called him pretty.

She gives me a sheepish grin. "Can I let him out?" Again, she bites the corner of her lip.

I want to bite it too.

"He'll probably jump all over you. He's always a little worked up when I first get home," I state quickly, but don't stop her from reaching for the latch.

Quinn opens the gate and barely has time to prepare herself before being attacked by doggy kisses. "Jack, sit," I tell him with authority.

My dog does as instructed, but it's hard. His butt is practically scooting across the floor to get closer to Quinn, his tail thumping a frantic beat on the hardwood. His tongue dangles from his chin, and he keeps leaning forward as if he's going to get up, before glancing my way and thinking better of it. He's extremely well trained, but still has a lot of playfulness in him.

"Jack," I warn, when he acts like he's going to get up a third time. I shake my head and exhale a laugh.

I can't help but wonder if this is exactly how I look whenever she's near too.

"Come on, buddy. Let's go outside," I state. The moment I say the last word, he takes off for the back door like a shot from a gun.

Quinn giggles, wiping the doggy drool off her face with this happy, content grin. In its place is the most breathtaking smile I've ever seen. "He listens well."

I nod. "He does. He's a good dog." I offer her a hand and help her off the floor. "But if I don't get back there quickly, my *good* dog will eat a hole in the back door. He loves going outside." To confirm my point, Jack barks in agreement.

She steps beside me as we head in the direction of my eager dog. I unlock the door, barely getting it open before he darts through. I grab the leash off the hook, take her hand in my own—because I can't seem to stop wanting to touch her—and head out to join Jack.

"We shouldn't need the leash. He's pretty good at obeying commands."

I watch as she takes in the back deck for the first time. It's covered, which helps keep the hot tub out of the elements. Suddenly, all I can think about is the number of women I've had in that very hot tub. Though I've never actually counted, it's an embarrassingly high number, and the thought of adding Quinn to that list actually turns my stomach. She's way more than a fuck in a hot tub. I'm still not prepared to delve into *why*, but I'm man enough to acknowledge it.

Turning my head away, I watch Jack sniff and eventually pick his place to mark. It's always a process with him, determined to choose the right spot to piss. Quinn takes a tug rope from the porch and looks my way. "May I?"

I nod, releasing her hand, even though I'd rather be touching her. As she steps down, Jack notices what's she's carrying and runs her way. His tail is already wagging, ready to play. "You can toss it, and he'll bring it back," I tell her, leaning up against the railing and watching.

Quinn gives it a decent throw, and Jack takes off to retrieve it. He stops once to smell a large boulder at the back of my property, before bringing the toy back. "Good dog," she coos to my pup, patting his head and scratching behind his ears.

"You keep that up, and he'll never want you to leave." My gut clenches.

What I wanted to say was *If you keep that up,* I'll *never want you to leave.*

If she notices my slight panic, she doesn't say anything. She just gives me a happy grin and snatches the tug rope from Jack. She gives it a second toss and watches as he darts off to get it.

Unable to just stand here any longer without touching her, I join them in the grass. My yard isn't big and it slopes, but it's enough for a dog to run and play. When Jack sees me step up beside Quinn, he quickly brings the toy to me. I reach for it, but he moves it just out of my reach. I chuckle as he slowly moves it toward my hand once more. I'm quicker the second time and latch onto the rope. As soon as I do, it's game on.

Jack tugs, but I don't relent. I pull back, playfully trying to take the rope from him. Quinn giggles beside me as I get lower and Jack mirrors my movements. We've played this game for three days, and it seems to never get old. We pull against each other, trying to steal away the toy. When I finally wiggle it free from his jaw, I throw it all the way to the boulder in back.

"He's a smart dog," she says, her arms crossed over her chest as she watches him play.

"He is. I got pretty lucky finding him," I state, as Jack comes back and plops down on my feet. He just lies there, contently chewing on the rope toy.

Quinn gazes down with the softest smile on her lips. "I'd say you were both lucky."

We stand there, both lost in our own thoughts and enjoying the warm night air. My thoughts go from the crazy contentment I feel having her here to wondering what she sounds like when she comes. It's wildly broad, on two opposite sides of the spectrum, actually, but imagining her coming undone around me feels as natural as the comfort that surrounds me just by her presence.

"Do you want to have a seat on the deck?" I ask, not really knowing what to do. My cock wants me to take her inside and fuck her four ways to Sunday, but another part doesn't want to rush this. That part reminds me of how easy it is to talk to her and how much I enjoy our relaxed banter.

"I'd love to."

"Would you like a drink? I have water, beer, or orange juice." She gives me an odd look. "I use it as a base for smoothies," I add, realizing OJ is probably an odd thing to offer someone I brought home.

"Ahh," she replies, taking a seat in one of the Adirondack chairs. "I'd love some water."

"Coming right up," I reply, heading inside. Jack stays out, dropping down and covering Quinn's feet with his big body.

I grab two bottles of water and take a few cleansing, deep breaths. I don't know what it is about this woman. Having her here feels so fucking good, yet so fucking terrifying at the exact same time. A part of me craves a shot of something strong to help calm my frayed nerves, but I don't want any more alcohol in my system. The few beers I had earlier in the evening weren't enough to mess with me, yet I feel a little drunk anyway.

On Quinn.

I slip back outside and laugh. Quinn has her heels off—something that looks all too good, seeing them thrown off to the side like that—and my dog has his head resting on her knees. She leisurely pets his fluffy ears, and I swear, when he sees me walk out, he smiles.

"You're spoiled," I tell my pup, as I set the two bottles of water down on the little table between the chairs.

Jack barks, as if he agrees.

"He's perfect," Quinn whispers, a soft coo that resembles a mother talking to her child.

I open up her bottle and set it within her reach before I open my own. "You sound like a dog lover," I say before taking a big swig of cold water.

She shrugs. "I never really saw myself as a pet owner, but if I had a dog like Jack, I think I'd be okay."

Jack whimpers in agreement.

I can't help but shake my head. "He's not all sunshine and roses, Bestie. The first night I had him, he ate the twenty-dollar stuffed squirrel I bought him. The second night? He gnawed the corner off his water dish. It no longer sits flat on the floor. And sometime today? He somehow got ahold of one of my socks and turned it into confetti." Looking over, a bubble of laughter spills from my throat. Jack is just staring up at her, as if she hung the moon and stars, and she's looking back at him like there's no way he could have done all that.

"He's in a new home and learning how to push your buttons," she responds, scratching him right behind the left ear. I swear I can see his eyes roll around in his head from ecstasy.

Speaking of ecstasy, I haven't forgotten about the beautiful woman I brought home. If anything, I'm more aware of her here than I was at Pork's. Here, she's in my space, sitting in my chair, and petting my dog. Even though we haven't so much as spoken of anything sexual since we got out of my truck, I'm still hard as nails and uncomfortable as fuck.

But she looks the complete opposite.

She looks at ease, comfortable, and so fucking beautiful it makes my chest hurt.

That's why I haven't moved to kiss her yet. I'm letting her set the pace and make the first move. I think it's important to her, to let her take the lead. No, she doesn't necessarily look like an "in charge" kinda woman—and yes—I've met a few of those in my time. Quinn is nothing like those women. The ones who know what they want and take it, usually on top. A little reverse cowgirl, if you will.

But Quinn isn't like that.

Even though I'm struggling not to picture her right now in a reverse cowgirl.

What I mean is she's the type who dates and probably has some bullshit rule about not sleeping with someone until the third date. She thinks everything through, probably too much so at times. And she never leaves the bar with a stranger, despite how attracted she is. I've only known this woman for less than a week, but I already know all these things.

There's also a shit ton of other stuff I'd like to learn as well. How she takes her coffee in the morning, and what kind of music does she listen to? What does she do when she can't fall sleep at night, and how long does it take her to shower? All little details I've never once given a shit about in regards to a woman, yet here I am, dying to know her story.

To know her.

When my eyes meet hers, there's a shift in the air. It's thick and heady, much like the heat on the dance floor. Quinn reaches for her water bottle and takes a sip, those intoxicating blue orbs holding my gaze the entire time. I'm actually a little jealous of that bottle and the sweet way her lips wrap around it. She slips the lid back on top and sets it aside.

Then she moves.

Jack moves to the side so she can get up, but we both ignore his sad whimper as he lies on the floor by her chair. I'm not sure what she's thinking or where she's going, but I'm not about to ask. I'm letting her take the reins, remember?

Quinn slips one knee along my outer leg and the arm of the chair. When she moves to do the same with her other leg, I reach up and place my hands on her hips, guiding her down on my lap. My cock is screaming in my pants, begging to be released from its confines, as she adjusts her weight on my thighs.

"Hi," she whispers, placing two tentative hands on my shoulders.

"Hi," I reply, flexing my fingers on her hips, but holding myself completely still. I won't move until I know what she wants.

"Can I ask you something?" Her fingers dance along my collarbone and the neckline of my T-shirt before touching bare skin. I have to swallow hard over the lump in my throat.

"Sure." My voice barely sounds like my own.

"Are you going to kiss me?" There's a vulnerability in her eyes as she sits on my lap and waits for my answer.

"I've thought of nothing else since the moment I saw you across the room," I tell her honestly.

She swallows and licks her bottom lip, nibbling on the corner of it as she considers my words. "I've pretty much thought of the same thing, Royce."

My fingers grip her hips as she leans forward just a touch. "You want me to kiss you, Bestie?"

She nods. "More than anything." There's a flush to her cheeks that's cute as hell and a glimmer of desire reflecting back in those sapphire eyes.

I slide my hand around to her back and pull her to my chest. "Your wish is my command."

Then I kiss her.

I finally kiss Quinn.

My Bestie.

I already know I'm never going to be the same again.

Chapter Twelve

Quinn

I'm not sure I'm breathing. As he gently presses his lips to mine, little zaps of electricity spark through the air and my body. It's tentative at first, light, as if we're testing the waters, but these waters are already rushing. Warmth spreads through my veins like lightning, and we've barely moved our lips.

I take the lead, opening my mouth for him. Royce wastes no time, his tongue delving in deep, licking and tasting me for the first time. His hand cups the back of my head and slightly tilts it to the side, giving him better access.

The kiss goes from zero to sixty in less than five seconds. I scoot forward to get closer. Closer to the heat of his body. When I do, I connect with his erection. It's big and hard in his pants, and the sexiest little hiss slips from his lips as I grind against him. His kiss turns ravenous as his left hand spans wide across my back and his right hand holds my head hostage.

Not that I'm complaining.

This kiss is probably the best kiss of my life.

Considering I'm thirty-eight years old, that's a sad realization.

Instead of focusing on my lackluster kissing past, I put everything I have into this particular kiss. And to be honest, it's so easy. Royce takes the lead and is an expert at it. His mouth is firm, yet gentle, as he nips and sucks at my swollen lips.

"Jesus, I think I could kiss you all night," he whispers, tracing my mouth with his tongue before slipping it inside in a slow, sensual dance.

"I think I'd like that," I gasp, sucking in greedy breaths of oxygen. "But…" My words are lost in the moan of pleasure.

"But?" he asks, slowly kissing across my jaw and down my throat.

"But we could move this inside."

He sits back just a bit and gazes into my eyes. They burn dark with desire, a wild yearning that matches what I feel coursing through my body.

"Are you sure?" he asks.

His question catches me off guard. Didn't he want this? I thought by inviting me here, by basically telling me in the hallway we were going home together, we were on the same page. Why is he asking me this now?

He must catch the flicker of worry in my eyes, because he quickly goes on. "I really, *really* want to take you inside, Quinn. I've thought of nothing but you since we officially met earlier today, and when I spotted you at Pork's?" He closes his eyes for a brief second and groans. "I've been hard ever since. I want to take you inside more than I want oxygen, but I also want to take this at your pace. I'd be fine with just more kissing, if that's what you want," he says, giving me a smirk that makes warmth flood between my legs.

"You'd be okay with just kissing?" I whisper with a tinge of shock, yet when I think about it, I'm not that surprised. Not from Royce. He's gone out of his way to make me feel comfortable, and I don't see him stopping anytime soon.

"Of course," he replies, swallowing hard, as if over a golf ball in his throat.

I scoot forward, rubbing against his erection once more, and give him a coy smile. "Are you sure?"

He huffs a laugh. "Well, I'm not saying it wouldn't be *hard*," he quips, lifting his hips just a little. "I imagine I'd be taking an ice-cold shower after you left."

The thought of leaving here after only kissing Royce feels more criminal than anything. God, the man can kiss like it's his job, but I really want to experience more. The kissing is just the tip of the iceberg.

Wrapping my arms around his neck, I lock my gaze with his and murmur, "Take me inside, Royce. I'd definitely like to do more than just kissing."

Suddenly, he stands up. I wrap my legs around his hips and hold on tight. A giggle spills from my lips as he grips my butt and carries me to the back door. He whistles and Jack is by his side a second later. We slip through the doorway and I'm pressed against the wall. I can feel every inch—every very hard and very long inch—of his body as he devours my mouth with another searing kiss. I whimper, melting into his embrace.

"You are going to be the death of me," he states, grinding his hips between my legs. I swear he could make me come just by rubbing against me like this.

Jack barks, breaking through the lustful haze. I rip my lips from his and try to focus on the dog sitting just off to our left. He's sitting pretty, his tail wagging eagerly, but his bark lets us know he's not too happy with waiting.

"Shit. I need to take care of Jack," Royce mutters. He keeps his hands firmly locked on my butt and starts to move. He carries me over to the kitchen counter and sets me down. I hate to let go but need to in order for him to feed and get fresh water for the dog.

Jack sits beside his food bowl and watches as his owner fills up the dish. He starts eating the moment Royce is out of the way and takes a break only long enough to get a drink when it's set down.

Once everything is set, the man with golden hazel eyes returns his attention to me. He walks across the kitchen, licking his lips as he approaches. He slides his large palms up the outside of my legs and slithers between them. He takes my lips with his once more and carefully pulls me forward. My legs hitch around his lean hips as he picks me up and walks me backward.

In the living room, he gently lays me down on the couch. Even in the semi-dark room, I can see the dark desire pooling in his eyes. Royce comes down on top of me, covering me with his large body. "So here's the thing. I need to hang out here for just a little bit. Jack'll need to use the lawn once more before bed," he says, nipping at my lip with his teeth. "But I can't hold off getting you naked for even another second, so we'll improvise."

Improvise? What does that mean?

Royce hops off the couch and crouches beside it. He keeps his gaze locked on mine as he reaches down and unbuttons my jeans. I suck in a harsh breath, but only out of nerves. They've returned and are making it hard to focus on anything other than the fact I'm about to get naked with who could possibly be *the* sexiest man alive.

"Is this okay?" he asks. The moment I nod my head, he starts to slide them around my hips and down my legs. Once I'm free of my pants, he tosses them over his shoulder and sets his sights on my top. "I've been dying to see what you're wearing beneath this tank top," he croaks through a dry throat, as he pushes the purple top upward. I sit up, and he makes quick work of making my top disappear as rapidly as my pants.

I'm practically panting like a dog the moment my shirt is gone, leaving me in my black tank and panties. Funny, I thought I'd feel way more exposed than I do right now, but with that look in his eye—the one that says he's about to devour me like a Thanksgiving Day turkey—there's no way I can feel anything but wanted.

After his eyes feast on my body, he reaches for the tank and starts to slide it up my torso. Cool air kisses my skin as his fingers burn a trail up my abdomen. I extend my arms over my head as I'm removed of that article of clothing as well.

"Fuck, you're even more beautiful than I imagined." He groans as he takes me in, my simple satin with lace overlay bra and panty set that seems to do a lot for him in this moment. I don't have a lot of lingerie but do have a few panty and bra sets. All of them are light colors and make me feel feminine and sexy. They cost a pretty penny too, despite using Sabrina's employee discount, but nothing could have prepared me for how I'd feel as Royce gazes down at me wearing this simple white set.

Nothing.

When his eyes finally return to mine, there's a touch of wild reflecting in those golden orbs. I feel the rough pads of his fingertips brush against my inner thighs as he parts my legs. His touch feels like fire dancing along my skin, and I realize quickly I'm completely helpless against it.

And I'm okay with that.

The pad of his thumb brushes against the apex of my legs. With the layer of satin covering me, it sends me into sensory overload. It's coarse and gentle at the same time. I suck in a deep gasp of air as his thumb slips beneath the material and comes in contact with my swollen, wet flesh.

"Those little noises? I've wondered what they'd sound like when I do this," he says, pressing and rubbing my clit. Shock waves of lust bolt through my veins as he continues to expertly touch my body.

Just when I think I can't take any more, he slides one finger inside my body, and I lose all ability to think. All I can do is feel, and right now, I feel everything. Including that second finger he's slipping inside.

I gasp at the tightness of just two fingers.

"Spread your legs, beautiful," he whispers, his eyes soft as he watches me.

The moment I do, the stiffness eases a bit and feels incredible. Royce moves his fingers in and out, a slow and steady pace that drives me wild. But the real pleasure hits the moment he lowers his head and swipes his hot tongue over my swollen flesh.

"Damn," I gasp, my eyes practically rolling back in my head.

Without lifting his mouth from my body, he growls, "I love it when you cuss, Bestie. It's so unexpected from the school principal."

The rawness of his words causes a new wave of moisture to flood my core. "I only cuss when the situation warrants it," I tell him, rocking my hips and taking his fingers as deep as I can.

"I want to know how many I can get you to say while you come." I swear his devil horns are showing as he smirks up at me from between my legs, a wicked grin on his handsome face.

Then he starts to work his tongue, and I know it won't be long until I'm coming.

Royce alternates between sucking on my clit and flicking it with his tongue, all while his fingers pump into my body. I can feel my orgasm looming on the horizon, and all it'll take is that one little push over the edge until I'm flying. I'm not sure I'm ready for this to end, but I know I'm not strong enough to stop it either. There's no stopping this freight train of desire from overcoming me completely.

With both fingers still buried deep, he curls them upward and slides them along this magical spot within. The result is like fireworks on the Fourth of July. Blinding lights that burst behind my eyelids as my orgasm crashes through me. His mouth is latched on to my clit, sucking and milking every drop of release from my body. When I finally start to ride the waves down, my throat is dry, and my body shakes uncontrollably.

Royce removes his fingers, but gently laps at my clit with his tongue. "That was the sexiest thing I've ever witnessed." He places open-mouthed kisses along my trembling thighs.

My entire body burns with a blush as I glance down. He's between my legs, his lips glimmering with my wetness, and his eyes burning with the intensity of a thousand suns.

I want him.

Bad.

Before we're able to further our evening, we're interrupted by Jack's wet, cold nose pressed to my outer thigh. I gasp and try to cover myself with my hands. Royce chuckles this low, gravelly sound that only causes more wetness to flood between my legs. He's so casual as he looks between my exposed body and his dog. "You have horrible timing, Jack," he says, as he pushes up off the floor and stands. "We're going to have to work on that. Come on, let's go outside one last time."

Jack takes off for the back door, but Royce makes no move to join him. His eyes are locked on me as he licks his lips and wipes his chin with his palm. "We're not finished." He gives me a pointed look before turning and leaving me lying on the couch.

In my mangled panties.

I try to right them, but they're too stretched out to fit properly. A giggle spills from my lips as I think about how exactly they got in this particular condition. I just let Royce Rigsby go down on me, and if his parting words were any indication, I'd say there's more to come.

I sit up on the couch just as he returns. Jack comes over and gives me a kiss on the hand before heading over to his bed and dropping down on the plush pillow. He settles into his spot and rests his head on his paws, exhaling deeply.

Royce approaches and reaches for my hand. "As amazing as you look in nothing but your underwear, how about we head back to my bedroom and take those off?"

Nibbling on my lip nervously, I nod. "I'd like that." And I would. I know this is the step I want to take, even if it's one I'm not familiar with.

He takes my hand and pulls me to his chest. Our fingers link as his lips descend to mine in a lazy kiss I feel clear down to my bare toes. With our lips locked, he guides me down the short hall and to what I assume is his bedroom. It isn't until I feel something firm, yet forgiving, hit the back of my knees that I finally open my eyes, gasping for air.

I glance around through hooded eyelids and take in the room around me. Faint light filters through the windows, spilling across the large bedroom, which is decorated in earthy tones and dark wood accents. I can see a bathroom through an open doorway with a large garden-style tub. I'd love to explore his space further, but when my eyes meet his, I can tell the only exploring will be of each other.

Taking the initiative, I reach down and grab the hem of his T-shirt and pull upward. When his abdomen is exposed, I almost groan in pleasure. Abs. Like real, honest to goodness abs. Eight of them. I toss the shirt over his head and trace each hard ridge with my fingertips. His flesh is warm and soft and there's a dark, thin happy trail that disappears behind the button of his jeans.

I want to explore it...with my tongue.

"I'd be okay with that," he grunts as I score my nails over his skin.

"What?"

"The tongue thing. You whispered it, most likely not intending for me to hear, but I wanted you to know all the same I'm game for some tongue action," he says, waggling his eyebrows suggestively. "Shall I take off my pants?"

Pressing my palms to his abs, I give him a grin. "Yes, I think that sounds like a superb idea."

He smiles widely as he unbuttons his jeans. "Superb, huh?" The sound of his zipper sliding down echoes through the room as he bestows upon me another of those panty-wetting smiles, like I won some big prize. "Know what else is superb?"

A bark of laughter spills from my lips as I shake my head at his playfulness. Yet, I know he's not exaggerating. I felt his erection pressed against me, several times. I know it's...superb. "Maybe instead of telling me, you can show me?"

He drops his pants, underwear too, and meets my gaze. "Oh, Bestie. I plan to show you. A lot." Royce toes off his shoes and rips off his socks, tossing them somewhere into the room.

When he stands before me, completely void of any clothing, all I can do is stare at the sight. He's simply amazing. Cut, hard, and smooth from head to toe. This is a man who takes exceptional care of his body, and suddenly, I feel very lacking. I try to eat on the healthier side and participate in yoga whenever I can, but my workout routine is nothing compared to his. That much shows.

A part of me wants to hide my own body. I've never been big on displaying it, even during sex. Lights are usually off or down low, and I don't wear revealing clothes. But there's something in his eyes, as he practically devours me from head to toe, that makes me feel...alive. Wanted. Sexy. Even with my less than perfect body, Royce doesn't seem to notice it, which helps alleviate some of my nerves.

My fingers itch to touch that dusting of dark hair on his chest. He holds completely still as I graze along his pecs and trail them down the valley of his abdomen. When I get to that happy trail, I hesitate. I've never just reached down and grabbed a man so boldly, but now isn't the time to hide behind my shyness. Now is the time to take the bull by the horns.

Or *horn*.

I skim a finger across his balls and pause when he hisses. My eyes meet his, and I immediately know it's not out of pain or discomfort. It's out of desire. The look in his eyes fuels me on. I work my hand up and wrap it around his shaft. My fingers don't touch, and my mouth goes dry. Without giving it a second thought, I drop to my knees and work my hand from root to head.

I've never wanted to take a man into my mouth more than I do right now. I've always found enjoyment in giving oral pleasure, even if it was always more of a one-way street. My previous boyfriends definitely enjoyed receiving more than giving. One of them wouldn't go down on me at all, saying he didn't like the taste. For the longest time, I wondered if there was something wrong with me, but then I think back to Royce, and the raw pleasure he received from giving.... Well, let's just say some men definitely enjoy it more than others.

I lick the tip of his erection, savoring the salty taste of the little beads of moisture. With one hand still wrapped around him, I take him into my mouth as far as I can, which, considering his size, doesn't seem like it's that much. Another hiss pulls from his throat as I work my way down, licking and sucking.

"Jesus, Quinn," he groans. The sound is loud and carnal. It also goes straight to the apex of my legs and spurs me on. My hands start to slide easily, my grip tight. I pump hard and suck even harder. His hips thrust, and I swear I can actually feel him get harder and thicker.

Suddenly, he pulls back, his penis popping from my mouth with a loud smack. I gaze up, confused. "What's wrong?"

Was I doing it wrong?

His face is tight as he stares down at me. "Nothing's wrong, Quinn. In fact, that was *very* right." He crooks his finger and extends his hand. "Come here."

The moment I'm on my feet, he moves me to my back, laying me out on the top of his bed. His lips press firmly against mine, his tongue coaxing my mouth open so it can dip inside. I completely melt against him, my legs wrapping around his naked torso. His erection presses into me, and I'm reminded of the fact I'm still wearing panties and a bra.

Royce runs his hands down my sides, as if he can't touch me enough, eventually working his way to where the stretched material sits. "These must go," he whispers, trailing his lips along my collarbone.

"Definitely," I choke out over my very dry throat.

He sits and slowly starts to remove them. It's a tad bit embarrassing because I know they're completely soaked. Royce doesn't seem to notice or mind, however. His eyes are riveted to my body as he slides them down my legs. Once they're around my ankles and discarded, he sets his sights on my bra.

I giggle at how easily he reaches behind me and just flicks the double closure open, exposing my breasts. "Wow, that was fast."

He gives me a smirk as he reaches for his bedside table and opens the drawer, pulling out a condom. "Not my first rodeo," he replies, ripping open the foil package with his teeth.

I watch in complete rapture as he slides the protection over his length and comes back to cover my body with his own. His touch is gentle, yet there's an eagerness written in his eyes that tells me all I need to know. Those hazel orbs burn with lust and something that makes my insides tingle.

"Quinn?" His voice sounds scratchy and strained as he holds his erection at my entrance.

"Yes. Do it," I gasp.

"You sure?" he asks, searching my eyes with his own.

"More than anything I've ever been sure of," I reply honestly. "Please, Royce."

He closes his eyes, as if the sound of his name on my lips is too much to take, and presses forward, filling me completely. I feel the stretch, the slight burn, but it's the sense of utter fullness that is my undoing. I know in this moment, the one where he's entirely seated inside of my body, things have absolutely changed.

Changed the relationship I have with Royce.

There's no going back now.

Not that I want to.

I'll never be the same.

Chapter Thirteen

Royce

I have to stop and take a deep breath the moment I'm seated inside of her warm, tight body. The urge to thrust is intense, but I push it back and focus on her. On Quinn.

My Bestie.

The look on her face is my undoing. It's part ecstasy, part amazement as she adjusts to my size. I've had women compliment my cock before, but nothing compares to the way Quinn looked at it. Let's be honest, praises for my dick are pretty much life. I'm a guy. But there's more to it with her. It's as if I'm the only guy in the world. The only one who can give her what she needs.

And that's the best fucking compliment I could ever receive.

I keep her gaze as I gently pull out. My body wants to drive back inside, but I hold back. Not until she's ready. A sweat is already breaking out on my body, but I ignore that too. I won't move until she gives me the cue. With just the tip inside her sweet pussy, I wait. Her legs fall open just a bit, her heels poised on my hips. The look in her eyes tells me everything I need to know, yet I hold back until I hear the words.

The ones that tell me she's mine.

Quinn reaches up and slides her warm fingers across my pecs. They jump under her touch as heat spreads through my veins. "Why'd you stop?" she asks, a flash of insecurity in those heavenly blue eyes.

"Making sure you're okay," I say through gritted teeth. The sex-part of my brain is demanding I move. Take. Yet, I hold back.

"I'm more than okay, Royce," she replies with the slightest smile. She looks down between her legs, and I follow her line of sight. It's erotic as fuck, seeing how her body stretches around mine. "Please." That single word a plea, a song, a beginning to the end.

That one word triggers every animalistic part of my body and my brain.

I hold my position above her, my eyes meeting hers one more time, as I thrust forward. White-hot lust pushes through my blood as I bury myself completely. My hips piston, my pace hard and fast, but Quinn doesn't seem to mind. She opens herself up farther and hangs on tight, rocking her body to meet mine.

The sweetest pants and moans of pleasure spill from her lips as I drive into her. My hands need to touch her skin, *need* to feel her against me. I cup a breast in my palm, sliding a thumb across her peaked nipple. She arches up, as if seeking out the contact. My hips move entirely on their own as I trail my hand down her stomach to her clit. With the slightest brush of my thumb over that sensitive part of her, I feel her pussy tighten. She gasps as I grind my pelvis into her, her eyes fluttering closed in ecstasy.

"Oh God," she whispers, her body starting to shake. I know she's about to come a second time.

I can feel it.

I thrust forward once more, rubbing her clit and grinding my hips. Quinn detonates like the most beautiful firework I've ever had the pleasure of witnessing. "Royce," she gasps, riding out her orgasm.

I'm too distracted though to follow, not ready for this to end.

Before she has a chance to catch her breath, I change our positions, rolling her over and pulling her up on her knees. Her ass is poised high in the air. My cock twitches at the sight. Quinn goes up on her elbows and glances over her shoulder. "I'm not done with you yet, Bestie." Her eyes flare with desire as I line myself up from behind. "Ready?" I ask, teasing her entrance with the head of my dick.

"God, yes," she groans.

I thrust forward, balls deep in one stroke. It's fucking heaven.

She's fucking heaven.

With my hands on her ass, I rock my hips, filling her with each stroke. She's so damn tight, so wet. All I can think about is making her come one more time. My body takes over, driven by lust. My hands glide up her back, my fingers tracing the divots of her spine. I never knew a woman's spine could be this fucking sexy, but it is.

Speaking of spine, there's a tingle at the base of mine, and I know the end is near. There's no way I can stop this freight train, barreling out of control and heading for the crash. The sound of our bodies slapping together fills the room, mixed with the sweet chorus of her gasps. I need to hold off, make sure she gets off a third time, but I'm not sure my body is listening anymore.

Suddenly, she reaches between her legs. I can feel her fingers graze against my cock as she plays with her own clit. "Fuck," I groan, picturing her soft, delicate fingers sliding along her pussy. My fingers dig into her hips as I thrust harder, the start of my orgasm imminent.

My balls tighten and my cock thickens. Quinn pushes back against me as she starts to come again. Her pussy tries to choke me in the best possible way, and I'm unable to ward off my release. She screams my name, riding out her own orgasm as I empty myself into the condom. I swear I blackout. It's almost too much. The feel of her tight pussy, the way she reaches back and grips my balls between our legs.

Too much, yet not enough.

It may never be enough with her.

We both fall forward, a heap of sweaty, boneless limbs and heavy breathing. I pull out of her body, even though I'd much rather stay there forever, and tuck her against my side. Her hair hangs limply in her face, and when I gently push it aside, the sweetest, most satisfied smile plays on her lips. It makes me feel like the king of the world.

"Am I dead?" she whispers.

A bark of laughter fills the room as I cup the side of her face. "God, I hope not. If you were, we wouldn't be able to do that again."

Her eyes open, slightly hazy and unfocused. Her smile is genuine and sated as she gazes up at me. "Again, huh?"

"Well, not right now. I'm gonna need...six, seven minutes to recover," I tell her, though I know that's probably not true. I'm gonna need a little more time than that. My body and my brain aren't on the same page yet. My brain says yes, let's go again, yet my body is too busy floating down the post-orgasm river, completely satisfied and exhausted.

"Six or seven minutes huh?" she asks, reaching down and gripping my balls in her delicate little hand. They're still hypersensitive and ticklish against her touch. My cock, however, starts to get blood flow again as she trails a finger over the thick vein that runs to the head. It jumps, suddenly eager to play.

"Maybe less, if you keep doing that," I tell her, tucking her into my side and pulling her close.

I realize quickly the mistake. This feels a lot like cuddling. I don't cuddle. After sex, I'm usually pretty quick to close myself off.

Sometimes, they hang around for round two, but most of the time, the women I'm with will head out to meet back up with their friends or home. After all, they were here for one thing, and one thing only.

Sex.

But right now, having Quinn in my arms feels too fucking good. Dangerous, but good. That's why I tell myself it's okay to relax and rest for a bit.

After a few minutes, I adjust my position. I need to get rid of the rubber, and I'm sure Quinn could use a warm washcloth. She doesn't say anything—hell, she barely moves—as I slip from my bed and make my way to the bathroom. I remove the condom and toss it into the trash before grabbing two clean cloths from the closet. I use the first on myself and notice under the unforgiving lights the faint scratch marks across my chest. They're not deep or anything, but just red enough I see them. Flashbacks of her hands touching me, her nails digging into my skin, parade through my dirty mind.

And my cock already starts to respond.

I ignore the rapid blood flow to my favorite appendage and smile when I think back to my first text exchange with Quinn. I called it just that—a favorite amongst appendages. She completely ignored my comment and just went on about unwanted dick pics.

A smile spreading across my face as I wet the other washcloth and return to my bedroom. The moment I see her, my heart stops beating in my chest and the smile is wiped off my face. My God, she is without a doubt, the most stunning creature I've ever seen. Her blonde hair is a wild, tussled mess and the thin blanket I use in the summer is tangled around her legs. She looks like an angel. An absolutely gorgeous angel lying in my bed. Never have I wanted to forget all about the commitment hang-ups I have and just snuggle up to her and never let her go.

But I know that can't happen.

Sure, maybe for a night or two, but the new, the *shiny*, will wear off. All relationships end in pain, which is exactly why I don't do them. Pain now or pain later, it doesn't matter. Pain is pain, and it's inevitable.

That's why I have to convince Quinn to just enjoy our time together, for as long as we have it. Could be a week or two, maybe a few months if I'm lucky, and then we move on. No harm, no foul.

Only, I'm not sure Quinn is built that way. I can already tell she's a relationship girl. No doubt a white picket fence, two kids, and a dog kinda woman. Looking for that one person to spend the rest of her life with.

The thought of someone else coming home and receiving her smiles does something funny to my heart.

I push it aside, though. No way am I digging any deeper into whatever the hell *that* was. The fact remains she'll move on, probably get married and have some kids—and I'll do the same—minus the marriage and kids part. I'll move on. I'll be fine.

With the warm washcloth in my hand, I head over to my side of the bed, where a beauty sleeps. She barely stirs as I move the blanket and whisper her name. Quinn doesn't move, just burrows into my pillow. I should probably wake her up, but the sight in front of me has my brain malfunctioning. Instead of doing what is right, I toss the cloth into the hamper and crawl into my bed.

My arm reaches for her and she comes willingly. Quinn nestles into my side, tossing her arm over my chest. Her soft hair tickles my neck, but not enough for me to move it. Instead, I hold her close and close my eyes, breathing in the scent of her shampoo.

This doesn't feel wrong.

Not at all.

***

Bacon.

I can definitely smell bacon. The rich, maple aroma of my favorite pork product has me wide awake just after seven. I glance around, spying the ball of wrinkled sheets—the very ones I threw off the bed around four, as Quinn climbed on top of me and rode me until I could barely breathe from orgasmic exhaustion.

Speaking of, she's nowhere in sight, which tells me she's probably in my kitchen right now, fixing breakfast. That domestic image is wildly appealing, but not the reason I climb out of bed. No, can't be. It must be my full bladder.

Has to be.

Yet, that doesn't explain why I'd rather head to the kitchen, find Quinn, and kiss the fuck out of her until she's ready for round...whatever. I've lost track. I force my legs to carry me to the bathroom to take a leak. While washing my hands, I discover one of the new toothbrushes I keep in the bottom vanity drawer sitting on the counter. Used. I grab the brush and examine it, as if it could produce answers to world peace and child hunger, but all I see is a simple brush. One used by a woman who spent the night. No, not the first time, but this feels...different.

After I brush my own teeth and slip on a pair of shorts, I head out to find the source of the amazing smell. What I wasn't quite expecting is the vision of Quinn that almost brings me to my knees. She's wearing my T-shirt from last night, which hits mid-thigh. Her long blonde hair is cascading down her back, and her feet are bare. Since when are bare feet so fucking sexy? And my dog is sitting at her feet, his tail wagging against the hardwood as he waits for her to drop some food.

I lean against the counter and watch as she takes the bacon from the oven and sets it on a potholder before grabbing a spatula and removing what looks like French toast from the skillet. She hums along to the tune in her head, and startles when she turns around, seeing me. Jack barks a greeting. "Oh, I didn't know you were there," she says, the cutest blush creeping up her neck.

"I figured that much," I offer with a grin. "Whatcha got there?"

"French toast," she replies proudly, setting the platter in the middle of the counter, my dog trailing her like a shadow.

While she retrieves the bacon, I fill up a cup of coffee and spy hers sitting just off to the side. With a quick top off, I take our cups to the counter and have a seat in one of the barstools. "Jack, go lay down," I command. He hangs his head and whines, but heads over to his bed and dramatically flops down. "Black coffee?"

"A splash of milk and one scoop of sugar," she replies, taking the seat beside me, "But I don't mind black either."

I shove a piece of crispy bacon into my mouth and chew. The moment I swallow, I add, "I would have thought you were a latte girl."

She shrugs, swiping her bacon through the maple syrup on her plate. "I'll drink those too."

I take a big bite of French toast, savoring the blend of egg and maple syrup. "This is good," I tell her, shoveling in a second forkful.

"Thanks," she replies with a shrug. "Your syrup is amazing."

"It's from Canada. I have a friend who moved there a year ago. He sent me that fancy jar shaped like a leaf." Honestly, I've never opened the jar. Hell, I had forgotten I even had it in my cabinet. I'm not much of a sweet breakfast kinda guy, but I'll admit, her homemade French toast and the Canadian maple syrup hits the spot this morning.

When Quinn has finished her food, she gets up, taking her plate to the sink. “Leave it. I’ll take care of it later.”

“I don’t mind,” she insists, turning on the water to rinse her plate.

I take the last slice of bacon and hold it out toward Jack. His ears perk up as he sits, not moving until given the cue. “Here,” I state. Jack jumps up and scampers over to retrieve the food in my hand, scarfing it down in one bite. Once he’s licked my finger clean of residual bacon grease, I head over to where Quinn stands, enjoying the hell out of the view of her legs as I go. When we’re side by side, I take the fork from her hand and drop it in the sink. “I said I’d get it.”

She sticks out her chin and huffs. “And I said I didn’t mind helping.” When she places her hands on her hips, all I can think about is kissing that defiance off her plump lips.

So I do.

I slide my hands around her waist and settle them on the globes of her ass as my mouth descends to hers. “No panties?” I ask against her sweet mouth, taking the opportunity to slip my tongue inside the moment she answers my question with a “no.”

Having sex with this woman should be the last thing on my mind right now, yet it’s the only thing. Her nails dig into my scalp as she pulls me down to her mouth, her fingers slipping through my hair. I back her against the counter and feast, as if I hadn’t just eaten a plate full of food. I’m famished for her, and only her.

“Fuck,” I grumble, ripping my lips from hers and sucking in a big gulp of oxygen.

"Yes, that. Let's do that," she begs, scoring her nails down my chest and across my abs.

"I don't have a condom with me."

A look passes through her blue eyes as they meet mine. "I'm on birth control."

My heart skids to a halt in my chest and my throat becomes dry. I've never—and I mean never— gone in without suiting up. Even in high school, when all my friends were *slipping in the tip,* I refused to risk it. Now, I do everything in my power to make sure I'm in control of the situation and my future. That means I wear a rubber one-hundred-percent of the time.

Yet, there's something promising in those deep blue orbs that has me reconsidering my stance on protection and willing to risk years of self-discipline and self-respect just to know what her body feels like against mine. It's a dangerous game. One I'm not sure I'm ready to play.

"I should grab a condom," I tell her, running my thumb down her jaw.

Instead of arguing with me, like I expect, I'm surprised when she says, "Then you better hurry up, huh?"

Like someone lit my ass on fire, I take off for my room. Jack thinks it's time to play and runs to catch up with me. I dive for my nightstand drawer, grabbing two from the half-empty box. When I turn around, I see man's best friend sitting there, eagerly waiting to join the game. I crouch down and pet his head. "Listen, buddy, I'm gonna need another half hour or so, okay? Then we'll play outside. Promise."

At the word *outside*, Jack barks.

"Yeah, you're not gonna like me right now, but I promise to give you plenty of attention in a little bit," I tell him, scratching behind the ears and standing up.

When we get back in the kitchen, I tell Jack to go lay down again, which he grudgingly does. My eyes return to the woman wearing my shirt. Well, actually, I take that back. My shirt is being tossed on the floor. I take her in a bruising kiss, my hands skimming across her hot, naked flesh. Her tits fit tailored in the palm of my hands, her nipples hard and begging to be sucked.

Of course, I oblige. My tongue dances across the hard nubs, causing her to gasp and moan in pleasure. My cock is hard enough to pound nails, and when my hand drifts down to her pussy, I find her wet and ready. I go ahead and slip two fingers inside, just to be sure, and then I spin her around to face the cabinets.

"Hang on tight, angel. This is gonna be a bumpy ride." I sheath myself in latex and line myself up from behind. I have to squat a little, considering she's so much shorter than me, but I make it work. The moment she arches back, I press forward, filling her sweet pussy in one thrust.

"Holy ahhhh," she gasps, turning and glancing at me over her shoulder.

That right there.

That look. It's part wonder and euphoria mixed with desire and trust.

It's my undoing.

I'm so very screwed, and I don't mean the sex.

I mean my heart.

Chapter Fourteen

Quinn

"What's your plan for today?"

His question startles me, as I didn't realize he was lying on his bed, waiting. I step all the way out of the bathroom dressed in last night's clothes. I've never completed a walk of shame, and I admit, it's slightly embarrassing as he sits there and watches me, no doubt noticing my wrinkled shirt, stretched out jeans, and makeup-less face. Not to mention my wet, limp hair from a quick shower.

With Royce.

"Umm, I think first up is to change my clothes and find some underwear," I tease, referring to the mangled panties I ended up throwing in the trash.

His eyes darken even more as the most wicked smile stretches across his mouth. He sits up and crawls off the bed in this sexy manner that makes my body start to hum. Royce stops directly in front of me. "Don't wear them on my account," he whispers, his fingers dancing against my side as he pulls me into his chest.

I swallow hard. "I usually do my grocery shopping on Sundays."

He seems to think for a few seconds, and I can't help but wonder if he's going to offer to go with me. Clearing his throat, he has another suggestion. "Well, how about you do what you need to complete today. Jack and I will be going for a walk later. Maybe we can stop by and say hello."

I wrap my arms around his waist. "Maybe I'll cook dinner?" I mean for it to be a suggestion, but for some reason it comes out a question. Probably because I've never been this bold before, and it's something for me to get used to.

His eyes light up. "Dinner? I like dinner," he replies just before his lips glide across mine. "Do you want me to bring anything?"

"Just Jack."

Royce snorts. "Oh, you know he'll be there. I think he likes you better than he likes me anyway," he says, running a hand through my hair. "Can I give you a ride home?"

Man, not only do I need to do a walk of shame, but he has to take me home too. That or call an Uber, which I'm not keen on. Those apps always scare me. Too many people say their card is charged for trips not taken or food not delivered. I'll stick to the old-fashioned way and do it myself.

Except in this case.

"Yes, that would be helpful, thank you." I grab my purse and phone, realizing it died sometime between last night and this morning. "Shoot."

"Problem?" he asks, leading me out of his bedroom and toward the front door. He stops and puts Jack in his kennel before locking up the house and escorting me to his truck.

"How long do you have to keep him in the kennel?" I ask, as he opens the passenger side door ignoring his original question.

"Actually, I probably won't keep him in there too much longer. He's trained well. They recommended it for the first week or two, just to see how he adjusts. He's out at night and while I'm home. I only put him in there when I'm gone," he says, closing the door behind me. The cab smells like him, all rich and musky, and is neat and organized.

Just like the owner.

I take in the cabin with fresh eyes. Last night, I could tell it was a great place, but in the light of day, I see it's well maintained and has great landscaping. I can almost picture Royce—shirtless—while mowing the yard, trimming the shrubs, and watering the plants. It's not all that unappealing. In fact, it's a pretty nice image.

He backs out of the driveway and heads in the direction of my place. I start to mentally make a list of things I'll need from the store, both for dinners throughout the week and for tonight. One of my favorites is salmon with lemon and asparagus with Parmesan cheese, but that doesn't mean Royce is a fan. "Can I ask you a question?"

"Shoot," he replies, keeping his eyes on the road.

"Do you like fish and seafood?"

"Love it, why?"

"I was just thinking about dinner tonight. Is there anything you don't like?" I ask, as he turns down my road.

He pulls his truck in front of my little white house and throws it in park. He turns those hazel eyes my way, looking deep in thought. "Well, let's see, I'm not a fan of chickpeas, peaches, Funyuns, or grape jelly. Oh, and pumpkin spice." Royce sticks out his tongue and gags. "That shit's nasty."

A bubble of laughter pulls from my throat. "Pumpkin spice is weird. I don't get the craze. But grape jelly? Really?"

"Strawberry, all the way, baby," he adds with a wink.

"I spent my entire childhood eating grape jelly and peanut butter sandwiches with Doritos on top."

He just stares at me from across the cab. "I think I just fell in love with you."

I know he's teasing, but tell that to my heart, which kicks up a few hundred beats per second.

"Yes, well, if I'd had known you were this easy to please, I'd have made you a few sandwiches for breakfast."

Another wolfish grin breaks out across his lips. "Oh, I'm very easy to please."

Yeah, he's definitely not talking about food.

Clearing my throat, I reach for the door handle. "Wait, I'll help you out."

Royce jumps out of the truck and meets me on the passenger side. With his hands on my hips, he practically lifts me off the seat, depositing me on the ground in front of him. He doesn't move his hands, as our gazes meet. "Thank you for everything." My words are just above a whisper and I can feel the heat creeping up my face.

Instead of saying anything right away, he places his hands on the sides of my head and plants his lips on mine. It's a quick kiss, but still packs quite a punch. "I had a great time."

Clearing my throat, I ask, "Would you still like to come for dinner?"

Why am I so nervous?

He lifts the corner of his mouth in a smile. "I'd love to. What time would you like Jack and I to arrive?"

"Any time after five? I'll have dinner ready at six."

"Sounds perfect," he says before kissing me soundly once more. In fact, he does such a thorough job, I'm on the verge of inviting him inside. "I'll see you around five."

With one final chaste kiss on my lips, he heads back to his truck, leaving me standing on the sidewalk. My legs feel shaky as I make my way to the door, the weight of his stare heavy on my back. The moment the door is open, I turn and wave, letting him know I'm good. He throws me a smile and wave of his own before starting his truck and driving off. I watch him go, and stand there for a few minutes after his Chevy has disappeared.

Then, I finally step inside.

First thing I do is plug in my phone. It takes a few minutes before it charges enough to turn on, and the moment it does, it practically blows up with texts and voicemail messages.

"Shit," I mumble, scanning through the dozen messages from my best friend. They start sweet and encouraging, but as the night rolls into early morning, they get progressively more concerned. I had never thought to check my phone while I was with Royce, and now I realize the damage I've caused.

I worried my friend.

Hell, I probably even terrified her.

Just thinking of the shoe being on the other foot makes my heart race. If Sabrina had gone home with some guy and I couldn't get ahold of her, I'd be a little panicked too.

I dial her immediately and hold my breath.

It doesn't even finish the first ring. "Holy shit, Quinn Michaels. I thought you were lying in a ditch or already sold as a sex slave in Mexico!"

I cringe at her words and the tone of her voice. "I'm so sorry, Rina. My phone died, and I didn't notice until a little bit ago."

"You better be sorry, missy. You can't just disappear like that. I've been worried sick!"

Groaning, I lean against the counter and close my eyes. Memories of being pressed against a certain countertop earlier this morning flash through my mind, creating a vivid porno-like parade of naughty recollections.

"What? Are you okay? You just moaned," Sabrina asks, her voice calming down a few decibels.

"Oh, uh, yeah, I'm fine." My throat feels dry.

Sabrina gasps. "Oh my God, you had sex with the hottie, right? You totally did! I can tell!" She whoops and hollers, making me laugh. "Tell me all about it, and don't leave out a single detail. He's hung like a Clydesdale, right?"

"Sabrina! I'm not talking about *that*," I insist, that all-too familiar burn sliding up my neck.

"So, that's a yes. I knew it. I totally pegged him for an eight, maybe a nine-incher. He's tall and big, but not in that gross, bulky way, but what really gave it away was his hands. Huge hands and long fingers, Q. Hands never lie."

"Big hands mean big penises?" I ask, smiling because she's spot on when it comes to Royce Rigsby.

"You tell me, Miss I Had Sex With A Gorgeous God last night."

"And this morning," I mumble.

I have to move the phone from my ear as she screams into the device. "I knew it! I totally knew it! Start at the beginning. Was he the King of Foreplay?"

Sighing, I close my eyes and try not to picture how our evening began. Instead, I focus on grabbing a sheet of paper so I can start my grocery list. "I'm not telling you all the dirty details, Rina."

"So, he's dirty. Yeah, I can totally see that. Does he have a playroom?" she asks, way too eager for juicy details.

"No," I reply with a chuckle. "Though, he does have a game room in his loft."

"Probably not the kinky games I'm imagining right now." She sighs, the phone line filling with silence for several long seconds. "So you're okay?"

"I'm...perfect. He's coming over for dinner tonight." You couldn't wipe the smile off my face with a putty knife.

"Really? It must have gone really well. I'm excited for you."

"Thanks, but don't get too excited. I'm not really sure this'll lead anywhere."

"Well, it's already led to orgasms, which is the most important direction to head."

"True, except, you know what I want in this life."

"Orgasms get you there."

"Technically, yes," I start, but she cuts me off.

"Orgasms lead to babies, as long as he's got good swimmers."

"Yes, I understand biology, Rina, but you're missing my point."

"Well, then make it already."

I sigh. "I don't think Royce is the marriage and family kinda guy."

She's quiet on the other end. "Why do you say that? Did he say he didn't want it?"

"Well, no, we didn't exactly reach the 'what do you want out of life' discussion this weekend."

"That's because you were still in the 'make you forget your own name from too many orgasms' discussion," she adds with a giggle.

Even though she's right, she's missing the point. "What I mean is everything about him screams wham, bam, thank you, ma'am."

"But...didn't you say he's coming over for dinner?"

Sighing, I realize she's right. "Yes."

"That doesn't scream very wham bammy."

"No, I guess it doesn't," I concede, still feeling a little confused.

"Listen, Q, I know you had this plan that involved a husband and kids. I also know it hasn't exactly happened the way you thought it would. I don't know if Royce is husband material or not, but there's nothing wrong with having a little fun until the right one comes along."

"But what if the right one comes along while I'm having fun with Royce? And I miss him?"

"Then he wasn't the right one, Q. You know I don't believe all that Hallmark bullshit on soul mates and whatnot, but I also know you do. There's no way fate would put your Mr. Perfect in front of you, only to have you miss him because you're having fun with Royce. I say, let loose and have fun with Mr. Nine Inches and when you're done having fun, move on. Mr. Minivan and Picket Fence will probably appear just when you think he's already passed you by."

She does make sense. Kind of.

I may not know much about Royce, but I think I've learned enough to know he's not really looking for the same things I am, long term. It's nothing he's said, so much as the vibe he gives. He has that one-night stand feel. The guy who plays hard, has fun, and moves on. The one who's declared to be single until the day he dies and will probably follow through with his plan.

The one who could really hurt a girl like me, if I were to let him.

Good thing I already know that can't happen.

Getting involved too deep with Royce Rigsby isn't in the game plan, which might be why staying away altogether is the best option.

But then I think about how dark his hazel eyes got when he was close to coming, and how his masterful hands played my body like a musical instrument. It's details like those that have me actually contemplating her idea of having a little fun now, while I wait for Mr. Forever.

"You're quiet, which means you're thinking. I hope it's about what positions he'll do you in later tonight."

"You have a filthy mind for someone raised by a preacher," I tease.

"It's the sheltered life talking. There was nothing to do in Wednesday night Bible study but think about sex," she replies, and I'm not entirely sure she's joking. "Anyway, my point is this: have fun with Royce. Enjoy a few more orgasms while he's willing to provide them, and then move on. You may not get so lucky on the orgasm front with your forever, Q. Daphni Simmons was telling me she hasn't had one in four years. Four. Years, Quinn. Can you believe that? See what marriage does to you?"

I roll my eyes, even though she can't see. "Maybe it's because Mr. Simmons is too busy sleeping with his secretary to worry about his wife's sexual needs?"

"Probably," she replies. "Listen, I gotta go. Now that I know you're not dead, I'm going to meet Decker at the coffee shop."

"Oh yeah? How'd that go last night?" I ask, hating I didn't ask before now.

"Good. I mean, not as good as your night, obviously, but we agreed to meet up today when he gets off work. Maybe, if I'm lucky, he'll show me how the coffee grinder works in the back room, if you know what I mean."

A smile crosses my lips. "Well, be safe, friend. Make sure you suit-up before he does any grinding demonstrations."

Sabrina laughs. "Will do. And you make sure to think about what I said. Just because Royce isn't the endgame doesn't mean you shouldn't play ball."

"Play ball?"

"It's a sports metaphor. Sheesh, catch up."

"No, I got it. I just don't think I've ever heard you say play and ball in the same sentence without referring to testicles."

She laughs again. "I love it when you say testicles. So proper."

"Goodbye, Sabrina," I say, essentially cutting her off.

"Just say big hairy balls once, will you?"

"Goodbye!"

I hang up and set my phone on the counter, trying not to giggle at her antics, and make sure the phone is still plugged in. Then, I grab my notepad and start making my list. I start with breakfast items, before moving to lunch and dinner. Only when I have my week planned out, do I turn my focus to this evening.

Dinner with Royce.

It's been awhile since I've made dinner for someone of the opposite sex. Paul always preferred to go out for dinner. When he would allow me to cook for him, I had to do it at his place because it was roomier than mine. The truth was, Paul was a bit snobbish and cared way too much about appearances.

But now is not the time to think about Paul.

Now is the time to plan my menu, get ready for the day, and head to the store before it gets too crazy-busy with Sunday afternoon shoppers. Once that's done, I'll be able to turn my focus to Royce and the dilemma he creates.

Do I consider spending more time with him, even if he's not possibly looking for the same things in life I am? Or do I cut my losses now to avoid the potential heartache later?

Even after I unload my groceries, I'm still not any closer to making a decision.

***

I get more nervous with each minute that passes five o'clock. I have a salad ready in the fridge, the asparagus cut, seasoned, and placed on a baking sheet, potatoes ready to be baked, and the salmon marinating. All I need is my dinner date.

Or companion.

Not a date.

Not really.

I start to pace and fret, which is not a good look on me, but I can't help it. What if he doesn't come? What if I went to all this trouble for him to not show? Or worse, what if I burn the vegetables or the fish doesn't turn out?

I groan in frustration, hating how I'm letting worry get the best of me. And fortunately, I'm saved from further torture by a knock on my front door.

The door is open, so the moment I round the corner from the kitchen, Royce comes into full view. He's wearing a fresh T-shirt and shorts, his feet adorned with running shoes, and a ball cap perched on his head. In his hand is a leash, which leads to his dog. Jack is sitting like the good boy he is at his feet, tongue hanging in excitement.

"Hi," I greet, offering a smile as I push open the screened door.

Jack barks in greeting, his tail thumping hard against the porch. The moment I crouch down, I'm awarded with a wet, slobbery kiss across my cheek. "Jack, behave," his owner instructs, but the dog doesn't seem to listen. He places his big paw on my knee and bumps my shoulder with his head.

I laugh at the same time Royce does, and shake the dog's hand. "Come on in," I tell them both, standing up and holding open the door.

"Are you sure you want him in here?" he asks, grabbing the door and holding it for me. "We can just hang out in the backyard."

"No, it's okay. I don't think there's anything he can get into," I reassure as we both step inside. Jack instantly starts sniffing everything, pulling against the leash. "You can release him."

Royce seems hesitant at first but ends up removing the leash from his dog. Jack bolts into the living room, smelling everything within reach. I glance at his owner and find his eyes scanning my living room as well. "You have a nice place."

"Thanks. It's small but suits me just fine."

Suddenly, Jack must catch a whiff from the kitchen. His nose shoots up as he sniffs hard and bolts toward the food. "Jack," Royce hollers, turning and following the eager pup.

"It's okay. I have everything put up or out of his reach," I assure.

We step into the kitchen together and laugh as Jack tries to find the source of the amazing scents. "Wow, smells good in here," Royce says, glancing at the covered pan of fish on the stovetop.

"It's salmon," I reply hesitantly. I know he told me he likes about anything, but I can't help but still feel worried about my choices tonight.

"I love salmon," he confirms, a smile spreading across his face.

"Well, that's a relief. I was afraid you wouldn't. Fish is one of those entrees where you either love it or hate it, and even then, people are very picky about their fish. My grandma loved bluegill but disliked pretty much any other type. My grandpa would take her to Wisconsin every summer to fish, and she'd only keep the bluegill," I tell him, realizing I'm rambling. But when I look his way, I only see his grin. "What? Sorry, I get a little long-winded sometimes."

He shakes his head. "No, I like hearing about your family. Are they still alive? You're grandparents?" he asks, popping his hip against my counter and crossing his arms. The T-shirt pulls snuggly against his biceps, which makes my mouth drier than the Sahara.

"No, they've both passed. My parents live in Sevierville and my older brother is in Alaska."

"Alaska?" he asks, leaning his elbows on the counter as if he's totally engrossed.

"Yeah, he's in the Army, stationed at Fort Wainwright. He's a lifer, serving twenty-two years."

"Wow, that's commendable. Twenty-two years makes him..." he trails off.

"Quentin turned forty earlier this year."

He looks to be deep in thought. "So, if he's older than you, and he's forty, that makes you...thirty..."

I giggle. "Eight."

"Huh," he says, straightening up and giving me a long, perusing glance from head to toe. "I'd never have guessed you were a day over thirty-two."

I roll my eyes. "Right. So why didn't you just ask me my age?"

He sobers. "My mama always told me never to ask a lady their age. It angers them."

I giggle. "Your mama taught you right." I grab the food from the fridge to go in the oven and glance his way. "Do I want to know how old you are? You almost sounded shocked when I said I was thirty-eight."

"Shocked, yes, but not in a bad way. I'm thirty-five." Those hazel eyes shine brightly under his ball cap.

"Thirty-five, huh?" I state aloud, as if trying it on. He's younger than me, though not nearly as cradle-robbing as the coffee house guys were. Three years isn't much of a difference at all. Though, I have to admit, I always pictured myself with an older guy. Funny how life happens, right?

I mean, not that we're *together* or anything.

Just friends.

Who hang out.

And have amazing sex.

Let's definitely not forget that part.

"Where'd ya go there, Bestie. Your smile was a little wicked," he teases, the tone in his voice laced with something dirty.

"Nowhere," I insist, turning my rapidly blushing face away from his knowing gaze.

"Mmhmm," he sings with the brightest smile ever on his gorgeous face. I busy myself at the stove, getting the salmon ready to grill, when I feel his body press against my back. A gasp slips from my throat as his erection sort of nestles right above the cleft of my rear. It's not completely hard, but he's working on it. "I think your mind was in the gutter, Bestie."

I glance over my shoulder and watch his lips trail a line of kisses across my shoulder. When his eyes meet mine, I simply shrug and say, "Maybe."

His grin is devilish as he wraps his arms around my waist and holds me against his body. "Mine has been stuck in the gutter since I dropped you off earlier. All I can think about is a repeat."

My blood zings through my veins and wetness floods my panties. I find myself pushing back against him, his now very-hard erection sandwiched between us. I want to turn around, drop to my knees, and worship at the temple of Royce Rigsby.

But the moment is broken when he lightly pats me on the ass and steps back, severing our connection. "Maybe I'll let you have your dirty way with me later, Bestie Tami with an I. Right now, I think we start with food and maybe a drink or two." His eyes burn darker and practically draw me in, like a moth to a flame. "You're going to need your nourishment for later."

Later.

Yep.

Moth to a flame.

Chapter Fifteen

Royce

"That was delicious," I tell her again, dropping my napkin on the table beside my empty plate. I look to my side where Jack snores, his belly full from the kibble I brought along for his dinner.

"Thank you," she replies, reaching for the plate in front of me.

I grab them before she can and stand up, heading for the sink.

"You don't have to clean up. I can do it later," she says, setting everything beside the empty sink.

"It won't take too long. We can do it now," I offer, but she shakes her head.

"No, let's go sit on the porch. It's a gorgeous evening."

We quickly clear off the table, setting the dirty stuff aside. While Quinn puts leftovers in the fridge, I grab two bottles of water and head for the front door. Jack stirs, realizing I'm about to go outside, and jumps up to follow. I set the bottles on the bistro table and watch as my dog runs out and starts to sniff every corner of her small yard. When he finds the perfect place, he finally lifts his leg and takes care of business.

"I love sitting out here," she says, as she steps out on the porch to join me.

"It's a great neighborhood," I agree, looking around, the sun starting to dip below the tree line. Quinn lives in the middle house of three on the street, with the same number on the opposite side of the road. She doesn't have the view I have, considering she's at the base of the mountain, but it's a quiet, somewhat remote area. The only traffic is local, but with only a few houses on her block, that traffic is limited.

"I always thought I'd love to live down at the bottom of the mountain, but after spending some time last night out on your deck, I'm seriously considering relocating," she states with a chuckle as she takes the empty seat across from me.

"I got lucky with my place. It was an older couple who built it. They didn't like driving up and down the mountain in the winter anymore."

"I purchased my house from an older couple too. They wanted to move closer to their daughter and her family. I believe they called this place their home for like forty years. I just realized I didn't give you a tour. That's rude of me," she says, her eyes apologetic.

"It's okay. You can show me the bedroom. Later." I wiggle my eyebrows suggestively and watch as one of those blushes darkens her cheeks. I take a long pull of water and watch as Jack continues to sniff and mark different places in the yard. Since I'm out here, I don't have him on a leash, but so far, he's staying on Quinn's property. "So have you ever visited your brother in Alaska?"

"I have, actually," she replies, leaning back in her chair and looking up at the sky. "Not too long after he transferred up there, my parents and I went for a visit. We stayed in Fairbanks, which was nice, and we were there in the summer, so the weather wasn't horrible. The unit he's in is combat ready forces, so he can be deployed anytime. It's hard on his wife and kids," she says, a note of sadness in her words.

"I bet that's hard. I did a couple of tours but didn't have the baggage he has." I think back on how my deployments always affected my own parents. After my dad died, that was part of the reason I stepped back from that life. The last deployment really took a toll on my mom, according to Rueben, and I didn't want to lose my only remaining parent because I was off fighting wars on foreign soil and she was home worrying herself to death.

"His wife knew what she was signing up for," she states, glancing my way. "They met in high school. She went off to college when he joined the Army. They dated long distance for four years before they got married, and she moved to where he was. Alabama, I believe it was at the time. I always wondered how they make it work, but they do. My nieces were born in different states, but Quentin and Lydia wanted them to be as stable as they could through school. So they've stayed in Alaska for fourteen years."

"Wow, that's admirable," I reply, and it is. They put their kids first, or as close to first as you can with a job like his. I know it's not easy to do, so he must be fairly high up in rank.

"My parents go visit every year. I always say I'll go again, but it's hard to do sometimes." When our eyes meet, there's guilt there.

"Do they ever come here?" I ask, finishing off my water.

"They do. Most years, Lydia and the girls come. Sometimes Quentin too, if he's not overseas."

I don't know why, but I reach over and take her hand. To offer comfort, maybe? She seems sad, and maybe a little lonely talking about her family like that. When I was overseas, I missed the hell out of my own family, but I was always so focused on my job, I didn't let it get to me too much. Not until that last tour after Dad died.

That's also the reason I never settled down. I couldn't imagine leaving my wife and kids back at home and going off to fight. I'd constantly be wondering what was happening, worrying about them. No way could I focus on my job, which is what was asked of me every time I strapped on my helmet and grabbed my gun.

Needing a redirect from the heavy shit, I ask, "So where's your dream vacation destination? You've already been to Alaska."

She sighs deeply. "The history buff in me would love to go to Rome or Egypt. Somewhere with culture and a story, you know?"

"That would be cool. I was able to do a little sightseeing while I was in New Zealand," I tell her.

Her eyes dance with excitement. "That would be amazing. I'd love to see the Waitangi Treaty Grounds and the Olveston Historic Home. Not to mention the Larnach Castle."

"I think I have some photos on my laptop still. Not the same as seeing it in person, but definitely beautiful sights and country," I add. I find myself just smiling over at her, loving the way her blue eyes sparkle with excitement as she mentions historical places around the world.

Her breathing seems to change, right before my eyes. Her face goes from joy to something a little darker, a little dirtier. Suddenly, I'm pretty sure she's not thinking about historical places at all. Which is good, because I'm abruptly thinking about her, naked. Maybe even at those places she mentioned someday. But right now, it's here. On her bed. Her underneath me.

Movement on the porch catches my attention as Jack plops down at her feet and sighs. Quinn reaches down and pets his thick coat, yet keeps her eyes locked on mine. The air thickens around us, a sexual haze that makes it hard to see anything but her. I've felt desire plenty of times, but this is...different. Yes, it starts in my crotch, but it spreads through my veins like fire and kickstarts my heart and short-circuits my brain. It's scary, actually, how I respond to her, and no, not just my dick.

Though, I'm still ignoring those other responses.

"How about that tour now?" I ask, reaching for my empty bottle and her half-full one.

She jumps up and almost trips over the dog at her feet. I reach out, grabbing her arms and pulling her into my chest. She fits so fucking perfect against me. My arms wrap around her tiny frame, so slender and right for my bigger body.

I lift her over Jack, but set her back down on the ground, take her hand, and lead her inside. I whistle for my dog, who comes eagerly. Inside, Quinn locks the door and looks around. "Will he be okay in here by himself?"

I glance around, not really seeing anything he can get himself into trouble with. "I think so." I turn to my pup and say, "Lie down, Jack." He walks over and plops down on the rug in front of the fireplace, his eyes closing instantly for a nap. "He'll be good for a bit."

Quinn nods and then pulls me down a short hallway with three doors. She points to the first one on the left and says, "Bathroom." To the farther door on the left, she adds, "Guest bedroom." Then, she turns to the only door on the right and steps inside.

Her room is exactly as I'd pictured it. Spacious, feminine, and pretty with a floral print comforter and cheerful décor. Even as the sun fades in the sky, I can tell this place is her sanctuary, her solace after a long day.

"There's a small en-suite bathroom and walk-in closets. I don't have a lot of clothes, but those babies are what really sold me on this place," she says, turning to meet my gaze, a bright smile on her face. I can almost picture her initial excitement at discovering those deep storage spaces along the back wall.

"It's perfect," I tell her, pulling her back into my arms. "This space is very much you."

She smiles the most genuine grin I've ever seen, and the result causes my heart to thunder in my chest. I swear she can probably hear it pounding, but if she does, she doesn't say a word. I silence the noise by kissing her soft lips. My hands skim around her waist and land on her lower back. She presses her chest to mine, her delicate body molding against me.

Quinn reaches down and grabs the hem of my T-shirt, pulling it up and over my head in a quick motion. Her eyes—fuck, the way she looks at my body—devour me, as her soft fingers trace every ab, every ridge on my chest. "You're very pretty to look at," she confesses sweetly, blushing as she meets my gaze.

"You're not so bad yourself, Bestie. In fact, I'd rather enjoy the view of you wearing less clothing, if you don't mind," I reply, grabbing her own shirt and pulling it over her head.

"Better?" she whispers.

I reach around her back and unfasten the closure on her bra. The material slides down her arms, and she drops it on the floor. "Now it's better."

She giggles, throwing her arms around my neck, and plasters her bare chest to mine. "Even better yet."

I take her lips with mine as I move her to the bed. My mind starts to spin with all the different positions I want her in. I know last night wasn't enough, and if I'm being honest, I'm certain tonight won't be either. She's the drug I crave, a desperate shot of alcohol to a recovering alcoholic.

Laying her back, I come down on top of her. I position one knee between her legs and can feel the heat of her body. She rocks into my leg, as if seeking out precious contact where she aches for me. My mouth waters at the thought of tasting her again, and as sweet as her mouth is, there's something I want more.

I start to make my move down her body, tickling and sucking on her soft flesh. She arches her back, pressing her glorious tits up into my face. I take the first nipple into my mouth, my cock getting painfully hard when she moans in pleasure. "Fuck, I love your tits," I tell her, licking and toying with the little buds.

She gasps when I draw one hard nipple into my mouth. "I think they love you too."

Chuckling, I pay a little more attention to her chest before continuing on my voyage downward. When I reach the buttons on her simple khaki shorts, I glance up and make sure she's all right with what's coming next. Her eyes are eager, her mouth gaped open as she lightly pants. She doesn't tell me to stop, nor discourage me any, so I go ahead and pop the button. Her eyes flare with desire as she watches me remove her shorts.

Glancing down, I spy basic pink panties with lace trim around the legs. "I see you found some underwear," I state, recalling how mangled the ones she wore last night ended up.

She blushes even harder. "I did. The others had to be scrapped, no thanks to you." I know she's teasing, but there's something primal that flares to life in my chest.

"Let's see if we can keep these in a little better shape," I state, slipping my fingers under the waistband and moving them down her legs. "See? Perfect condition. You may be able to wear them again."

She hums. "Except those are all *wet*."

Fuck. I knew they were, but now that she's drawn my attention to them, all I can think about is how soaked that cotton is and how badly I want that taste in my mouth. Refusing to deny myself any longer, I bend down and bury my mouth between her legs. My tongue delves into her pussy repeatedly, her body starting to quiver and shake as her hips rock.

I slide a finger over her clit, lightly pinching it as I fuck her with my mouth. The only sound in the room is her panting and the occasional slurp from me. With each pump of my tongue inside her pussy, she gets closer and closer to coming. I start to work my fingers faster and can feel the pressure building. Her orgasm is right there, within reach. All she needs is to be tipped over the edge.

I'm like a man possessed, hell-bent on feeling her come around my tongue. With a few more pumps and flicks of my fingers, she detonates, coming in the most beautiful way I've ever felt. Her pussy squeezes against my tongue as her hips rock, riding my face. Experiencing her orgasm could almost trigger my own, but I hold back, needing to be inside her when I finally blow.

"Jesus, I could watch you come all day long and never get tired of it," I confess, wiping my mouth with the back of my hand.

She's spread out across the top of her bed, the comforter still gripped in her hands. "I think you should put your money where your mouth is and do it again."

I laugh hard. "My mouth was just all over your pussy."

Her blue eyes sparkle like sapphires under the sun. "Any chance you brought a condom with you on your outing this evening?"

I reach into the pocket of my shorts and toss it on the bed beside her. "Just like the American Express card. Never leave home without it."

I shove my shorts and underwear down in one swoop and toe off my shoes. I grab my socks and toss them in the pile of discarded clothes and reach for the protection. Quinn takes it before I can and sits up, ripping open the package with her teeth.

"May I?" she asks.

Stepping forward, I aim my erection at her and wait. "Be my guest."

With gritted teeth, I try to hold absolutely still as she palms my cock, her hand sliding along the entire length. She fumbles a little as she pinches the tip and positions it over the head. I'm pretty sure my blood is all south of my waist because I can't seem to think straight. All I want to do is thrust and drive into her body, letting myself be overtaken by the sensations.

When it's in position, she gives me a smile, like she's proud of herself. "I've never done that," she says. Something primal erupts in my chest at the thought of being her first anything.

"You can do that anytime you want," I say, crawling over her body. "Scoot up a little." She does, moving to the middle of the mattress.

I take her legs and position them over my shoulders. I'm already lined up perfectly. Before I thrust, I get a good look at Quinn, lying there, ready and waiting. She places her hands on my knees, a touch that seems to calm my racing heart and spur me on. So I don't deny either of us what we want.

I press forward.

I don't thrust, even though the pleasure threatens to completely override my brain. I make my movements slow and deliberate, savoring the feel of her tight body stretching around me. With her legs up, almost together, her pussy hugs my cock even firmer.

Gently, I pull out, but my hips start to do all the talking. I push in, my movements more hurried than before. Her eyes are wild as I hold her legs straight up, creating a tighter fit that threatens to steal my breath. Her little gasps of pleasure are like lava in my veins. Blue eyes lock on mine as her hand reaches between her legs. My gaze follows, zoning in on the delicate motions of her fingers as she strokes her clit.

I swear my cock swells even more. I couldn't look away if I wanted to. Her noises fill the space around us as her pussy squeezes hard. Her second orgasm is triggered, a beautiful eruption that spurs my own release. I can't think, can't breathe. I can only feel.

So. Fucking. Much.

Her legs are still in my hands, and the moment I release them, we fall into a heap of boneless limbs. "Wow," she whispers, her warm breath tickling my shoulder.

I grunt in reply, unable to formulate words, apparently.

"You okay there, Slugger?"

"I'm fantastic. You?"

She giggles and kisses my bicep. "I can't feel my legs, but it's so worth it. Soooo, worth it," she sings, a tender smile on her lips.

"Mind if I use your bathroom?"

"Of course not," she replies through a yawn.

I find myself smiling as I get up, my legs a little shaky, and step into her bathroom. I dispose of the condom, wash up, and grab a warm washcloth for Quinn. Funny, I was doing the exact same thing last night.

And, again, early this morning.

There's no sign of slowing down anytime soon.

The moment I slip back into her bedroom, Quinn hops up and excuses herself into her bathroom. I stare at the bed, wondering what I'm supposed to do now. This feels a bit like déjà vu, and I realize, this is the exact moment I'd slip on my jeans and leave. Yet, all I want to do is climb back inside and hang out a little more.

The door opens behind me, and her delicate fingers slide across my upper back and wrap around my arms. “Do you have to head out?” she asks. It’s a simple question, yet feels loaded as hell.

Do I *have* to head out?

Nope. I could stay another hour or two, maybe give her a third orgasm. Hell, we could even talk for a bit, and I’d be completely content with it.

Which is why the answer to her question needs to be yes. It’s way too comfy and cozy here. Without realizing it, I’m entertaining ideas I have no business entertaining. This is fun. Nothing more.

Yet, for some foreign reason, my mouth and brain don’t communicate, and I find myself replying, “I can stay for a little bit.”

Shit.

Chapter Sixteen

Quinn

His warm, wet tongue slides across my cheek. I can't help but smile a little, even as his tongue glides across my ear. A giggle slips from my throat, and he nuzzles into the crook of my neck, the hair on his head tickling my chin.

"Quinn?"

My eyes crack open, but it's not Royce's now-familiar ones I'm staring into.

It's Jack.

He's lying on my side of the bed, his tongue hanging out. When he realizes I'm awake, he gives me another kiss across the face, this one right across my eyes. "Oh, Jack," I grumble, wiping doggy drool off my face.

I feel Royce shift behind me, my back pressed against him. "Jack. Down."

The dog just looks at him though. I swear Jack's eyebrows arch in question, like he wants to know what Royce is going to do about it.

"Shit, he probably has to go outside," Royce mumbles against my ear.

The moment the last word flies from his mouth, Jack jumps up, his tail wagging. He's practically spinning circles in excitement. "I think you're right."

Royce groans as I glance at the clock. It's just after eleven. "I need to go," he whispers, but doesn't make an immediate move to get up. Instead, he tightens his hold on me and kisses the side of my head. Jack must agree, because he barks.

I laugh, until Royce moves and starts to crawl out of bed. Then, my amusement turns to sadness. I knew he couldn't stay, but a part of me really wishes he would. There's still so much we haven't talked about, but I'm trying to just go with the flow, even though a part of me wants to know what his intentions are where we're concerned.

I watch as Royce gets up and stretches, his erection isn't fully hard, but I know all it would take for it to be is to throw my covers back and invite him to return to bed. Jack lies beside me, patiently waiting, as his owner slips on his underwear, shorts, and shirt. I stroke the dog's soft fur as I take in the man before me. His...hardness—and no—I'm not just referring to what's in his shorts. He's fit in a way I've never really cared about before; not that I care about that now. I never really thought I'd find it so...attractive.

When he slips his socks and shoes on, he stands up and turns my way. He shakes his head at Jack, who seems just as content to lie beside me than go home right now. "Come on, Jack. Let's go home."

The dog perks up but doesn't immediately jump off my bed. Instead, he nuzzles his wet nose against my arm and licks me. I scratch across his ears. "Good night, Jack. I'll see you soon."

Jack barks.

Royce laughs, places a knee on the mattress, and leans over to give me a kiss. It's a slow, lazy one that makes my nipples hard. "I'll talk to you later," he whispers, placing one last peck on my lips.

I reach for the comforter, but he stops my hand. "I can see myself out and lock up. You stay in bed," he insists, getting up and heading for the door. Before he steps through, he adds, "I have to work late tomorrow evening, but maybe we can grab dinner this week?"

There's a nervousness in his voice that's usually not there, which makes me wonder why? Is it because he's concerned about my answer, or the question? I've already determined Royce isn't a relationship guy, so does he see dinner as getting too close to something he doesn't want? Right now, he's far from the cocky, confident man I've come to know. Maybe that's because he's slightly out of his element.

"That sounds great. We have a book fair fundraiser at the school Thursday, so that's the only night I'm not available," I tell him.

He rocks back on his heels and gives me a grin. "Okay, I'll text you." Royce throws me that wink and any apprehension I saw moments ago is long gone. "Good night, Bestie Tami with an I."

My heart literally skips a beat when he uses that nickname.

"Good night, Rigsby."

He waves as he adds, "I'll lock up. Come on, Jack."

I listen as they make their way down the hall. Royce talks to Jack as he puts his leash on him and grabs the small bag he brought earlier. Then, the front door opens and closes, and I'm left in silence.

I toss and turn for about fifteen minutes and swap out my pillow for the one Royce was using. It smells like him, and even though I should be ashamed of myself, I can't stop from stuffing my nose into the material and inhaling.

After another few minutes, I toss my blankets off and get up. My first stop is the bathroom, followed by the kitchen for a glass of water. The bowl Jack was using is set in the sink with the other dirty dishes, and even though I know I should just go to bed, I end up loading the dishwasher and handwashing the pans.

When our dinner mess from earlier is finally taken care of, I turn off the overhead light and head to the living room. There on the couch, are splotches of dog hair. I can't help but laugh as I walk over and check out the mix of dark and light hair from the German Shepherd and Golden Retriever mix. After a quick stop in the bathroom for my lint roller, I rid the couch of dog hair; surprised I'm not upset about it at all. In fact, I kind of like the traces of Royce's dog left all over my house.

Double-checking to make sure the front door is locked—which it is—I grab my cell phone and head back to my bedroom. Once I'm settled in the blankets, my head resting on the pillow Royce used, I lift my phone, debating on whether or not to send the message. I mean, the polite thing to do would be to verify he made it home, right?

Pulling up the texting app, I fire off my message.

Me: *Did you make it home okay?*

His reply comes instantly.

Royce: *Safe and sound. Jack scared off all the boogiemen lurking in the night.*

Me: *I'm glad. Thank goodness you have him to protect you.*

Royce: *Definitely. I'd be a quivering pile of scaredy cat if not for him.*

Me: *Your secret's safe with me, Rigsby.*

Royce: *Thank God, Bestie Tami with an I. I don't know what I'd do if people found out.*

Our conversation goes from light and teasing to talks of work and family. I've never been able to talk to someone as easily as I do Royce. Even from the very beginning, before we had met, he was fun and engaging. He's the lighter side to my more serious one, if I'm being honest with myself, but I have to warn myself not to head down that trail of thought.

Next thing I know, I yawn and glance at the clock.

Me: *Holy cow, it's after one!*

Royce: *Well, look at that. Good thing I don't work until noon tomorrow.*

Me: *You mean today.*

Royce: *LOL! I do mean today.*

Me: *Well, I have to get up in like four hours.*

Royce: *Man, sucks to be you!* *insert grinning devil emoji*

Me: *Not funny, Rigsby. Five is going to come quickly.*

Royce: *You're right, it is. I'm sorry for keeping you up so late.*

Me: *Not your fault. Besides, I was the one who texted you first.*

Royce: *That's right, you did! It's your fault I'm not getting my beauty sleep right now.*

Me: *You don't need any more beauty sleep.*

Royce: *Are you saying I'm pretty?* *insert batting eyelash gif*

Me: *You know you are. Stop fishing for compliments.*

Royce: *LOL! You do wonders for a guy's ego, Bestie.*

Me: *I'm sure you'll live.*

Me: *I really should go to sleep.*

Royce: *Sweet dreams, Bestie.*

Me: *You too, Royce.*

I set my phone on the nightstand and turn on my alarm, dreading the thought of it going off in just a few short hours. I can't believe we just texted that long. I don't think I've ever had a conversation via text message for that long, continuously, even with Sabrina. In fact, I know there's no way that would happen. Her attention span maxes out at ten minutes.

Snuggling into my spare pillow, I slowly start to drift, images of Royce's smile and the scent of his shampoo lulling me to sleep. The last thing to cross my mind isn't the worry of what my lack of sleep will do to my workday. No, it's of hazel eyes that turn a dark gold color as he's about to get off, and the way he whispers my name so softly in that moment, I don't even know if he realized he did it.

***

Monday night, Royce worked until closing. He texted me as soon as he got home and was preparing to take Jack for his nightly walk and jog. That's why I'm slipping out onto my front porch with a glass of water, waiting.

I changed from my pantsuit into a soft cotton tank top and lounge shorts but left my hair up in the bun I threw it in this morning while it was still wet. I don't think I've ever gone to work with wet hair, but that's what happens when you spend half the night texting and don't get to sleep at a decent hour.

I start to wonder if maybe Royce took a different route tonight when I see a man running this way with a dog on a leash. A smile instantly breaks out on my lips. Standing up, I step over to the stairs and wait for him to approach. He moves fluidly and effortlessly, his long, muscular legs carrying him toward me.

As he reaches the edge of my property, he stops running, a warm smile spreading across his face. "Hey," he says, barely panting, even though he's been running. Jack spots me and barks, pulling against the leash. "Settle down," his owner says, as he crouches down and releases the leash from the collar.

Jack takes off, heading my way fast, his tongue hanging out of his mouth. I take a knee on the edge of the porch and brace myself for the blow. He flies up the stairs, his tail wagging, and I can tell by the look in his eye he's about to jump. Royce must sense it too, because he hollers, "Jack, don't you jump."

If the dog hears him, he doesn't listen. Jack launches himself at me, plowing straight into my chest. I lose my balance and fall to the side, my shoulder thumping on the hard wood, the big dog practically landing on top of me.

"Shit! Jack, no!" Royce yells as he joins us on the porch, reaching under all the hair to help me up. "I'm so sorry, Quinn. He's still young," he sputters as he helps me stand.

"It's okay," I assure him.

"It's not okay," he says, a look of mortification on his handsome face. He turns to Jack and shakes his head. The dog just sits there, a sad look on his face, like he knows he did something wrong, even without Royce saying anything.

I place my hand on Royce's arm to stop the criticism that's coming. Instead, I step over to where Jack sits, his nose cast down. "Jack?" I ask, squatting right in front of him. He watches me, lifting his paw to shake. I grin and take his paw, giving it a slight shake.

When he sets it back down, I scratch behind his ears. "Jack, jumping on people is bad, okay? You're a big guy, and you could really hurt someone, you hear me? No jumping." He drops his nose again, but I keep scratching his head. "Come on, Buddy. Give me a kiss."

Jack lifts his head and meets my eyes. He leans forward and licks across my face.

I stand up and face Royce. "He didn't mean to do it."

"I... I know, but still. He could have injured you. Does your arm hurt?" he asks, moving my arm to see if there's anything wrong with it.

"It's fine, truly. It doesn't hurt," I insist, bending my arm to show him.

Royce glances over at Jack, who still sits stoically on the porch. Royce kisses me on the forehead before turning to his dog and squatting in front of him. He reaches out and runs a hand over the pup's back. "Jack, Jack, Jack," he says, exhaling. "You know better than to jump, right?"

The dog whimpers, as if answering the question.

Royce gives him a smile. "No more jumping, you hear?"

Jack barks.

When his owner stands back up and turns to me. "I'd hug you, but I'm all sweaty from my run."

Ignoring his comment, I throw my arms around his waist and draw him near. Sure, I can smell sweat and feel the dampness against my cheek, but I don't care. I'm too comfortable in his arms to be disgusted by a little man sweat.

Royce throws his arms over my shoulders and kisses the top of my head. "I'm getting you wet."

I know what he's referring to, but I can't stop myself from saying, "I've been wet since the moment you stepped onto my front lawn."

His chuckle is like the sweetest music to my ears. "Naughty girl, Tami with an I."

After I run in and grab a bowl of water for Jack, we sit outside and visit for a little bit. He tells me about a young couple who came to zipline earlier today. The guy was trying to be all tough and excited in front of his lady, but Royce could tell he was sweating bullets on the outside. "He ended up chickening out the moment we went to hook up his harness. He was all pale and clammy. Dusty ended up taking him back down the mountain."

"And his lady?" I ask, a hint of humor in my voice.

"Oh, she went down and loved it," he answers with a chuckle.

"Is that some innuendo?" I ask, teasing.

When his eyes meet mine, the laughter dies. "No, of course not. I didn't mean she went *down.*"

I smile. "I know, I was just giving you a hard time."

His face is a bit stoic as he holds my gaze. "You know, Quinn, we haven't really talked about us much, but I want you to know, I'm not seeing anyone else."

My heart flutters, not only from his words but the look on his face. It's so serious, and that's not something I'm really used to from Royce. He's more of a good-natured, lighthearted guy. Plus, there's the fact we're teetering at the edge of something we've never dipped our toes in yet.

Us.

"Oh, okay. Well, I guess that's good. I mean, I'm not seeing anyone else either," I stammer, hating how off balance I sound.

He gazes straight out at the roadway, but I'm not sure he's really looking at it. "And I know we're probably on two different paths in life." He turns and meets my gaze. "You seem like the type of woman who wants marriage and kids."

It's almost an open-ended statement, so I go ahead and confirm. "I do. I hope someday to have both."

He nods thoughtfully. "I suspected. And that's great, really, but I don't think I want that. I'm more of a *fun* kinda guy. I don't see myself settling down, married, and all that jazz," he replies with a shrug.

Even though I suspected as much, it still kinda hurts a little to hear him say it. Mostly because I *like* him, and I could easily see myself getting completely caught up in him, liking him more than *like*. We have fun together, whether talking on the phone or hanging out. And let's not forget about the sex. I don't have the experience I know Royce has, but that seems pretty fantastic too.

So now I have the choice I suspected I'd have to make.

Do I cut things off with him because we want different things, or do I have a little fun with Royce, knowing it won't go any further?

He pins me with a sharp look that borders on dirty. "I do really like hanging out with you, and I'm not just talking about in bed, though that's fucking phenomenal," he states, his hazel eyes turning that sexy shade of gold I associate with him being aroused.

"I like you too, and yes, that part is...amazing." My cheeks burn, and my grin is so wide, it hurts my face.

"So, what do you say we keep having fun until one of us, or both, decides it's not working anymore? Then, we can go our separate ways without all the weird entanglements and drama," he suggests.

I wish I could say I don't know what my decision is going to be, that I need time to think about it. But that would be a lie. The moment the words were out of his mouth, I knew where my decision lay. I enjoy spending time with Royce too much to walk away now. I'm not ready for it to end, even though I know someday it will.

"I'd like that," I blurt out, knowing it's going to hurt.

Because there's one thing I know as well as my own name.

This will end.

Chapter Seventeen

Royce

The plan was to pick her up at her place at six thirty on Tuesday, by five thirty, I was practically walking a hole in my hardwood floors. So, here I am, just after six and walking up to her front door. I just want to see her.

My hand knocks harder on the door than intended, but for some reason, I just feel...edgy. I saw her last night and texted her throughout the day while we were both at work, but it still doesn't calm this anxiety I've felt off and on throughout the day. Like I might not get to see her again, and that bothers me.

I don't know why, though.

We talked last night, and it went exactly as I'd hoped. We'll continue to see each other and spend time together, but without the weight of having a relationship. We'll hang out, go to dinner, fuck a little, and when it stops working for either of us, move on. That's exactly what I wanted.

Yet, ever since she agreed to this, I keep picturing her going off with some faceless dickhead, and that makes me ragey. I actually got up earlier than normal today and went for a run to try to burn off some of the excess fretfulness I had, to no avail.

No, all I want to do is see her, and maybe steal a kiss or two.

The moment she opens the door, all thoughts of *just a kiss* go right out the window. She's wearing sensible blue shorts, a white lacy top that hangs off one shoulder, and these little tan sandals that cross over the top of her feet. Suddenly, I'm practically hard as a rock and all I want to do is see that gorgeous shirt thrown on her bedroom floor.

"Hey," she greets with a smile. "You're early."

"Yeah," I stammer, running my hand across the back of my neck, "I'm sorry, I hope you don't mind."

Her eyes light up as she pulls open the door. "Not at all. I was just touching up my makeup. Come on in."

I place a kiss on her cheek as I slip inside her house, inhaling the floral scent on her skin. She smells absolutely fucking delicious. Like normal. Like Quinn. My heart starts to hammer, a combination of excitement and fear. It's both calming and alarming in a way I've never experienced.

Never even wanted to.

"I'll be out in a just a few minutes. Make yourself comfortable," she says, placing a kiss on my cheek before scurrying down the short hallway to her bedroom.

I just stand there, like an idiot, with the residual sizzle from her kiss on my cheek. I force my feet to move farther into the living room. There are a few decorative framed photos on the walls. A field of wildflowers, the sun rising over the mountains, and one of it setting over the ocean. It's a beautiful display of elegance and simplicity. A reminder to stop and see the beauty that surrounds us.

Like Quinn.

She steps out of her bedroom at about the time my palms start to sweat. I have no idea what the hell is wrong with me. Suddenly, she's all I see, all I think about, and not in that "I want to fuck you senseless" way I'm accustomed to.

Although, seeing her in that outfit does cause a certain reaction in my pants.

“Ready?” I ask, my throat dry and scratchy.

“Ready,” she confirms, grabbing a small bag and meeting me at the front door. “Where are we going?”

“It’s a surprise.” I offer her a wink and a smirk, which causes her to just roll her eyes.

“You’re lucky I enjoy surprises.”

With my hand on the small of her back, I lead her outside and wait while she locks her door. Once it’s secured, we make our way to my truck. She hops up without assistance, making me grin at her eagerness. I head over to the driver’s side and join her in the cab.

“Any hints?” she asks, blue eyes shining.

I glance her way and shake my head. “We’ll be able to see the Smokys,” I tease, starting the ignition and backing out of her driveway.

We really do head toward the mountain, specifically in the vicinity of where I work. Quinn tells me about her day, and my thumb taps uncontrollably against my thigh. I try to pay attention, really I do, but I’m so anxious, it’s hard to concentrate. What if she doesn’t like what I have planned? Am I making a big mistake asking her to step out of her comfort zone?

“Hey, are you okay?” she asks, reaching over and placing her hand on top of mine.

“What? Oh, yeah. Fine.”

She gives me a soft, knowing smile. “You seem a little…not yourself,” she says, wrapping her soft hand around mine. The strumming of my thumb stops immediately the moment her skin touches mine. Relief replaces my earlier anxiety, another foreign concept hard for me to fathom.

I take a deep breath and give her one of my best grins. “I’m good, sweetheart. Promise.”

Sweetheart.

I've never used a nickname.

Turning my hand face up, I lace my fingers with hers and maneuver through traffic. It's not too heavy for a Tuesday night, but it's still tourism season, so it makes getting to where we're going more difficult. Before too long, I'm pulling into the employee lot of Elevate Sky, the SkyLift sister-company to the zipline business I run.

"The SkyLift?"

"Have you ever been?" I ask, parking the car in one of the available spots and turning off the ignition.

She glances around, but there's not really anything to see yet from where we're parked. "Actually, I did go once when I was younger, but not since...like junior high."

"Well, I'm sure tonight's experience will be a little different than it was back in sixth grade."

I hope.

"Ready?" I ask grabbing my keys and waiting for the cue.

"Totally."

I hop out and meet her around at the passenger door. She places her hand back in mine and jumps out. We make our way to the office, where I spy the manager waiting. Tito is a big guy with tattoos covering his arms. He looks intimidating as hell by appearance but has a heart of gold and is the biggest softy.

"Tito," I say, reaching for his outstretched hand for a bro-hug.

"What's up, little Rigs. This y'er lady friend?" he asks, giving Quinn his best smile.

"Keep your paws to yourself there, buddy. But yes, this is Quinn. Quinn, this is Tito Masters, manager of the SkyLift."

"Pleasure to meet you, Quinn. When you get tired of this guy, you give me a call," Tito adds with a wink.

Quinn giggles. "Nice to meet you too, Tito. I'll definitely keep you in mind," she states with a wink of her own.

"All right, all right. You take care of me, Tito?" I ask, taking Quinn's hand and following behind the manager.

He guides us to the lines for the skylift, moving us around the ropes where customers wait for their ride up the mountain. No one says anything as Tito steps up and waves to the attendant manning the lift. "Your chariot awaits," he says, as a trio disembarks the lift and the chair swings around to where we wait.

"Thanks, Teet. I owe ya one," I say, taking his hand and giving him another one-armed bro-hug.

"You do. I'll collect soon." Tito throws Quinn a wave and takes off, probably to head back to the office.

"Here we go," I say, guiding her to turn around as the cart approaches.

"When you feel the seat at your knees, have a seat and enjoy the view," the slightly bored attendant says just as the bench seat hits the backs of our knees, causing us both to fall back and sit.

Quinn glances around, a touch of apprehension in her body language. I reach over and take her hand again and relax into the seat. I've taken a skylift a million times since my time in Tennessee, so this is no big deal for me, but someone like Quinn, who's more reserved and likes both feet safely on the ground, well, she might not be as excited about the experience as I am.

Knowing I need to take her mind off the fact we're slowly climbing up the mountain, I start telling her about the history of the business. I already shared some of the key points during her zipline trip, but nothing about the company that owns a huge part of the mountain. "Have you ever been up to the city?" I ask, referring to the small tourist trap at the top of the mountain.

"Would you think less of me if I said I hadn't?" she asks, glancing my way, yet keeping an eye on the landscape around her.

"No way," I reply quickly.

"When I was younger, we went up the small lift. At the time, there wasn't much up there, and I was too chicken to get off the lift and explore around at the lookout. My friends teased me relentlessly," she confesses.

I squeeze her hand. "Well, I won't tease you," I reassure her, giving her a smirk as I add, "much."

She smiles widely and seems to relax a little more. We're already more than halfway up, so I go ahead and point out some of the landmarks in the scenery, including where our zipline appears beneath us. We actually get to watch someone coming down one of our lines. "That's pretty awesome," she says.

After a few more minutes, we finally approach the platform at the top of the mountain. The attendants are there, giving us the directions I already know by heart, one happily assisting Quinn out of her seat. There's a ghost of a smile on his lips as he helps her move out of the way of the lift, which starts to turn to pick up riders heading back down.

The moment I'm clear of the lift, I give the guy a pointed look and practically drag Quinn away, like the caveman asshole I suddenly am. All I need to do is pound on my chest and smash her over the head with my club to complete the image.

I don't, of course.

"Come on, let's head over to the lookout. If you're feeling brave, you can see the city from one of my most favorite spots," I say, as we head in the direction of where dozens of people gather.

"I can't believe I'm doing this," Quinn mumbles, more to herself than to me.

"You got this, Bestie Tami with an I. You're fierce. You've ziplined," I tell her, as we stroll past the masses of tourists and head for the private area for staff.

She looks a little confused as we bypass the spot she thought we were headed, but she doesn't say anything. Quinn follows along, tentatively glancing over the edge of the mountain or taking in the spectacular view. When we reach the gate, I use my keycard to open the latch, and help guide her through. The moment we're past, I spy the set-up Tito helped arrange.

"Wow," Quinn says, stopping in her tracks and taking in the breathtaking scene in front of her.

The landscape of the Great Smoky Mountains is on full display, the sun slowly dropping in the clear, blue sky. We got lucky there's hardly any wind today, which definitely helped my plans for this evening. "Come on, let's go check it out," I say, leading her toward the blanket and basket on the small platform. The concrete platform won't be the most comfortable, but I'm hoping the blanket helps.

"Is this for us?" she asks, happiness reflecting in those eyes. Not only does it cause a stir in my pants, but in my chest as well.

"It is. Tito helped me set it up," I confess, as she kneels down on the blanket and sits. When she's situated, I drop down beside her and reach for the basket. Inside, there are grapes and strawberries, as well as chips, ham and cheese panini sandwiches, and two bottles of water. All things sold at the walk-up food stand in the heart of the city.

"This looks delicious," she says, once I have everything set on the blanket.

For the next thirty minutes, we sit and eat, chatting about things that happened during the day at work. I still can't quite believe how easy it is to talk to her or the fact I actually look forward to it. I've come to realize she's the best part of my day, when we can text or chat about the little things that happened.

"This view is breathtaking," she says, staring out at the landscape in awe.

"It sure is," I agree, though I'm not talking about the same scene she is. I'm referring to the woman before me, the one who in a matter of days, has embedded herself into my life so easily I didn't see it coming.

"I come up here sometimes after work. This particular area is a staff platform for breaks and whatnot, but no one ever says anything about me using it. I think in the last year or so I've been coming up here, I've shared it twice with a staff member. But they have to provide them with an area for breaks. Most just hang at the foot stand or head out to the treehouses."

"Treehouses?" she asks, her eyes sparkling.

"Yep. Complete with rope ladder walkways and everything."

"Can I see?" Her enthusiasm makes me laugh.

"Of course. They don't close for another hour tonight, so we're in no rush to head down," I say, gathering up our trash and making sure it's secured in the bin. I place the basket along the gate and reach for her hand. The wind picks up at that exact moment, sending tendrils of blonde hair sweeping around her head like a mini halo. With the setting sun behind her, I can't help but stop and just stare. She's the most beautiful woman I've ever seen.

And not just on the outside.

I reach for my phone before I can even stop myself. The old bachelor in me would be ashamed at the thought of taking a selfie, but here I am, flipping my camera around, pulling Quinn into my side, and smiling for the picture. My arms are long, so it's easy to get plenty of the gorgeous backdrop, even though what's snuggled into my side might be my favorite view of all.

And she is, snuggled in close, that is.

The top of her head barely hits my shoulder. Her arm snakes around my waist as she grins up at the phone camera. I snap a few different ones, some with her eyes closed and some with mine. I turn my head and nuzzle my nose into her hair, inhaling the scent of her floral shampoo. I don't even realize I'm still tapping the button, even after she looks up and places her lips against mine.

The kiss ends much quicker than I'd like, and we move in the direction of the treehouses. They're always a huge draw, especially for the kids. There are several treehouse platforms with rope and wood bridges between them. And the views are outstanding. Even though I haven't checked them out in a while, they're still a fun part of the mountain experience.

We jump right in and move from platform to platform, holding hands the entire way. Once or twice, I pull her into my arms and kiss her under the shade of the big trees and then we laugh at the little ones running in and out of the treehouses, their carefree laughter washing over us. When the sun finally starts to drop below the horizon, we head toward the lift to go back down the mountain. There's a small line, so we spend the time holding hands and stealing kisses. I've never been a fan of public displays of affection, but as long as it's Quinn's lips I'm tasting, a little PG PDA doesn't seem so bad.

The moment we settle into the lift, she turns and says, "This has been the best date, Royce. Thank you."

I slide my thumb over the top of her hand. "You're welcome. I'm glad you've enjoyed seeing more of my mountain."

"*Your* mountain?" she teases.

"Yep, mine."

Like her.

Mine.

Chapter Eighteen

Quinn

"This is a great turn out, Quinn," Eloise, Grace Private School's office manager, says.

We're standing in the doorway of the office, watching the gym fill up with families and city residents, all visiting our school's book fair. The school spends quite a bit on newspaper and radio advertising, in addition to plastering flyers on just about every flat surface we could find.

And the result is amazing.

"You did a great job on those publicity flyers, Eloise. They're attractive and appealing to the eye. I'm sure that's a huge factor in the draw to our event," I say, taking in the dozens of families wandering through the gymnasium, viewing the racks and racks of books. Several have a few already in hand, which is always a good thing for our profits.

"Oh, definitely attractive and appealing to the eye," Eloise mumbles, which catches my attention.

I turn her way, but notice her gaze is locked on something in the gym. Trying to follow her line of sight, I realize what she's seeing isn't so much something.

But someone.

Royce.

A slow smile spreads across my lips and I start to move before I give myself time to think about it. He's looking at one of the display tables we set up to showcase some of the featured books available. Funny, he doesn't look as out of place as I would suspect. He looks rather cozy—and definitely rather gorgeous—as he browses books at a children's book fair.

I notice several moms glance his way, their eyes lingering a few seconds longer than deemed appropriate, but he doesn't seem to notice or pay them an ounce of attention. "Fancy meeting you here," I say as I step up beside him.

His hazel eyes dance when they land on mine, that sexy smile spreading widely across his lips. "Hey, you."

"What are you doing here?" I ask, rearranging a few of the books in the display that got knocked down.

He seems almost uncertain. "I, uh, you mentioned this was going on, and said it was open to the public?" His statement comes out as a question.

"It is," I reassure him, placing my hand on his arm. It's warm to the touch and tanned from his time outdoors every day. "I'm just surprised, that's all."

He shrugs, and I swear, I see a blush creep up his neck. "Well, I was headed home from work and remembered you had this event. Thought I'd stop by and see what it was all about."

"Well, then, let me give you the grand tour." I place my arm in his and guide him around the room. I show him the many racks of books, from chapter to picture ones, and everything in between. I make sure to smile brightly—maybe with a little extra satisfaction—as we go. I can feel eyes on me, and all it does is make me lean into his warmth just the slightest bit. Not enough to make anyone uncomfortable, but enough for those watching to know he's with me.

"Thank you for the photo," I say, as we stroll throughout the gym, referring to the photo of him and Jack I received last night while I was setting up for tonight's book fair. I don't tell him I made it my cell phone background the moment I got it.

Royce shrugs. "Jack insisted. He told me my selfie game needed some work."

I can't help but laugh. "Well, having him in the photo did add a little something extra."

"Well, we missed you and didn't want to call since we knew you were busy."

Gosh, isn't he just the sweetest?

"And what's this?" he asks, as we approach the large table with bins.

"These bins hold the books the teachers have chosen for their classroom libraries. They select books, and families can purchase them for the classrooms. After the book fair is complete, the school uses the funds we've raised from the sales to purchase as many of the remaining books as possible."

"Wow, that's cool," he says, thumbing through a few bins. "Have many been purchased?"

"A few," I state, glancing at the bins. Some classrooms have more than others. It just depends on the parents and whether they have extra disposable income tonight or not.

Royce takes his time and scans the books in the kindergarten bin. When he finds one with a dog on the front, he pulls it out and smiles. I watch as he moves on to the first grade bin and does the same thing. He makes it through all of them, choosing a book for each and every classroom. "Now what?"

I give him a questioning look and realize he means with the books. "Are you..."

"I want to buy each classroom a book."

Tears suddenly prickle my eyes. I stare up at this incredible man, and no, I'm not referring to his looks—though, those are pretty impressive too. I'm talking about his huge heart. The one who is stepping up and helping every classroom in my school. The man who spent time to pick the perfect books, most of them with dogs on the covers.

I turn away so he can't see the wetness threatening to fall and scan the cashier's table. One of the parent volunteers is there, and the line isn't too long. Slowly, we head for the table. "That's very generous of you, Royce. You don't have to do that."

He shrugs. "I know, but the teachers deserve it. I've heard a lot about how funding for school gets worse and worse, and I know you're a private school, but that doesn't mean your school couldn't use a little extra help like any other, right?"

"Right," I reply, giving him a small smile.

"So, I just thought if I get each teacher a book, that's one less supply that comes out of their own pockets."

Suddenly, I hug him. Right there in front of my students, their families, and the faculty of my school, I throw my arms around his shoulders and hug him. Awkwardly, of course, because he's holding a stack of books, but surprisingly, he doesn't drop one. "Thank you, Royce." My eyes meet his. "I mean it. Thank you."

He leans in and I swear he's going to kiss me. Part of my brain is screaming not to do it. Not in the middle of a crowded gymnasium. But then there's the other part of my brain, the one who knows I'm falling in love with this incredible man. As much as I've tried to avoid it, told myself falling for him isn't what either of us want, I went and did it anyway.

I've gone and fallen in love with Royce.

He doesn't actually kiss me but brushes a lock of hair off my forehead. Most of it is pulled back in a tight bun, but there's a piece that's fallen from its confines. "Any chance you might care for a visitor later this evening?" he whispers, as we move up closer to the front of the line. "I'd love to have you at my place, but I know you have to work early in the morning, and it would probably be more convenient for you to get up and ready at your place."

"We could try at your house," I reply with a casual shrug. "I mean, you have Jack and he's comfortable there."

He turns to face me, those intoxicating hazel eyes boring straight into my soul. "You want to stay at my place?"

I give him the slightest grin. "I wouldn't mind, if it's all right with you."

It's our turn at the front of the line to purchase his books. He steps forward and hands over his purchases. He pays with his debit card and takes the offered bag. We step aside to get out of the way, and the moment we're out of earshot, I add, "You *do* have a hot tub I haven't been able to experience yet."

Royce's eyes burn dark and a wolfish grin takes over his face. "We can't have that."

"No, definitely not. The fair will wrap up at eight, but it'll take a little time to clean up. I can run home, grab a bag, and be at your place by nine thirty."

He steps forward, the musky scent of his cologne tickling my nose. "I'll be waiting."

With a knowing smile, I point to one of the smaller tables by the door. "That's where you can place the purchased books. Each teacher has their own basket by grade."

He takes his new books out of the bag and makes sure each one is in the correct basket. "Well, I should probably get home and clean up the running clothes thrown on my bathroom floor," he says with a chuckle.

"I'll see you in a little while," I reply, unable to hide the grin I'm wearing.

Royce leans in again, this time, brushing his lips across mine in a sweet, simple kiss. "I'll be waiting."

***

Royce: *I know you're working, but I have a question.*

Royce: *My brother Rueben and his fiancée Cricket invited us over for dinner. Nothing fancy or anything. Just something on the grill.*

Royce: *I know we had talked about dinner. If you'd still rather go to a restaurant, we can do that. This is just an option.*

It's just after lunch on a Friday afternoon, and this is the first time I've been able to glance at my phone. I spent a big part of the day reviewing the financial reports for last month, including the one for the book fair last Thursday night. The one where Royce surprised me, showing up in support of a school function and buying books for the classrooms. Not only did I meet him at his home later that evening, but we've pretty much been together ever since.

I've tried not to look too much into it, but it's hard when he holds me so tightly while he's sleeping. I never would have thought Royce to be a snuggler, but by God, he's always reaching for me and pulling me against his naked body. I'm not sure he even realizes he does it, to be honest. He sometimes seems a little shocked himself when he first wakes up.

Smiling, I type out a reply.

Me: *Sounds good to me. Should I bring anything?*

The bubbles appear right away.

Royce: *If you're sure. He's been hounding me all week to come over, so he sicced his fiancée on me.*

Me: *I'd love to meet them.*

Royce: *They're boring and completely gross with PDA. You'll regret saying that by the end of the evening.*

Me: *So, maybe we just one-up them...*

Royce: *insert smiling devil emoji* *I like the way you think, Bestie.*

Royce: *Off at 6. I'll run home and shower. Jack and I should be at your place around 6:30.*

Me: *See you then.*

I set my phone back in my drawer, unable to hide the little grin on my face, and get back to work.

***

"Did Royce ever tell you about his senior prom?" Rueben asks, causing Royce to groan.

"She doesn't want to hear this," he argues, to no avail.

"I'm pretty sure she does," Rueben insists.

I glance over at Royce. Even though he's arguing with his brother, I can see he's not really bothered at the fact Rueben is going to share whatever story he's about to tell. He just shakes his head and relaxes into his seat. Jack is sleeping at our feet, his front paws draped over my feet and his back ones over Royce's.

"Royce here went to his senior prom with a girl in a wheelchair."

Wait, what?

That was definitely not where I thought Rueben was going with his opening.

My eyes meet his, and he gives me a little shrug. I swear I can see a slight pink in his cheeks that wasn't there a moment ago. Royce tries to hide it behind his water bottle, but I saw it nonetheless.

"What was her name?" Rueben asks.

"Julie."

"Julie! That's right, Julie. She's the girl who took the line drive to the leg."

Royce nods. "Yep, at a softball game about two weeks before prom. She was pitching when the batter cracked a line drive straight into her upper leg. I wasn't there, but they said you could hear the bone snapping from the force."

My mouth falls open. "Seriously?"

He nods. "Yep. She had surgery the next day to set the bone. She was in a cast all the way up to her hip with her leg extended out straight."

"Holy cow," I reply. "And she was your date?"

"Nope, his date was Sydni with an I."

I crack up laughing at Rueben's description of her name, mostly because of the correlation with the name I gave him when we were first texting. But also because it's a little fitting for someone dating Royce.

"Ah, yes, Sydni. With an I," he says softly, throwing me a wink for good measure. "She was fun."

I roll my eyes. "Of course she was, Casanova."

"So, if Sydni was your date, why did you take Julie?" Cricket asks, leaning in to hear the answer.

"His date dumped him before the dance," Rueben throws out there.

"No, that's not true. Well, maybe. Technically, I dumped her when I found her fucking Julie's boyfriend in the back seat of his Camaro. Even after I caught them, they still tried to deny it. I told Syd to find a new date, which apparently, she already had one. Matt didn't want to take Julie because of her injury, so he cheated on her with Syd."

"Two douchebags," Cricket points out.

"That they were. Julie was heartbroken, upset because he cheated, but also felt bad for herself because of her injury. Blamed herself a little for his cheating too."

"That's bullshit," Cricket hollers.

"So he took her," Rueben chimes in.

I glance over at the man beside me. He's sweet and caring, despite trying to hide it behind humor and a bad boy smirk. Of course he would take her as his date. He didn't care whether she was in a wheelchair or not. She was hurting and sad, and he wanted to make her smile. That's the man I've come to know and love.

Yes, love.

But I'll keep that tidbit of info to myself, considering that's the exact thing I was trying to avoid. I learned it's really hard to avoid it when you're sleeping next to him almost every night or when he's always sending these sweet little messages or even leaving surprises on my doorstep. How could I not fall in love with the guy, honestly? He's perfectly imperfect, and that's perfect for me.

"She didn't have a date, and neither did I," Royce says, focusing on the tabletop to avoid our gazes.

"She was way prettier than Sydni anyway," Rueben adds.

"Totally," the older brother replies. "Red dress with that slit straight up the side."

Rueben snorts. "It was because of her cast."

That ornery gleam sparkles in Royce's hazel eyes as he replies, "She still let me get to second base."

We all laugh as he waggles his eyebrows suggestively.

"You're a principal, is that right?" Cricket asks, sipping her drink.

"I am. Grace Private School over on Hanson Drive."

"Yes! I've heard of it. I work in the tourism department for the Chamber and spend all of my time promoting mostly the sights and businesses affected by tourism, but I've been thinking of doing a video series on some of the non-tourism-based businesses, like churches and schools. Maybe even a walk or something, like they do at cemeteries."

"Cemeteries? What do they do there?" Royce asks.

Cricket explains what a cemetery walk is, how they even have historical figure ones with actors who speak about that person's life and death. They can happen at one particular graveyard, or even spread out between several. I've heard of them, but never actually participated.

"Weird. And people pay money to go stand at someone's grave to learn about their life?"

"They do," Cricket says. "The historical society has been doing them for years with great turnouts."

"How would you do that for churches and schools?" I ask, completely intrigued now.

"Well, churches are easier because there's a lot of history and architecture in so many throughout town. Schools would be a little trickier to incorporate, but I think we could do it. Let me think about this some more and get back to you," Cricket says, giving me a decisive head nod.

"Sounds good," I reply, giving her a little grin.

"By the way, I can't believe you actually enjoyed ziplining," Cricket says to me, shaking her head and changing the subject.

"I mean, it wasn't completely horrible," I reply, taking another sip of the sweet white wine she served with dinner. This is actually my third glass. For someone who isn't a big drinker, I should be a little concerned about how I'll feel in the morning. Yet, all I can think about is how much fun I'm having with Rueben and Cricket, and Royce, of course.

"Not everyone is terrified of heights like you," Royce teases his soon-to-be sister-in-law.

"I'm not terrified," she argues, making both men laugh. "What? I'm not."

"You screamed the entire way down," Royce says, a broad smile on his handsome face. He looks completely relaxed in his shorts and T-shirt, a pair of flip-flops on his feet. He's sitting beside me, a bottle of water in one hand and my shoulder in the other. Ever since we finished dinner, there have been little touches. My arm, my neck, and now, my shoulder. Just the faintest graze of his fingers against my skin, but it's like someone threw a bucket of gasoline on a smoldering fire.

"You did," Rueben confirms. "I could hear you." He takes Cricket's hand and brings it to his lips to try to hide the smile on his face. I can definitely see the resemblance. The brothers both have hazel eyes with dark hair, and their jaw and cheekbones are cut the same, but Rueben is leaner and wears glasses. Hot in that boy next door way, but my eyes only see his brother.

"Anyway," Cricket says, dragging out the word, "it was a little scary when I went—"

"A little scary?" Royce asks, interrupting.

“Yes, it was a little scary,” she jumps right back in, giving her future brother-in-law a pointed look. “It all ended up pretty well though, because Rueben asked me to marry him. So I guess if I have to fly down a mountain, fearing I’m going to die, well, it was worth it.” Cricket smiles ear to ear as she leans over and kisses her fiancé.

“Knock it off with that mushy shit,” Royce interjects, drinking the rest of his water bottle. He gets up to throw it in the trash and nods to my glass. “Ready for another?” Jack whines at being woken up from his nap, but curls back up around my legs, licking my calf before closing his eyes once more.

“No, I think I should probably lay off the wine. After this glass, of course,” I say, smiling sweetly over the rim of my glass.

Royce laughs and heads for the house.

“Yeah, sure, I don’t want another drink,” Rueben hollers as the screen door slams shut. Sighing, he stands up and adds, “I better go help him before he takes all my good beer.”

I watch as he follows his brother into the house, mumbling about what a pain in the ass he is. Their banter makes me smile. Rueben and Cricket have been fun and welcoming the entire evening, and I can’t help but feel so at home here with them.

And with Royce.

I’ve already gone and done the one thing I told myself I wouldn’t do, and now, there’s no going back.

I’m in love with him.

Chapter Nineteen

Royce

I'm just shutting the fridge when the entry door opens and shuts. I know it's my brother, but he doesn't say anything. Even when I turn around and face him, Rueben just stands there and watches me. Clearly something's on his mind, so I just wait him out, propping my hip against the counter and staring back.

"Have you told her yet?" he asks, crossing his arms over his chest.

"Told her what?" I ask, popping the lid off my water bottle and taking a hearty drink.

"That you love her."

The water still in my mouth goes flying across the room. If he were any closer, he'd be wearing it. "The fuck?" I whisper-yell, glancing toward the still-open door. I can hear Cricket and Quinn faintly, Quinn's laughter carrying through the screen on the door. "What the hell, Rueben?"

My asshole brother just shrugs. "So, that's a no. Looks like you haven't even told yourself yet."

"I'm not..." I sigh. "I'm not in love with her, Rueb. We're just having fun."

"Right, because you bring a lot of the women you have *fun* with home to meet your family," he states, all cocky-like. Fucker.

"You invited us," I point out.

"I've invited you before too. In fact, I usually invite you and whoever you're having fun with, but you still only come solo. Why is that?"

"You're a nosy fucker, you know that?" I retort, looking for a redirect.

"I know. You tell me often. So? Why didn't you ever bring them around?"

I sigh deeply again. He's never going to let this go until I just answer the damn question. "Because they've always been just that. Fun."

"And Quinn is..."

Not just fun.

That's what I almost say but am able to keep the words from flying at the last possible second. Mostly because it's true. She's way more than just someone I'm having fun with, even if that's what I keep telling myself. She's...amazing. She's kind and generous and so fucking smart. Not to mention sexy, alluring, and more spontaneous than either of us suspected. Maybe that comes with comfort, like you relax enough with a certain someone that you start to let your guard down. When I first met Quinn just a few weeks ago, spontaneous wasn't a word I'd use to describe her. Now, it's one of my favorite ones.

"Quinn is?"

I glance at the floor. "She'll make someone very happy someday."

"But not you?"

I'm already shaking my head. "No, not me."

Rueben sort of lets this frustrated growl fly. "That's dumb, Royce."

The shrug I give him feels sad. So does the weight settling on my chest. "That's how it is. We want different things."

"Cricket and I wanted different things," my brother says, reminding me of the time he had to put her on a flight back home to California, even though he wanted her to stay.

"No, you and Cricket wanted the same thing. You just lived in different states."

"And we were both willing to compromise to make it work."

"I'm aware, Rueb. I was there for the entire nauseating experience, remember? Listen, I'm not in love with her, okay?"

He gives me a shocked look. "Why not?"

I shrug. "I told myself not to."

Rueben laughs. He actually laughs at me. "That's not how this works, Royce."

"Yeah, well, it's how it's going to work here. She wants...things I don't want."

"Like?"

"Kids. A marriage." Saying those words used to cue the heartburn, but now, they feel...good. That's why I can't fall in love with her. Good only lasts through the honeymoon phase, and suddenly, you're left trying to coexist with someone who's secretly trying to change you into someone you're not, bitching at you for staying out too late with your buddies and leaving the toilet seat up. I've seen it a lot, especially from my military buddies. They go off to war, come back, and everything's just different.

"You know, if you'd get out of your own head for five seconds, you'd see you'd actually make a really great husband and father someday," he says, walking to the fridge and grabbing a beer. "It doesn't have to be right now, and frankly, it doesn't have to be Quinn, but you at least have to be open to the fact."

The thought of it *not* being Quinn causes a pain in my chest I can't describe. It's like a thousand knives piercing my soul and leaving me bleeding on the kitchen floor.

The truth is, I'm already falling. My brother knows it, and even though I try to fight it or hide from it, I know it too. That's why this won't work between us. We're supposed to be fun, not serious. No feelings. No heartache.

And that's exactly where this is going.

"I'm going to head out. I work early tomorrow," I say, throwing my now-empty bottle into the trash can and walking to the back door.

"It's okay to be scared, Royce. I get it. But don't push her away because of it. Let her help you work through that fear. You might actually be surprised and happy with the results."

I don't turn back around and look at him, just nod once to let him know I heard him. I push through the door, my heart practically tripping over itself the moment I see Quinn on the deck with Cricket. They're laughing so easily, so naturally. She's already roped in my future sister-in-law, carrying on as if they're long lost friends. Hell, even my dog fucking loves her.

Do I? Do I love her?

Probably.

That's why I need to end this now, before either of us falls any deeper into the trap of relationship hell. Heartache, pain, and resentment. I've seen it happen all too often. Hell, with almost everyone I've met. Even with my mom. Dad died, leaving her behind to pick up the pieces and carry on with her life as if she didn't lose half her soul.

Even if you're one of the lucky ones to find happiness for a short time, it never lasts.

"Ready to head out?" I ask, suddenly feeling like I'm suffocating.

She turns my way and her smile falters just a bit. It's as if she can read my body language and probably the apprehension on my face, but if she does, she doesn't say anything. "Thank you so much for inviting me to dinner," Quinn says politely to Cricket as she stands.

"I'm so glad you could come. We'll have to grab lunch one of these days. Maybe an upcoming Sunday," Cricket says, and I start to feel a little lightheaded.

"I'd like that," Quinn replies, as she steps up beside me and places her hand on my forearm. Like the balm her touch is, I feel my heart rate drop and a calmness settle in. I hate I've let it come to this, because I know what happens next.

I wave goodbye to my brother and give Cricket a kiss on the cheek, thanking her for dinner. Quinn and I make our way to my truck, Jack hot on our heels. The moment I open the back door, he jumps in and settles on the seat, while Quinn hops in the front. As I move to the driver's side door, I take a few deep breaths, though it doesn't seem to help. Not really.

"That was fun." She practically beams as I start the truck and pull out of my brother's driveway. We have a short drive back to Gatlinburg, and I'm not looking forward to it. Fortunately, Quinn fills most of the time by chatting eagerly about my brother and his fiancée, all while completely oblivious as to what's about to happen.

As I approach town, she reaches over and takes my hand. I didn't even realize it was sitting on the console between us. "Are you okay?" she asks, her fingers dancing along my skin, making it hard to think straight.

"Fine, yeah."

I can feel her eyes on me, but I don't glance her way. I keep them trained on the road, for once, grateful for the Friday night traffic in town. She doesn't say anything else as I drive to her house. We had never discussed later tonight, but it was insinuated. Quinn has a bag on the floorboard behind her seat.

When she realizes we're heading to her house, she watches me out of the corner of her eye. I know because I'm watching her out of the corner of mine. I pull behind her car in her driveway, but I don't turn off the engine.

Quinn unbuckles her seat belt and turns to face me. "So I guess we're staying here tonight?" There's a glimmer of hope reflecting in those soulful blue eyes.

"Actually, I'm not feeling so great, and I have to work early tomorrow. I thought maybe I'd just head back to my place." I hold her gaze, trying to act calm and collected, even though my heart is racing out of my chest.

"Oh. Okay." She sits for a few more seconds, waiting for me to say something else. When it's clear I'm not going to, she reaches for her door handle.

Automatically, I jump out and head to her door. It would be easier if I had just stayed in my seat, but no, I had to climb out of the truck to be a gentleman. The problem is now she's directly in front of me, I want to touch her.

And kiss her.

And go inside with her.

"Well, thank you for taking me to dinner with your family. They're nice." She looks up at me with those bluest of blue eyes, and I swear I can actually feel my heart crack under the hurt. As much as I've tried to avoid it, I've fallen in love with Quinn Michaels.

"You're welcome," I reply, running my hands through my hair to keep from reaching for her.

"I hope you feel better." She steps forward, bewilderment and dejection written plainly across her face, as she waits to see what I do.

I'm a weak man. This is only a new development in regard to her. That's the only explanation as to why I step forward, intending to kiss her cheek, but I catch a whiff of her floral scent. My lips turn at the last minute and take hers, slowly and seductively. Quinn groans the sexiest sound ever, which goes straight to my cock.

This is easy.

Effortless.

This crazy passion consumes me when she's near. I could kiss her for hours, days even.

Forever.

That one word dances through my mind, causing me to rip my lips from hers. We're both panting, her eyes glazed over as she looks up at me. The invitation is there. She wants me to come inside, and a big part—specifically, the part controlling my dick—really wants to go. But the other part, confirms I'm getting too close.

And I don't want that.

"Listen, Quinn," I find myself saying, almost on autopilot.

Before my eyes, I see realization set in. Her spine stiffens as she takes a step back, seeking space. Instantly, I want to draw her back to me.

But I don't.

I can't.

"You know, we said we'd have a little fun until it didn't work for one of us anymore." Fuck, I hate this.

Quinn nods, but doesn't say anything.

"And, well, I've had a lot of fun with you, but I'm thinking it's time to end this."

"End this," she parrots, her mouth falling open as she gapes at me.

"Yeah, you know, we've had fun," I start, but she interrupts.

"Fun, yeah, you've said that already." Her tone is a little annoyed, which sort of grates my nerves.

"You're right. My point is, we agreed that once this didn't work for one of us, we'd end it."

"And so you're saying it's no longer working for you," she says, filling in the blanks.

"That's right."

Why does it taste like I'm trying to swallow dirt?

"You're right," she replies, taking another step back.

Wait, what?

"I'm right?"

She nods. "You're right. This was our agreement, and if you're ready to move on, have more fun somewhere else, then this is where we part ways." There's a strength in her voice, a resolve in her words I wasn't prepared for. My heart sinks when I realize she thinks I'm ready to just move on to someone else. She has no clue how deeply she's embedded in my soul.

And that's my fault.

Because I'm too afraid to tell her.

When I meet her eyes, there's a flash of hurt and sadness, but she covers it quickly.

"I've had a great time with you, Bestie Tami with an I," I tell her honestly, drawing a smile to her lips.

"I've enjoyed my time with you too, Rigsby."

Then, she steps forward and throws her arms around my waist. Mine wrap around her shoulders, drawing her into my chest. I take one deep breath, committing the scent of her shampoo to memory. Something tells me I'll remember it forever.

Just like her.

I'll never forget her.

When I rest my chin on the top of her head, I just breathe her in. For the last time. "I hope you find everything you're looking for, Quinn." And I do. I hope she gets the husband who worships her, the house, and the kids who'll decorate the refrigerator with art and build blanket forts in the living room. Shit, she'll probably get a dog too.

She pulls back and looks up. There're tears in her eyes, but she doesn't let them fall. Instead, she gives me a brave smile, which causes my heart to ache even more. Quinn places her palm on my cheek, cupping my face. "I hope you find your happiness too. Whatever that is, I hope you find it." Quinn steps forward and places her lips against mine.

One last kiss.

Then she backs away, grabs her bag, turns quickly, and heads to her front door. She finds her keys and lets herself in. I watch as she sets her overnight bag down and turns to face me. Her hand is poised on the door, ready to close it.

To close this chapter of her life.

I wave and give her a smile, wishing it didn't have to be like this.

But it does.

I turn and return to my truck, hopping onto the driver's seat and throwing the ignition in reverse. As I back out of the drive, Jack whimpers, dropping his head on my shoulder. It's like he senses my despair, feels the growing distance between Quinn and us. Before I pull away one last time, I glance back up at the house. She's still standing there, her head resting against the door, watching me drive out of her life. I swear I can see the tears falling down her soft cheeks.

Jack barks as I finally pull away and head toward home. He hangs his head once more, his mood suddenly as miserable as my own. "I know, buddy, but this was for the best," I tell man's best friend. I'm not sure who I'm trying to convince more: him or me.

It only takes a few minutes before I'm pulling into my own driveway, Jack eager to get out. I watch as he marks his territory and sniffs every spot in the yard, chastising myself for doing the one thing I swore I'd never, ever do.

I fell in love.

And love is a bitch.

It sneaks up and blindsides you when you least expect it, leaving you in a world of hurt and pain.

I mentally scan my liquor cabinet, because there's only one way I'm going to get through this night, and that's with a bottle of something strong and unforgiving. Something that'll knock me on my ass and ensure I have a shitty day tomorrow. Something that'll help me forget, at least for tonight.

Just not tequila.

***

Seven in the morning comes awfully early when you haven't slept a wink.

I get to my office thirty minutes before the staff and slam my office door by accident, sending a photo on the wall flying, glass shattering as it hits the hardwood floor. *Figures.* I spend the next ten minutes looking for a decent broom, sweeping up the shards, and tossing the photo in the trash. When the mess is finally cleaned up, I drop into my chair like a sack of bricks and sigh, hands running through my hair in agitation.

I've slept on the hard, dirty desert, in a bunker with a dozen other men while bombs blew up nearby, hell, I even once slept standing up against a brick wall, but all of those times were more relaxing and comfortable than trying to sleep in my empty bed last night. No amount of blankets or pillows or Jack Daniels would help.

I even tried to run. Have you ever run at two in the morning, slightly drunk, up and down a mountain? Let's just say the cut across my shin is the result of that poor decision. I'm lucky I didn't cut open my head, though that'd probably serve me right for being a dumbass.

My phone chimes with a text, and I practically fall out of my chair trying to get to it. I'm both afraid and praying for it to be from Quinn. I've never wanted to see someone's name on my phone so fucking badly, yet dread it at the same time. And I've *never* prayed for it be someone I just broke up with.

Ever.

Until Quinn.

I glance at the screen, only to find my brother's name. Part of me wants to ignore it, but since it could be about my mom, I find myself swiping my finger across the screen.

Rueben: *How'd last night go?*

Me: *Fine.*

Rueben: *Fine?*

Me: *Yes, Rueben, fine. Busy. Just got to work.*

Rueben: *So, crabby and irritable. Got it.*

Me: *Fuck off.*

Rueben: *Don't need to. I gotta girl for that.*

Now, he's just trying to piss me off. I almost reply I have one too, but I realize that's not true. Not anymore. I pushed my girl away because...because we want different things. And you can't make it work long term when you're not traveling on the same path. Sure, we may be on the same road for a stretch, but in the end, she'll wind up married and happy, and I'll be me, as free as the wind blows.

Except, why doesn't that sound as appealing as it used to?

Rueben: *So how did things go with Quinn last night? You seemed a little freaked out when you left.*

Me: *Fine.*

Rueben: *insert eyeroll gif*

Rueben: *Fine, be a stubborn jackass and don't say anything, but listen up. I could tell by the look in your eye you're about to fuck this up with her. Don't do it.*

Too late.

Rueben: *I'm sorry I said anything last night. Just chill and see where things go with her. We really like her.*

I sigh and drop my phone on my desk with a thud. Yeah, he has no clue I already fucked everything up with Quinn, but do you know what? It's for the best. End it now before we both get in too deep.

Yeah, might be too late for that too.

What I need is a night out. Head to my old stomping ground and hang out with the tourists. Nothing cheers me up faster than a group of bachelorettes looking for a wild and memorable night together. That's something I can provide. Something I'm familiar with. Good Time Royce. That's me.

Except tonight, it doesn't sound like a good time. Tonight, maybe I'll just hang at home and have a few beers on my back deck with Jack.

And try not to think about Quinn.

Chapter Twenty

Quinn

I start to stretch on my mat, waiting for this morning's session to begin. It's busy for a Saturday morning, but that suits me just fine. The last thing I need is to be alone with my thoughts, because those aren't very forgiving right now.

Last night was hard enough to get through. First thing I had to do was wash my bedding. The sheets smelled like Royce and sex from the night before, and there was no way I was getting any sleep with those memories haunting me. That's when I found myself cleaning my entire house, top to bottom at midnight. Jack's hair was everywhere, and even though I didn't mind, if I was doing a deep clean, I might as well get rid of that too.

But that only made me miss them.

Both of them.

And then I got pissed off.

At Royce for being too chickenshit to give us a chance and at myself for not listening to my head when it said I would only get hurt. Well, head, you were right. I got hurt. I fell in love with a man who won't commit, but what makes it worse is he was nothing but honest the entire time. I knew there was no future, yet I went ahead and dove into the water. Without seeing the bottom or what dangers lurked within, I jumped, headfirst, into the deep.

And came out a little battered on the other end.

But I'm not broken. Oh, no. Far from it. It was about four in the morning when I realized I didn't need Royce Rigsby. I don't need him at all, even though my heart hasn't quite caught up with my head quite yet.

"What the heck? Did you get run over by a truck this morning?" Sabrina exclaims, as she unrolls her mat beside mine.

I roll my eyes and stretch out my lower back. "No, just didn't sleep very well," I reply cheerfully.

"Very well or at all?" my nosy best friend asks, as she plops down beside me and turns to face me.

I shrug in reply, feeling her eyes take in my frazzled appearance. I'm sure she sees my mismatched outfit, my unwashed hair pulled in a crazy knot on top of my head, and my makeup-less face. I wasn't exactly going for the homeless look when I left the house a little bit ago, but at this point, I don't really care.

"What's wrong?" she asks, starting to do her own stretches, all while keeping one eye on me.

Again, I shrug, anxiously wishing this morning's yoga instructor would begin the class.

"Everything okay with your family?"

I sigh, realizing she's not going to let this go. Again, that's my fault too. I should have realized showing up to yoga looking like I partied all night wasn't going to do me any favors where Sabrina is concerned. "My family is fine."

She makes a tsking sound and continues to scrutinize my appearance. "So, if your family is okay, then it can only be one thing. Man troubles."

I can't even stop the flinch before it hits my facial features.

"Ah ha! I was right. What did Royce do?" she asks as Crystal heads to the front of the room.

"Are we ready to begin?" Crystal asks, as she starts to lead the group in our first stretch.

"Shh, time to concentrate," I mumble, grateful for the temporary reprieve.

"Mmhmm, don't think I don't know what you're doing. We'll talk after class," Sabrina states, joining in the group stretching activities.

After the forty-five minute class ends, Sabrina launches at me like a cheetah. "Okay, spill."

I sigh dramatically and roll up my mat. "Nothing really to say. We agreed to keep it casual and we did. It was casual, and now it's over. End of story."

I can feel her eyes on me like a stabby knife. "Casual, huh? Then why do you look like you cried yourself to sleep? I've barely seen you, let alone talked to you in the last, like, two weeks. That's not casual."

"Well, it's over now, so why does it matter?"

Sabrina stands beside me and studies me. "Okay, so here's what's going to happen. I'm coming over with pizza, ice cream, and margaritas."

Tequila.

Great.

"I'm evoking the best friend breakup pact," she states, nodding her head and making a mental checklist.

"Is that really necessary?" I ask, mentally groaning at what this entails.

"Of course! Anytime you have a breakup, no matter how big or small, you evoke the pact!"

I let out another sigh and head for the door. "What time should I expect you?"

"Six!"

With a wave over my shoulder, I walk to my car and try to prepare myself for the chaos that will ensue tonight at six. If I'm lucky, it'll just be us. If luck isn't quite on my side—which, let's be honest, I'm not at all comfortable thinking it is—she'll only bring two additional friends. Hopefully, it's nothing like last time.

Last time I wound up half naked and very drunk while binge watching John Hughes movies.

***

The good thing about having company tonight is I didn't have to clean. My house was already spotless, thanks to my late night/early morning clean-fest.

After yoga, I showered and was able to take a nap. A nap that lasted four and a half hours. Now, I'm making some taco dip and cutting garden vegetables for snacks. Not that we'll eat too many veggies, unless we're dipping them into the taco stuff. Any best friend pact involves junk food, and a lot of it. I'm wearing a pair of navy yoga pants and an oversized T-shirt. That'll help with the bloating and expanding stomach that's on deck for this evening.

At six, a knock sounds at the door. I know it can't be Sabrina, since she's almost always late. Plus, she's the friend who never knocks, just barges in like she owns the place. When I open the door, I'm pleased to find my friend, Laura, there. I immediately pull her into a hug, close my eyes, and send a silent thank you to Sabrina for invoking the pact. "I can't believe you're here," I whisper, fighting to keep the tears at bay.

She pulls back and grins, wetness in her own eyes too. "Justin can handle the kids for a little while tonight. I get four hours of uninterrupted adult time, and I'm going to use it," she proclaims, stepping inside with a bag. She holds it up and says, "Ice cream."

Before I can shut the door, a second car pulls along the road and stops. I spy my friend Joy's raven black hair immediately. She comes running to the door wearing comfy clothes and a big smile, a stack of DVDs in hand. "I have movies and margaritas!" she proclaims when she hits my porch. Joy instantly throws her arm around my neck and hugs me tight. "I can't believe it's been, like, almost a year since I've seen you!"

I squeeze her extra hard. "Well, we've all been busy. How's work?" I ask, as I escort her into my home.

"Ugh. So busy. They have me traveling almost every week right now. The last six months have been so hectic," she says, reaching for Laura and giving her a hug. "How about you? You ready for baby number three?"

Laura laughs. "Well, maybe. Both of my other kids were conceived after a night of alcohol, so you never know what tonight might bring."

For the first time in what feels like forever, I smile my first real smile. Actually, no that's not true. There were real smiles last night too. You know, before Royce freaked and ended things.

My happiness must falter because Joy suddenly pulls me into her arms once more. "I'm sorry you're hurt, Q. Tonight, we're going to drink and eat and watch cheesy rom-com eighties movies until we're ready to explode."

I shrug. "Actually, I'd be perfectly content catching up," I tell her, leading them both to the kitchen. "When was the last girls' night we had anyway?"

Laura groans. "Almost a year ago, because I got pregnant with Mason that night."

"See? It's been way too long. I'm glad you're both here so we can catch up a little."

The door bursts open and my best friend flounces in, the scent of garlic and cheese filtering through the doorway. "I have pizza!" she proclaims, smiling when she sees Joy and Laura already here. "I'm so glad you were both able to come."

"Me too. I was supposed to be in Detroit this weekend, but it got pushed back a few weeks," Joy says.

"And you're not spending the night with Kale?" Laura asks, referring to Joy's fiancé. They met about a year and a half ago while traveling for the same company. Kale is in new agent recruits and Joy's in marketing for the same national insurance agency. They're able to work from home and travel between the different corporate offices, occasionally also hitting the small agent offices too. When they met at a corporate conference in New York, they hit it off so well, he was moving to Gatlinburg a few months later. Now, they're engaged to be married at the end of the year.

"I see him all the time," she replies, waving her hand dismissively. "We've been able to keep a very similar travel schedule, so where he goes, I go. It's been amazing." Joy practically beams with delight and happiness, and I can't help but grin back at her. It wasn't that long ago she was single and frustrated with the dating scene. She had a few long-term boyfriends, a handful of mediocre dates, and a couple of one-night stands before she stumbled into Kale at the brunch buffet.

"I'm really happy for you, Joy," I tell her honestly.

"Thanks. I've learned if you kiss enough frogs, you'll eventually find a prince," she says, starting to mix up the margaritas.

Sabrina opens the two pizza boxes on the counter and grabs plates and napkins. “I got you those nasty olives on half,” she tells me, picking one off and tossing it at me.

“Hey, now,” I holler, laughter bubbles up from my chest.

“At least you’re smiling. And showered. I’m glad. You smelled like the back end of a goat earlier,” my best friend points out with a grin.

“It wasn’t that bad,” I argue, reaching for a slice of pepperoni and olive pizza.

“I remember those days,” Laura says, taking the first margarita from Joy. “Actually, never mind. I still don’t get regular showers,” she adds with a chuckle.

“How are the kids and Rob?” I ask, taking a margarita.

“Good, good. Rob is in charge of Ag loans now, with his eye on taking over as president of the bank for his dad when he retires. JJ turns three next month, and Bennett is almost three months old already.” She practically beams with pride at the mention of her young children. It makes that part of me yearning for a family of my own rear its ugly head.

“Come on, let’s go to the living room,” Sabrina says, a plate of pizza in one hand and her margarita in the other.

We gather in my living room, Joy and Sabrina on the couch with Laura and me on the floor in front of the coffee table. “These margaritas are delicious,” I say, taking another healthy sip of my lime mixed drink.

“I made them extra strong to help Laura with conception when she gets home later,” Joy says, giggling. We all start to laugh, in fact.

God, this feels amazing to relax, drink, and hang out with my friends.

"I can't believe we haven't done this lately," I confess, feeling guilty I've also let our friendship fall by the wayside.

"Don't do that," Laura chastises, her mouth full of pepperoni pizza.

"Do what?" I fret confusion.

"Don't feel guilty. We've all been busy, Q. Our personal lives have pulled us in different directions, but I think that's okay. I know if I needed one of you, you'd be there for me in a second. Like tonight. Sabrina called and we all came," Laura says.

She's right. As we grow older, our lives become busier and more complex. That doesn't mean we're not friends anymore. Even if we don't see each other regularly, or even talk more than the occasional text exchange, I know my friends would be there for me when I needed them.

"You're right," I state. "Just because we don't see each other as much as we used to, doesn't mean we're not there for each other when we need to be. Life gets hectic, but I hope you all know I'm just a call away." My eyes burn as I look at the three women I've been closest to since college.

"Likewise," Joy agrees. "Now, tell us what brought us all together tonight."

I sigh, realizing I'm going to have to tell them about Royce. Not that I mind, it's just I know talking about him will remind me of how much of an idiot I was to ever think I could not let my heart get involved.

"I was seeing this guy, and it's over. It wasn't a big deal," I say, casually, even though it feels anything but.

"No big deal, my ass. She's in love with him," Sabrina announces.

"I never told you that," I grumble to my best friend.

"No, but I could tell. I've never seen her like this, guys. She was totally into him," Sabrina tells the girls, who in turn, give me their full attention, desperate for more details. "Tell them how you met."

I smile instantly, thinking back about that first text message. "I sent him a text, complaining about a dick pic I was shown on a date I had that night."

Everyone bursts into fits of laughter. "Seriously?"

"That happened to you?"

I nod. "I had gotten my new cell phone earlier in the day, but I couldn't transfer any of my contacts from my old device. I thought I remembered Rina's number, but apparently, I was wrong."

"So you complained about a dick pic?" Laura asks, her smile wide across her face.

"Yep, and he replied. Though, I thought it was Sabrina. We chatted, and it wasn't until the next day I discovered it was a guy."

"And they started dating," Sabrina adds before chugging some of her margarita.

"Well, not quite like that, but you get the point. We met face-to-face without realizing it. He ran by my house, and we chatted, but we had no clue it was the person we'd been texting. And we hung out for a couple of weeks," I add.

"And now you're done," Laura says, sadly.

I shrug. "It's okay. Royce was totally honest from the beginning. We decided to have some fun until it didn't work for either of us. I knew he wasn't looking for anything long term, and he knew I was. We were destined to fail."

Joy gives me a weird look. "Royce?"

"Royce Rigsby. He manages Elevate Zipline," I confirm, and watch as her face goes pale.

"Does he go by Rigsby?" she whispers, something that looks like shock and dread crossing her features.

"Yeah, actually he does," I reply tentatively, recalling our first conversation when he called himself Rigsby. "Do you know him?" I ask, a feeling of uneasiness starting to weigh heavily in my gut.

"Oh God!" she bellows, her delicate hands covering her mouth. "I know him."

"Know him?" Laura asks.

"Like *know him*, know him?" Sabrina adds.

She covers her eyes. "Kind of. I met him before Kale, like two years ago. He was new in town, I think."

"Umm, did you..." Sabrina starts, but can't seem to finish her question.

"No!" she hollers, her wild eyes meeting mine. "I didn't sleep with him. I mean, we almost did, but I ended up getting sick." She averts her eyes. "We, uh, kissed a little, and maybe got a little handsy, but when we got back to his place, I ended up puking from all the alcohol I drank. He ended up taking me home after I sobered up."

My heart hammers in my chest as I try not to picture one of my best friends with Royce. Unfortunately, all I can see now is him taking her home with the intent of sleeping with her. Worse, the only thing that stopped them was the fact she drank a little too much alcohol.

"Q, I'm so, so sorry."

When I glance up, there are tears in Joy's eyes. I can tell she feels a crazy amount of guilt for something that happened two years ago. Before I met him. The truth of the matter is it was before me, so how can I be mad at her?

I find myself standing up and going to her on the couch. Her wide eyes watch my every move, and she holds completely still as I pull her into a hug. It takes her a few seconds to realize I'm not going to hurt her or yell at her, and she returns it with a hard squeeze.

"It's okay, Joy. I'm not mad. You didn't know, and even if you did, you can't change something that happened two years ago. The truth of the matter is you met him first. If anything, I should be apologizing to you for sleeping with a guy you almost slept with."

She's already shaking her head. "No, please don't apologize."

"I guess it makes it a little awkward, but we'll both get over it, right? I mean, it's not like I'm going to see him again anyway. He broke it off with me so he can keep living his bachelor lifestyle," I tell her, lifting my shoulders in a shrug.

"I know, but still. I'm sorry I almost slept with the man you love."

Tears fill my eyes and slowly fall down my cheeks. "And I'm sorry I fell in love with someone you almost slept with when you were drunk."

This time it's her pulling me into a hug. She holds me while I cry, while I mourn the loss of Royce. Not only him, but his friendship. I think that's what I miss the most. Sure, we had crazy chemistry in bed, but it's more than that. I miss his texts, the witty banter, and knowing he's there, even when he's not.

After I finish crying on my friend's shoulder, we turn on *Sixteen Candles* and drink another pitcher of margaritas. By the time the movie credits roll, I'm completely stuffed from pizza and chips and dip, with a healthy tequila buzz, but feel so much better than I did before my friends arrived.

I pull out my cell phone and hand it over. “Since I lost all of my contacts, will you add yours back in?” I ask my friends. Both do it without being asked twice.

“Call us if you need us,” Laura says, giving me a hug before slipping out the door. Once she finished her margarita with dinner, she stopped drinking so she could drive home. Even though she’s not buzzed in the least, I’m confident there’ll be a little baby making later on when she gets home.

Joy’s next, and even though we’ve talked it out, there’s still apprehension in her face. “I’m sorry,” she whispers as she steps up beside me.

“Please, don’t. I’m not mad at you for something that happened before my time with him. If anything, it just proves the point he’s not interested in anything more than a little booty,” I state, the alcohol doing wonders for my loose tongue.

Joy giggles but shakes her head. “I know. But he did seem like a great guy, you know the few hours I hung out with him. When I got sick, he never tried anything and was very respectful when he took me home.”

I nod. “I’m sure he was. Too bad he’s a total commitment-phobe. He’d be the perfect guy for someone.”

Someone like me.

“His loss, though, because you’re amazing, Q. Your someone is out there. I promise he is. Don’t lose hope,” she whispers with one last hug before heading to her car.

“I’m out too, unless you want me to stay,” Sabrina says, coming to stand beside me on the porch.

“No, I’m good.” I turn and pull her into my arms. “Thank you for tonight. I didn’t realize how badly I needed this. You and them.”

"That's what friends are for, Q. Now, if you'll excuse me, I'm going home to dream about Jake Ryan standing outside my bedroom window," she replies with a wink. "I left you the leftover pizza in the fridge and the margarita mix and tequila on the counter."

My heart skips a beat at the mention of the alcohol.

"Thanks, Rina. I'll talk to you tomorrow."

She throws one last wave and climbs into her car. I stand on the porch and watch as she leaves, the silence suddenly surrounding me. It's a gorgeous night, one I could probably enjoy on the front porch, but I don't think I'm ready for that. Part of me still feels like Royce will come running down the street any minute, Jack on his leash and leading the way.

So, I head back inside and prepare for bed. It's late and I've drank enough to ensure sleep will come a little easier tonight. At least, that's my hope. After brushing my teeth and changing into pajamas, I slip into my bed, grateful for the cool, clean sheets. His scent is gone; it brings me both relief and sadness at the same time. I turn on my side, my back to the empty side of my bed, and sigh.

I think about Joy and Royce and how they almost slept together. I really am surprised I'm not more upset than I am. Sure, it might make it a little uncomfortable, but I refuse to let it. It's not like they're ever going to see each other in my presence, right?

He's gone.

Now I'm able to go out and find Mr. Right.

Time to move on and forget all about Royce Rigsby.

If only I could get my heart on board.

Chapter Twenty-One

Royce

I push my way through the Friday night crowd at Dave's Sports Bar, headed for the massive oak counter at the front of the room. I'm in desperate need of another drink, and maybe a little air from the girls' weekend group in back.

When I arrived just a bit ago, I jumped right back into my usual routine. Grab a drink, scope out the crowd, and throw a few cocky grins at the ladies. It didn't take long before the group of six was inviting me over to share a few drinks and laughs.

As I got to know them, I found it's their first night in Gatlinburg on a two-night girls' weekend getaway, and there are two singles in the group. A skinny brunette with long hair and bright green eyes, and a blonde with light blue-green eyes. She's the one who gave me the fuck-me eyes the moment I joined their table, but everything about her is all wrong. Her blonde hair is a little too dark and her eyes more almond shaped. Why is that wrong?

Because I'm comparing her every feature to those of Quinn.

That realization had me ordering a round of shots for the table, on my tab, of course.

The blonde, whose name is April, kept reaching over and sliding her hand suggestively along my jean-clad thigh. Usually, I'd be all over that signal like white on rice, but tonight, as much as I try, I just can't seem to appreciate what she's offering. And frankly, the feel of her hand on my leg was enough to cause me to retreat to the bar.

I'm next in line for a drink when someone bumps into me from behind. When he doesn't apologize, I turn around, only to find my brother standing there. I return my eyes forward and wait to catch Dave's attention. I'm enough of a regular here that he knows my drink of choice and will bring it over without asking what I'll have.

"What are you doing here? This isn't your usual hangout," I say, just loud enough for him to hear.

"No, but it is yours, so I took a chance," Rueben replies, as the guy in front of me moves aside.

I nod to the bar owner, who glances at my brother. Rueben holds up two fingers, signaling he'll have the same as me, and pulls out some cash. "Wow, you're even buying? How'd I get so lucky?" I ask, as Dave sets two beers down on the counter and takes my brother's money.

"Figured you could use a drinking buddy for a little bit. You got somewhere to sit?" he asks, glancing around at one of the busiest tourist hotspots in town.

"Back there," I state, signaling toward the table of six.

Rueben tsks, disapprovingly, and heads off toward the quieter back corner. The blonde waves me over, but my feet move in the direction of my brother, not her. When I catch up with him, I'm surprised he found a small bistro table for two along the wall. "Nice find. I might have to take you out with me more often," I reply, though usually I have no problem finding a table of ladies to join.

"So why are you here and not with Quinn tonight?" he asks between sips of his beer.

"Not pulling any punches, I see," I say, drinking more than half my beer in one long pull.

"You wouldn't with me, would you?"

"Fuck no."

"So answer my question. Where's Quinn?"

I shrug and glance over his shoulder, watching the growing crowd of people, but not really seeing them. "Probably at home? Not sure."

"What happened?"

"Nothing, really. We decided it wasn't working for us anymore," I say casually, though it feels like a jackhammer is pounding in my chest. I've had that same reaction for the last week since I walked away from her.

He arches an eyebrow and stares at me. "Not working for both of you, or just you?" he asks, no-so-delicately.

"Neither of us. We agreed to casual and that we'd move on once we had our fun. End of story, Rueb."

He shakes his head. "I don't buy that," he says, leaning forward, positioning his elbows on the table. "I don't buy the bullshit you're trying to sell, and neither do you. I saw you last Friday night, Brother. I saw the fear in your eyes when I mentioned the word love. You got scared and broke it off with her."

I open my mouth to argue, but nothing comes out. He just continues to watch me, his hard gaze staring straight into me, waiting me out. "Fine. I got scared. I was probably falling in love with her, and that's not what we wanted. So, I ended it."

"Not what either of you wanted, or not what *you* wanted?" he asks, practically the same question as before.

I sigh in frustration and glance away. "Listen, Rueb, she's a great woman, and someday, she's going to make someone a very lucky man," I start, hating the taste of my own words. They're bitter and sound hollow, even to my ears. Mostly because the thought of her with someone else, marrying some guy, makes me want to punch someone square in the face until my fist is raw and bleeding.

"Yeah, she is. Too bad it won't be you," he says. His words hit bull's-eye too, square in my fucking heart.

"It can't be me, Rueb," I find myself whispering, leaning in and resting my own elbows on the table. I'm fucking exhausted from a week's worth of lack of sleep and missing her like crazy.

"Why?" he asks, his question full of curiosity.

"Because I'll fuck it up. I'm not the type of guy you bring home to Mama. I'm the kind you use to make your ex jealous."

"That's bullshit, Royce, and you know it."

"You don't know what you're talking about," I start, but he cuts me off.

"No, you don't know what you're talking about. You think being in a relationship is easy?"

"Fuck no, it isn't. They're hard and messy and usually end with a shit ton of pain," I state.

"Well, you're partially right. They are hard and can be damn messy, but not all of them end that way. Look at me and Cricket. Hell, look at Mom and Dad."

I roll my eyes. "You and Cricket are still in the pre-honeymoon phase where everything is sleeping naked and random blowjobs. That shit doesn't last."

He sits up straight. "You're right, it doesn't last. But do you know what does? Friendship, loyalty, and a commitment deeper than anything you'll ever know. A love so pure you can't imagine spending one day away from them, let alone the rest of your life. You keep bringing up Mom and Dad and her pain. Why do you think she hurts so bad, Royce? Because their love was deep and true, but don't think for one day they didn't have to work on it. They made it look easy, but they worked hard on that shit. I know it because I live it. I spend every day trying to be the best me and do right by Cricket, to love her more than anyone else in the world possibly could. And if my time with her is short, then I know I did everything I was capable of doing to show her how much I loved her."

He looks me straight in the eye and adds, "Like Dad did for Mom."

The room feels heavy and dark, like I can't catch my breath.

"But now Mom is alone," I whisper, hating the weakness I feel, the vulnerability that weighs on me.

"Yeah, she is, but you should ask her sometime about it. I bet she'd tell you falling in love with Dad and being with him was worth the heartache, worth the pain. She'd do it all over again in an instant, just to feel that love once more. Do you know how I know that, Royce? Because I feel that every day. That's how much I love Cricket. If something happened to her tomorrow, heaven forbid, I'd go back and love her again and again, even with the same result. Do you know why?"

I glance up, knowing the answer. "Because you love her."

"With everything I am." He takes another drink of his beer. "Now, let's talk about your dumbass and how you fucked up the best thing to happen to you."

I snort. "Don't hold back, brother."

He grins. "Oh, I don't plan on it. I've been waiting for this day for years."

I laugh. "Well, let me have it then."

"You're in love with Quinn and you're scared. You're afraid of the fallout, of the hurt." He leans forward and gives me a pointed look. "Well, what if it doesn't end? What if it doesn't hurt? What if you actually live the rest of your life with a beautiful woman who wants to spend it with you too? It's hard to believe someone as smart as her would pick you, but by the looks of what I saw last weekend, I'd say she'd do it in a heartbeat, Royce, if you didn't already fuck it up."

I sigh, recalling the look on her face last weekend when I told her it was fun, but over. She tried to be strong, to not act like my words were affecting her, but that wasn't true. I saw the ache, the hurt in those blue eyes, yet chose to ignore it. I told myself it was for the best, even if it hurt like hell.

Fuck, did it hurt like a son of a bitch.

Still does.

"Listen, I don't know if this thing between you and Quinn is forever. I don't know if she's the one for you anymore than I knew Cricket was the one for me in the beginning. All I'm saying is you owe yourself the chance to find out, Royce. Don't be a fucking pussy. You've always been my big, tough brother, who fights in wars and changes the world. Don't make me take you off the pedestal I put you on when you were seven and chased that little shit of a dog away from biting my ass."

I snort out a laugh. "That dog was a dick," I add, remembering how the little ankle biter used to chase my little five-year-old brother around the neighborhood, barking up a storm. One day, I went outside to play and found that dog trying to bite Rueben in the sandbox. I grabbed a plastic shovel and chased it all the way back home. The owner finally put up a fence in her backyard after that, and Rueben wasn't scared to play outside anymore.

"He was," Rueben confirms with a grin.

I sit back and finish off my beer, thinking about what he said. Do I know Quinn is the one for me? Nope, not at all. But do I owe myself the chance to find out? Probably.

A shadow falls over our table, and when I glance to my right, I see blondie. April. "Hey, you. We were talking about heading back to our hotel and sitting in the Jacuzzi. Wanna join us?" she asks, batting her overly-done eyelashes and giving me the "I want to suck your dick" smile. A month ago, I probably would have already been out of my seat, but now? Now, all I can think about is Quinn.

"Sorry, but I think I'll pass tonight. Enjoy your evening," I tell her and watch as her face falls.

"Well, if you change your mind, we're at the Holiday Inn, room 620." She draws her finger across my shoulder and taps it on the back of my neck for good measure before turning and heading back to meet her friends.

"Why didn't you go?" my brother asks, looking at me as he takes the final swig of beer.

Shrugging, I answer, "I guess she's not my type."

Rueben snorts, no doubt not missing the resemblance between April and Quinn. "So what is your type?"

"Blonde with blue eyes," I reply, knowing I've just given the exact description of the woman who left our table. "But also funny and smart."

"I'm still wondering just how smart Quinn really is if she was with you," Rueben teases, making me smile. "So what are you going to do?"

"I'll think of something," I reply, pushing my empty bottle aside as my mind already starts to spin with ideas. "Something that tells her exactly how I feel about her."

"Which is?"

I just smile.

No way am I telling him I love Quinn before I've had the chance to tell her. Even if I take the leap and she sends me packing, at least I'll know. I won't spend any time second-guessing myself and my decisions.

But my brother's right, even though I'd never say it aloud.

What if I get to spend the rest of my life with a woman who wants to spend hers with me? As scary as it is, that really doesn't sound too bad.

Not bad at all.

Chapter Twenty-Two

Quinn

It's a lazy Saturday night as I make my way home from grocery shopping. Yes, that's me. Getting groceries on a gorgeous Saturday night so I can head home to watch movies and fall asleep. Alone.

As much as I've enjoyed living on leftover pizza and the measly contents of my refrigerator for the last week, I know it's not feasible anymore. I've eaten everything but a box of saltines and the bottle of ketchup. So I made the dreaded trip to the grocery store to fill my cabinets and fridge.

While there, I actually stumbled into a very nice man in the produce aisle. I was reaching for some avocados when I accidentally hit the stack and a few rolled away. He quickly grabbed them before they were able to fall on the floor, saving the green fruit from becoming bruised and mushy. I commented on his Superman reflexes, which resulted in a wide grin that could make even the happiest of married women blush.

We chatted for a few minutes, and I could tell he was flirting. A quick ring finger glance confirmed he was single, or at least not a ring wearer, and before I knew it, he was asking for my phone number.

A part of me was ready to decline the invitation that would soon follow the exchange, most likely dinner at some point, but then I remembered I'm single. I'm free to date and see men of my choosing whenever and wherever I wanted. It was a sobering realization, one that had me offering my cell number to be programmed into his phone for later. My heart was heavy as I waved goodbye and hurried to the check-out counter, needing to put just a little distance between myself and the handsome stranger who wants to take me on a date.

Sad, isn't it?

I have a perfectly viable dating option, one who seems eager to see me again, and all I can do is think of someone who doesn't want me anymore.

That's why I'll probably accept Robert's invitation when it comes one day this next week. To help push me over the hump of missing Royce and wishing things were different.

As I pull into my driveway, something catches my eye. A bag is sitting on my porch by the door. I wonder if Sabrina is returning something she borrowed or maybe even Joy dropping off those samples of the new brand of cosmetics she found and loves.

I slip out of the car and glance around. I'm not sure why. No one is here. I click the button on my key fob to pop the trunk and grab a few paper bags before stepping on the porch. As I get a closer look at the bag, my heart starts to hammer in my chest. It's an alcohol bottle, no doubt. I can see the top of it sticking out of the paper bag. In fact, it's probably the same brand that was left on my porch just a month ago.

Tears fill my eyes as I slip my key into the lock and open the door. I ignore the small bag and take in the first trip of groceries, ignoring it again as I exit the house to grab the rest of my food. Once that's safely delivered to my kitchen and it's all put away, only then do I step outside. The bag is like a neon sign, even though it's a plain brown bag. When I flip it over, there's no message written across the paper sack like the first time.

The wetness in my eyes falls down my cheek as I stare at the contents of the bag. Why is he doing this? What does it mean? Does he think it's funny to mess with me, toy with my emotions? He says he wants to move on, but this? This borders on cruel and mean.

A dog barks in the distance, the sound stealing my breath. I jump up and spin around, eagerly glancing down the road. Only when the dog comes into view, it's a small one attached to the leash of her female owner. My heart sinks like the *Titanic*.

It's been a week since he left and hasn't so much as called or texted. Frankly, I didn't expect him to, so why is he leaving this bottle of tequila by my door now?

Frustrated, I grab the bottle and head inside, locking the door behind me as I go. I head for the kitchen and pull the leftover tequila and margarita mix from the cabinet. When Joy left it behind, I didn't think I'd have a reason to drink it, let alone so soon afterward. But here I am, doctoring up my first margarita with an extra shot of alcohol, the new bottle of top shelf tequila staring at me from the counter.

Sighing, I slowly sip my drink. Wow, yeah, too much tequila, but I don't care. I'm drinking it anyway. Maybe it'll help numb the ache in my chest for just a little bit. I take my glass to the living room, but don't really feel like watching television. I could go through the paperwork I brought home to review this weekend, but that doesn't exactly sound like fun either, so instead, I head for the front door once more.

The night is a cooler evening, which lets me know fall is just around the corner. I take a seat on my swing and slowly start to rock. The motion is soothing, even though my gut is churning. I definitely should have eaten something before drinking, but oh well. I'll heat something up in a bit.

When the night air temperature really starts to drop, I slip inside and grab the throw blanket on the back of the couch. I probably should just stay inside, but for some reason, the outside is beckoning me. I toss the blanket over my legs, slowly sip the lime drink, and listen to the quiet night settle around me.

I catch movement out of the corner of my eye and my chest tightens. A man is running toward me, a big dog trotting beside him. I stand up to get a better view and drop my glass, spilling the contents of my margarita all over the porch. The man stops in the road and looks my way. My heart stops beating.

Royce.

He's here.

"Are you okay?" he whispers, his voice sounding deep and gravelly.

"I, uh, spilled my drink," I confess in what feels like poetic déjà vu.

Under the streetlight, I see the whites of his teeth as he smiles. Royce takes a step closer, Jack practically pulling him from the roadway to get to me. "Easy, Jack," he says, not moving onto my property without my permission.

"It's okay. He can come up here," I find myself saying before I can give it a second thought.

"You sure?" he asks, not making any move to release his dog.

I nod eagerly, suddenly so very excited to see Jack after only a week's absence. "I'm sure."

Royce reaches down and unclips the leash. He barely has the words, "Behave, Jack," out of his mouth before the dog takes off like a rocket. He runs toward me, his ears flapping and his tongue dangling. I move to the stairs and meet him as he leaps up and slams into me with all his weight behind him.

"Umph," I groan, as the air leaves my lungs and my ass hits the floor.

"Shit!" Royce hollers and is at my side a second later. "I should have known he'd be a little eager," he says, reaching down and helping me stand. The moment my hand is in his, a zip of electricity bolts through my blood, landing squarely between my legs.

"It's okay," I say the moment my feet are under me again. "He just missed me, isn't that right, Jack?" I ask, dropping to my knees to get down to his level.

I swear I hear, "He's not the only one," whispered from Royce, but there's a good chance I'm hallucinating right now, so I'm sure that was in my head.

"Jack, you know better than to jump, don't you?" I ask the eager pup. He gives me a sheepish look before licking me clear across my face. "Thanks," I mumble with a laugh as I wipe doggy drool from my chin.

When I glance up at his owner, he's wearing a broad smile. One that holds a touch of happiness and a pinch of relief. It's the first time I get a real good look at him too. Royce is wearing a T-shirt and shorts, along with his favorite running shoes. His hair is a touch longer and his facial hair a little more pronounced than usual. It's like he hasn't bothered with a trim in a few days.

But do you know what?

He still looks positively breathtaking.

"I was going to say the same thing," he whispers, reaching up and swiping my hair from my forehead.

"What?"

"You said I was breathtaking, and I was going to say the same. You look absolutely beautiful, Quinn."

Suddenly, I realize how very close he is. He's directly in front of me; close enough our bodies are practically touching. I clear my throat, intent on taking a step back, but my legs don't seem to want to work right. "Wh-what are you doing here?" I stammer, trying to clear my head.

"Well, Jack has been restless lately and wanted to go for another run. Apparently, he wanted to say hello, because he picked this route all by himself."

I can't help but grin. "All by himself, huh?"

Royce shrugs. "Well, maybe he had a little help," he replies with a smirk of his own. Then his face falls serious. "The truth is I wanted to see you."

"You did?" I ask, my heart hammering so loud, I'm certain he can hear it.

"I did. I have something to say to you, Bestie Tami with an I."

I gasp at the use of my nickname. All I can do is gape up at him and wait for whatever it is he has to say.

"I thought I could treat you like every other woman I've met. I thought I could keep it simple and fun and walk away. Turns out, I can't because you're not like every other woman at all. You're *the* woman, Quinn. *My* woman. The one who makes me laugh, who I can't stop thinking about, and who makes me want to think about a future I've never thought I'd have. You, Quinn, are the reason I want to throw every trick up my sleeve out the damn window, because I don't need lines or come-ons with you. I just need you."

I'm not sure when I started to cry, but it happened at some point in his speech. The large pad of his thumb swipes beneath my eye as he gently grabs my hip and pulls me close. "I'm sorry I was an idiot. I'm sorry I walked away and hurt you. But most of all, I'm sorry

I didn't just tell you I loved you that night instead of treating you like every other woman."

My mouth falls open and my eyes go wide. "You love me?" I whisper.

"So fucking much," he says, sliding his other arm behind my back. "The question now is how do you feel about me?"

I start to open my mouth to respond, when he cuts me off.

"It's okay if you don't feel the same, Quinn. I didn't say that to force you to say it back. You can say it whenever you're ready, but I wanted you to know, okay?"

"Know?"

"That I love you."

I smile again. "I just wanted to hear you say it again," I state with a giggle. Royce laughs, his lips making a slow descent toward mine. Just as they brush across mine, I whisper, "I love you too, Royce."

He freezes and pulls back, his eyes wide. "Yeah?"

I nod impatiently. "I knew I loved you that night too."

Royce closes his eyes and lets out a deep sigh. "Thank fucking Chr—" he starts, but stops himself. "I mean, thank goodness."

Another bubble of laughter slips from my throat. "So what was it you were about to do before I opened my mouth?"

"You mean this?" he asks, claiming my lips hard and fast in a dizzying kiss. His mouth is full of determination and love as he coaxes my mouth open and his tongue delves inside. It's like a homecoming, a celebration as peace and desire roll through me. His hands hold the sides of my face, as if it were a delicate piece of china, but he never deepens the kiss.

He pulls back and stares at my swollen, wet lips. "I'd really love to kiss you some more, but I need to get home."

Wait, what?

The corner of his mouth turns upward as he gazes down at me and slides this thumb across my bottom lip. "I can tell by your eyes you're confused, so let me explain. I'm not staying tonight, even though I want to. Fuck, I want to so bad, but I'm not rushing this."

"But what if I want you to rush it?" I ask, my hands gripping the back of his shirt.

A smile spreading from ear to ear. "Oh, I'm sure we'll rush it soon, but not tonight, Bestie." He places a chaste kiss on the tip of my nose and takes a step back and pulls a folded envelope from the pocket of his shorts.

"What's this?" I ask as he hands it over.

"Open it."

I pull open the flap and remove the paper inside. I scan the top and giggle at what I read. It's written out like an invitation with my name at the top.

"It's an invitation to join me tomorrow night at Elevate at the top of the mountain. Every night I work, I take the final trip down. I'd like for you to go with me."

"Down the mountain?"

He nods. "Yeah. Will you go? With me?"

I open my mouth, wanting to say yes, but still a little nervous, even though I've already ziplined once before.

"Come on, Bestie," he says, leaning in and whispering, "Double dog dare you."

I smile as warmth spreads through me. "I'll go."

He instantly grins. "Good. Be there at seven thirty, okay?"

I nod.

Royce grips my face once more and places a hard kiss to my lips. "I'll see you tomorrow, Quinn." And then he adds, "I love you."

Royce whistles for Jack, who's busy lapping up the remnants of my margarita off the floor.

"Well, at least he's not thirsty anymore," I say with a shrug.

"Great. Now I get to run home with a buzzed dog," he teases, whistling again. Jack barks and heads toward his owner. He seems completely fine, even if he did slurp up a smidgen of alcohol. Royce slips the leash back on, heading down the sidewalk.

Before he takes off, I holler, "Hey, Royce?" He stops and turns my way. When his eyes meet mine, I state, "I love you too."

I'm rewarded with the biggest grin before they take off down the road, eventually running out of sight. I'm all smiles as I pick up my empty glass and head inside, securing the door behind me as I go. I'm still grinning as I clean up the kitchen, flip off the lights, and make my way to my bedroom.

After brushing my teeth and slipping into a pair of pajamas, I crawl into bed, only to hear my phone ping with a message. When I pull up the screen, I see an image text from Royce.

Grinning, I pull up the message and click on the image to download. The moment the photo fills my screen, I bark out a laugh, my hand covering my gaping mouth. There, in all it's beautiful glory, is a dick pic. A really nice, really big, and very hard penis.

Royce's penis.

Royce: *Now you've received a REAL dick pic.* *insert devil emoji* *insert eggplant emoji*

Giggling, I fire off my reply.

Me: *Seen one, you've seen them all.*

Royce: *Ouch, Bestie. Ouch.*

Me: *You've got more than enough ego to pad your fall.*

Royce: *Are we talking about my ego or my "ego"...*

Me: *Both are big...*

Royce: *LOL. You're good for both too.*

Me: *Too bad your ego is all the way over there tonight.*

Royce: *Very tragic, actually. I'm reconsidering my stance on taking things slow.*

Me: *Well, no going back now. You have to work tomorrow, and then you're escorting me down the mountain.*

Royce: *That's right, Bestie, I am. Seven thirty, right?*

Me: *I'll be there.*

Royce: *Night, Quinn. Sleep well.*

Me: *You too, Rigsby.*

Royce: *Love you.*

Me: *Love you too.*

Royce: *I'll never get tired of hearing you say that.*

Smiling, I set my phone aside and snuggle into my pillow. Thoughts of how my day took a drastic turn for the better filter through my mind. I never expected to see Royce again, let alone find him standing in front of my house, professing his love. It's amazing how quickly you fall asleep when your heart feels a thousand times lighter and freer.

When it's finally home.

Chapter Twenty-Three

Royce

I've been watching the clock all day, waiting impatiently as it slowly ticked closer and closer to seven thirty. When it was finally time, I lock up my office and head outside, hanging back by the cluster of picnic tables. I'm only there a minute or two when I spy her walking my way. A smile breaks out across my face, and my cock jumps in my pants. I'm way too excited to see her.

She approaches with a hint of shyness in her grin, so I take the opportunity to kiss it right off her face. Hands threading in her hair, full-on kissing the ever-loving hell out of her. And I don't even care we're in public.

"Hi," she says, breathlessly, when I finally release her lips.

"Good evening," I reply, already smiling. "I'm glad you're here." I take her hand in mine and lead her to the UTV waiting by the office. "Your chariot awaits."

Quinn climbs in the front seat and buckles in while I do the same. We make the slow climb up the mountain just as the sun begins to dip near the tree line. "The last group already left, so the platform will be almost empty when we get to the top."

"Almost empty?"

"Yeah, Brian's up there. There's a remaining employee at each platform. As I head down, they close up their landing and jump on this machine," I tell her, slowly making my way up. "You're in for a treat tonight, Bestie. The sunset will be perfect as we go down."

Quinn reaches over and grabs my hand, entwining our fingers together. It's hard to believe I ever fought this. With her. Our connection and the powerful feelings she evokes just by being near. Sure, I'm still a little worried I'm going to fuck it all up, but my brother's right.

Don't be a pussy.

I'd rather spend my nights with her than without her.

When we reach the top, Brian's already prepared for our departure. They're all used to my nightly routine, but I threw them for a loop earlier when I told them to prepare for two. I endured a little razzing, but I didn't care. I'd take all their teasing on the chin if it meant I was with Quinn.

"Here we are," I state, as I pull the UTV into the clearing beside the platform. Quinn's unbuckled and jumping out before I can even get myself released from the seat. "Anxious?"

She nods as we meet at the front of the machine and walk toward the platform.

"All set?" I ask, even though I know he is.

"Good to go, boss," he replies, handing me my harness. I grab one for Quinn, already knowing what size she needs, and help her slip it on. Only when she's completely ready to go do I get myself ready for the ride.

It doesn't take long and we're ready to go, strapped in and hooked up to the line. Brian makes sure the system is set and gives me a thumbs-up. "Ready, Bestie?"

She gives me a wide grin. "Ready."

Brian releases the braking system and sends us flying down the mountain. Quinn squeals in delight as we fall, the sound echoing through the trees and making my heart so fucking full it hurts. The good hurt. The kind my brother was talking about. I watch as she sits back and spreads her arms out wide, enjoying the fall. She tips her head up and breathes in the fresh mountain air. There's no better sight in the world than watching the woman I love enjoy this moment together.

Well, maybe watching as she comes, but that's the last thing I need to think about right now. I don't need a hard-on.

When we reach the second platform, she's all smiles. We greet Sami, one of my employees, who does her thing and gets us ready for the next trip. As she does, I reach over and give Quinn a little tug. She's close enough I can touch her, so I take full advantage of the opportunity and kiss her sweet lips.

"What was that for?"

"Because I can," I tell her, grinning like a loon and not missing Sami shaking her head as she tries to secure our clips. "We ready?" I ask my employee, who nods as soon as the line is fastened.

"All set. Enjoy the ride," she says before doing her thing and sending us down again.

The sun finally drops just when we hit a clearing in the trees. I grab my phone from my pocket and snap a few pictures of Quinn, a content smile on her face as she falls and the sun setting behind her. I even flip it around and manage a couple of photos of the two of us, selfie-style.

When we hit each platform, I take the opportunity to steal a few kisses. My crew doesn't balk too much about the PDA, but I wouldn't care if they did. This is my favorite time of the day, and I'm sharing it with my favorite person in the world.

Finally, our ride comes to an end and we land on the last platform. Everyone is already down the mountain and clocking out when my feet touch wood. I release myself from the line and go straight to the woman I love. "Thank you for going down with me," I tell her, slipping my fingers into her hair at the bottom of the helmet.

"It was amazing. I can see why you love it so much."

"It's my second favorite thing," I confess, pulling her firmly against my chest.

"Second favorite?" she asks, pressing her hip into my rapidly growing erection.

"That has something to do with the first," I quip, kissing her lips once more. "But only with you. Always, only you."

"Want to come to my place tonight?" she asks, stripping off her harness and handing it to me to hang up.

"Love to. Give me five minutes to finish closing up here. I'll run home and grab Jack and some clothes for tomorrow," I state.

"Okay, I'll see you in a bit," she replies with one last kiss before she takes off for the parking lot. I watch her go, mostly because I'm hypnotized by the sway of her hips and the swell of her ass.

After she's in her car and pulling out of the lot, I finish locking up all of our equipment and making sure the UTVs are secured in the shed. I sign off on today's crew, flip off the lights in the front office, and lock the door. I'm all smiles as I make my way home to grab an overnight bag and my dog.

The moment I slip through my front door, a text message dings. Jack is running circles around my feet, anxious to see me and to go outside. "Let's go, buddy," I holler, heading for the back deck. Jack is there, hot on my heels, and bursts through the open doorway as soon as he can. I watch as he sniffs around and marks his territory, only then remembering I have a message on my phone.

I see her name and instantly grin. It's a picture message and only takes a second to download. When the image comes into view,

I gasp and almost swallow my tongue. There's my girl, naked from the waist down, the picture a close-up of my second favorite set of lips.

Me: *Jesus, Quinn. Give a guy a warning next time!* *inserts flame emoji*

Quinn: *Well, I heard those kind of pics are all the rage.* *insert winky face emoji*

Quinn: *Wanted to show you what's waiting for you here. At my place.*

I whistle for Jack, not giving a care in the world about cutting his outside exploration short.

Me: *I'm on my way.*

Quinn: *I'll be waiting…*

My cock is like steel in my pants as we head inside. I throw random clothes in a bag, grab my personal products from the bathroom, and toss Jack's things into another sack. I'm practically running for my truck, Jack excited for the ride and possible playtime.

Before I fire up the engine, I grab my phone and send off a quick message to my girl.

Me: *Keep my dinner warm, Bestie. I'm on my way, and I'm a starving man.*

She sends the winky face emoji as I toss my phone onto the passenger seat and take off like a bat outta hell. Off to see my girl.

The one I love.

The one worth giving up the meaningless existence I had before her. She may not know it, but she changed my life that day she sent me a text, complaining about a random dick pic.

That's the day I started to fall for my best friend.

Tami with an I.

Epilogue

Quinn

6 months later

"Thank you, all, for coming to the annual Grace Private School Family Reading Night. We have a great evening planned for you all. Each of the three rooms have a different book and activity planned. Afterward, please stop by the cafeteria for lemonade, cookies, and popcorn, furnished by the GPS Booster Club. We hope you all enjoy our festivities and, as always, thank you for your support. The entire Grace team appreciates you all very much."

My greeting to family and friends in the auditorium is followed by instructions from the teachers who helped organize our family event on which room to head to for which reading.

"Miss Michaels, we have a situation," our first-grade teacher, Dalia Daniels, says quietly and with a hint of urgency.

"What's up?" I ask, ducking away from the moving crowd so we may speak privately.

"We don't have a prince."

"What? I thought—"

"Yes, but apparently, Paul Rivers came down with the flu today. He's unable to read in the fairy tales' room.

I close my eyes and sigh. Of course, right before we have a fairy tale story for our youngest readers, our Prince Charming is MIA. "Okay, so we have the costume, right?"

"Yes," Dalia confirms.

"What about—"

"Mr. Reynolds is too big for the costume. We already checked," she interrupts, speaking of our fourth-grade teacher. Zack Reynolds is a large man, regularly busting out of his button-down shirt. I suspected he wouldn't fit into our rented costume, but it was worth a shot.

"What if—"

"I'll do it."

I stop and turn, instantly smiling at Royce. He's standing beside me, looking completely edible in dark jeans and a tight Henley, the sleeves pushed up to expose his forearms. In fact, I'm pretty sure my mouth waters just a bit at the sight of my boyfriend.

We've been together for just over six months now and have been talking about the possibility of moving in together. That's as far as it's gone, the talking stage, and believe it or not, it was actually Royce who initiated it. We rarely spend a night apart anymore, and it just seems logical to stop paying double everything and consolidate down to one household.

It's a huge step, not only for him, but for me too.

"What are you doing here?" I ask, going up on my tiptoes to give him a quick peck on the cheek.

"Well, I was in the neighborhood and wanted to stop by. Did I hear you're short one Prince Charming?" he asks, glancing between Dalia and me.

"Yes, I guess the man playing him tonight has the flu."

"I could help out," he suggests, as if it were the most logical idea in the whole world.

"You? Really?"

"Well, it's just reading a kid's book, right? I mean, I *am* practically one of them still," he jokes, giving me a smirky grin.

I look up at him, trying to determine if he's serious or not. "There's a costume," I say slowly, as if letting the words sink in.

He shrugs. "You don't think I can pull off Prince Charming?"

Now I'm the one smiling. "I think you'd be perfect."

He kisses my forehead. "Where's my costume?" he asks before being practically whisked away to somewhere else to get ready.

I visit with a few families slowly making their way to the reading rooms. I poke my head in *The Maze Runner* room and find it full of the teenagers and their families. The second room is geared more toward our third through fifth grade students with a theme of "Captain Underpants." The final room is the one I'm looking for. Prince Charming is making his way to the front of the room, a book in one hand and a plastic sword in the other.

"Can I have your attention, please? I am Prince Charming, and I'm going to read *Sleeping Beauty*," he announces.

With a loud voice that carries throughout the room, Royce transforms into Prince Charming. I can't stop from smiling as he stands there and reads, totally getting into the character. The kids all love him, giggling along as he reads the silly parts and hanging on his every word.

Suddenly, he thrusts the sword in the air and says, "Where is my princess? Where is Princess Quinn?"

My heart skips around in my chest as a few heads turn back to face me.

"Oh, there she is," he announces, heading my way.

"What are you doing?" I whisper as he approaches.

"Improvising," he answers with a shrug.

Before I know what's happening, I'm being pulled to the front of the room. Some of the students at my school are giggling and pointing. "Royce," I whisper-yell, trying to pull back against his grip.

"Ladies and gentlemen, I've found my princess. Please welcome Princess Quinn to the front of the class," he says to a round of applause.

My face burns as he helps me sit on the stool and reaches for the book. He flips through the pages dramatically, causing a few more bursts of laughter to fly around the room. Suddenly, he tosses the book over his shoulder and sighs theatrically. "Well, I've lost my place, so I'm going to have to ad-lib this part."

He turns to face me, getting into character as he lifts his sword and says, "My Princess, I've searched far and wide throughout the kingdom until I finally found you. You see, Prince Charming was an idiot for the longest time, frolicking about the kingdom and showing his sword to all the maidens."

My eyes practically bug out of my head, which seems to be a common reaction from approximately half the parents in the room. The other half giggles.

"But one day, the prince received a text message from the princess, and the prince hasn't been the same since. Even his trusty steed, Jack, was enthralled with the princess. So, one day, the prince decided he wanted to spend the rest of his life with the beautiful princess," he says, just before dropping down on one knee.

Gasps echo throughout the room, but all I hear is the swooshing of blood in my ears and my rapidly beating heart.

"Quinn Michaels, you're the best mistaken text message I've ever received. I want to spend the rest of my life with you, not only because I'm a better person when you're near, but also because I can't imagine living without you. Will you marry me?" he asks, pulling a small black box from somewhere in his costume. When he opens it up, a small, round diamond stares back at me.

There're several gasps and giggles from within the room, but I don't pay them any attention. My eyes are only for the man kneeling before me, asking me to spend the rest of my life with him. The only answer I can give is, "Yes."

Royce's grin is wide as he slips the ring on my finger and stands up, pulling me against his body. Applause and cheers fill the room as someone hollers, "Kiss her!"

His lips are soft when they slide against my own as I wrap my arms around his neck. When he pulls back, I whisper, "Your sword is poking me in the stomach."

He just smirks. "That's because he wants to come out and play."

I bark out a laugh and glance to the room full of students and their families. "I'm not sure this is the story they signed up for tonight."

"No, probably not," he replies, meeting my eyes with burning desire. "But do you know what?"

"What?"

"Both stories end the same."

I draw my eyebrows upward. "They do?"

He smiles that panty-melting grin that makes my heart flutter and my undergarments useless. "They do." He kisses me once more. "And they both live happily ever after."

I giggle and place my cheek against his chest. "I can't believe we're getting married. And you didn't even have to double dog dare me."

"Not this time, but maybe later tonight. When we're alone."

"You're on, Prince Charming."

And they both lived happily ever after...

The End

Don't miss a new release, reveal, or sale! Sign up for my newsletter at www.laceyblackbooks.com/newsletter

Also by Lacey Black

<u>Rivers Edge series</u>

Trust Me, Rivers Edge book 1 (Maddox and Avery) – FREE at all retailers

~ #1 Bestseller in Contemporary Romance

Fight Me, Rivers Edge book 2 (Jake and Erin)

Expect Me, Rivers Edge book 3 (Travis and Josselyn)

Promise Me: A Novella, Rivers Edge book 3.5 (Jase and Holly)

Protect Me, Rivers Edge book 4 (Nate and Lia)

Boss Me, Rivers Edge book 5 (Will and Carmen)

Trust Us: A Rivers Edge Christmas Novella (Maddox and Avery)

~ This novella was originally part of the Christmas Miracles Anthology

BOX SET – contains all 5 novels, 2 novellas, and a BONUS short story

With Me, A Rivers Edge Christmas Novella (Brooklyn and Becker)

<u>Bound Together series</u>

Submerged, Bound Together book 1 (Blake and Carly)

~ An International Bestseller

Profited, Bound Together book 2 (Reid and Dani)

~A Bestseller, reaching Top 100 on 2 e-retailers

Entwined, Bound Together book 3 (Luke and Sidney)

Summer Sisters series

My Kinda Kisses, Summer Sisters book 1 (Jaime and Ryan)

~A Bestseller, reaching Top 100 on 2 e-retailers

My Kinda Night, Summer Sisters book 2 (Payton and Dean)

My Kinda Song, Summer Sisters book 3 (Abby and Levi)

My Kinda Mess, Summer Sisters book 4 (Lexi and Linkin)

My Kinda Player, Summer Sisters book 5 (AJ and Sawyer)

My Kinda Player, Summer Sisters book 6 (Meghan and Nick)

My Kinda Wedding, A Summer Sisters Novella book 7 (Meghan and Nick)

Rockland Falls series

Love and Pancakes, Rockland Falls book 1

Love and Lingerie, Rockland Falls book 2

Love and Landscape, Rockland Falls book 3

Love and Neckties, Rockland Falls book 4

Standalone

Music Notes, a sexy contemporary romance standalone

A Place To Call Home, a Memorial Day novella

Exes and Ho Ho Ho's, a sexy contemporary romance standalone novella

Pants on Fire, a sexy contemporary romance standalone

Double Dog Dare You, a new standalone

Grip, A Driven World Novel

Co-Written with *NYT Bestselling* Author, Kaylee Ryan

It's Not Over, Fair Lakes book 1
Just Getting Started, Fair Lakes book 2
Can't Get Enough, Fair Lakes book 3

Acknowledgments

There are so many that helped me with this book!

Melissa Gill – Thank you for another beautiful cover!
Give Me Books – Thank you for your tireless work organizing the cover reveal and release.
Kara Hildebrand – Thank you for your editing expertise.
Sandra Shipman and Jo Thompson – Thank you for beta and alpha reading, and for your help in making the storyline consistent.
Karen Hrdlicka – Thank you for your proofing help.
Gel of Tempting Illustrations – Thank you for so many amazing teasers and images. I love showing off your pretties!
Kaylee Ryan – Thank you for just being you and always a call away.
Holly Collins – Thank you for always believing in me and for almost two decades of friendship!
Brenda Wright, Formatting Done Wright – Thank you for another amazing format.
My ARC team – Thank you for the early reviews and for sharing the book with the world.
Lacey's Ladies – Thank you for your continual support and for making me laugh every day.
My family, husband, and kids – Thank you for always standing by my side.
Bloggers and Readers – Thank you, thank you, thank you!

About the Author

Lacey Black is a Midwestern girl with a passion for reading, writing, and shopping. She carries her e-reader with her everywhere she goes so she never misses an opportunity to read a few pages. Always looking for a happily ever after, Lacey is passionate about contemporary romance novels and enjoys it further when you mix in a little suspense. She resides in a small town in Illinois with her husband, two children, and three broody chickens. Lacey loves watching old *Friends* episodes, shooting guns, and should only consume one mixed drink because she's a lightweight.

Email: laceyblackwrites@gmail.com
Facebook: https://www.facebook.com/authorlaceyblack
Twitter: https://twitter.com/AuthLaceyBlack
Website: www.laceyblackbooks.com

Made in the USA
Monee, IL
17 December 2022